WEDDING BELLS FOR THE VICTORY GIRLS

Summer 1945. After victory in Europe, best friends Lily, Gladys and Beryl are looking to the future. But even with this happy news, their lives are far from simple. Despite Lily's joyful summer wedding, she has doubts over what her heart wants now. As she adjusts to her role as a young wife, could this signal the end of her position at Marlows? The return of Gladys' husband Bill leads to conflict in their family life as he struggles to find work after the Navy. Meanwhile, big changes are afoot at Beryl's bridal shop. As the girls start to move on with their lives, they have never needed to stick together more . . .

JOANNA TOYE

◆

WEDDING BELLS FOR THE VICTORY GIRLS

Complete and Unabridged

MAGNA
Leicester

First published in Great Britain in 2022 by
HarperCollins*Publishers*
London

First Ulverscroft Edition
published 2022
by arrangement with
HarperCollins*Publishers*
London

This novel is entirely a work of fiction. The names,
characters and incidents portrayed in it are the work
of the author's imagination. Any resemblance to actual
persons, living or dead, events or localities
is entirely coincidental.

*A catalogue record for this book is available
from the British Library.*

ISBN 978–0–7505–4917–2

Published by
Ulverscroft Limited
Anstey, Leicestershire

Printed and bound in Great Britain by
TJ Books Ltd., Padstow, Cornwall

This book is printed on acid-free paper

For John, with love

1

June 1945

'Well? Will I do?'

Lily Collins hovered in the doorway of the small back parlour. Her brother Sid, blond, broad-shouldered, heart-stoppingly handsome in his full naval dress uniform, turned from the window.

Lily had the satisfaction of seeing a look that amounted to wonder cross his face before — typical Sid — he had to make light of things.

'It never is! It can't be!' He crossed the worn rug towards her, hands held out. 'My kid sister? Is it? She's been swapped in the night!'

'It's me. Every inch of me,' said Lily.

'Come on in then, and give us a twirl,' grinned Sid.

Lily did as she was asked, loving the feel of the silky bodice and skirt against her skin and the weight of the French lace over it. Stopping in front of Sid, she obediently turned around so he could get the full effect of the short train and the gleam of the locket that Jim had given her at her throat. Her blonde hair was curled back off her face in what they called a victory roll: her wedding veil was anchored with a spray of orange blossom. Her circuit completed, she stood to face him once more.

'Well? Cat got your tongue?' she asked.

For once, Sid didn't reply in kind. He simply took her hands, her engagement ring on her right hand for today, instead of her left.

1

'You look amazing, Lil,' he said. Was that a catch his voice? Surely not! 'It's just . . . I have this weird feeling of . . . déjà vu, they call it, don't they? When you feel you've been in the exact same situation before.'

'I haven't been married before,' Lily pointed out. 'I think I might remember!'

'I know, you daft ha'porth! What I mean is — it took me right back. Four years ago, I was sitting here, foot on a stool after I crocked it in training, and you came and stood in that doorway in your little summer frock and asked me what I thought. You were going for your interview at Marlows, remember?'

'Don't remind me!' Lily covered her eyes. 'Those dreadful ankle socks!'

'And look how far you've come, you're a silk stockings girl now.'

'I wish!'

'You know what I mean. It's been the making of you, your job in that store. And of you and Jim. You'd never have met him otherwise.'

Lily smiled.

'When I think how scared I was to go to the interview! And even when I got the job . . .' She tailed off. She looked up and met Sid's eyes, as clear and blue as her own. 'I'm a bit scared now, Sid.'

'What of? You and Jim are made for each other!'

'Oh, I don't mean like that! I mean . . . about me. I may look different, but am I really? Am I ready for this? To be someone's wife?'

'Here. Come here.' Careful not to dislodge her veil, Sid took her in his arms. She felt the comforting bulk of his body as he gave her a hug.

'Of course you're ready. You've grown up, Sis, and

not just on the outside. You've been through a lot these past few years. We all have.'

'That's what a war does for you,' said Lily wryly.

There'd been such times — worries about their brother Reg when he went missing; a bomb blast at the store that had come too close to home . . . But good times too — falling in love with Jim and knowing he felt the same; making the friends she'd keep for life; acts of kindness given and received; and laughter and fun despite everything.

'And now it's over,' said Sid simply. 'And you and Jim have your whole future ahead of you.' He stood back and Lily automatically smoothed down the skirt of her dress. Sid looked at his watch. 'He'll be at the church by now,' he said. 'And our car won't be long. How's Mum doing getting into her finery?'

As he spoke, they heard the front door slam.

'Ah, that's Beryl going,' said Lily. 'Mum'll be down soon. Beryl was doing her hair.'

Lily's dress had come from Beryl's bridal hire business and her friend was a dab hand at styling hair as well. On cue, they heard their mother's feet descending the stairs. But Dora Collins didn't linger in the doorway — widowed young with three small children, there'd never been much time in her life for lingering. She bustled in and made straight for the kitchen.

'Oy, oy, oy! Where do you think you're going?' Sid caught his mother's arm. 'I've done the breakfast washing up and tidied it away. The Admiral of the Fleet couldn't find fault with it! There's nothing for you to do in there!'

'I bet you haven't filled the kettle!' retorted his mother. 'That's the first thing we'll want when we get back, a cup of tea!'

Sid and Lily looked at each other and laughed.

'Mum, you are priceless!' said Sid. 'I think the war was won on your cups of tea — and all those blooming scarves you knitted, of course. Now stand still and let me look at you.' Lily looked on proudly as he scanned their mother up and down. 'Very smart,' he concluded.

Dora, her face a little lined perhaps, but slim and still pretty in her navy blue suit and matching hat, permitted herself a nod of acknowledgement.

'I'll do,' she said. 'Now, go and see if the car's on the way, will you, Sid? I know the bride's allowed to be late, but we don't want Jim to give up hope.'

'Nor lose the chance of getting this one off our hands!'

Sid moved too quickly for Lily's affectionate swipe — whatever else might have changed, their jokey relationship never would.

'So,' said Dora when she and Lily were left alone. 'How are you feeling, love?'

'Apart from the colony of butterflies I seem to have swallowed?'

'You look beautiful.' There was no mistaking the catch in her mother's voice and Lily knew the unspoken thought behind it: if only your father was here. She reached out and took her mother's hands.

'Mum, in case I don't get the chance to say it later, I want to say thank you. Thank you for everything you've done for me, the way you've always looked after me and loved me and sorted me out when I went wrong. If I ever amount to anything it's all down to you and your hard work. And you've done it all on your own.'

'What nonsense!' But Lily could tell from the way

her mother quickly swallowed that what she'd said had moved her. 'Taught you to walk and talk, that's all I did, then you did the rest! Never any stopping you after that, in either department!'

Lily thought back over some of the more impetuous — some would say madcap — things she'd done.

'I'm sorry for all the worry I might have caused you,' she said. 'But you can relax now — I'll be Jim's responsibility.'

'And the best of luck to him!'

But Lily knew the light-heartedness was only a front. There hadn't always been time for Dora to show much affection when the children had been growing up, but the hardships of war had brought mother and daughter closer together — an unexpected blessing. Lily clasped her in a hug.

'I do love you, Mum.'

'I love you too,' whispered Dora, glad her daughter couldn't see that her eyes were full of tears.

* * *

It hadn't been planned as a church wedding, nor as a summer one. Lily and Jim had booked the Register Office in their small town of Hinton for the first day of spring, but Dora had been rushed into hospital, and their plans had gone on hold.

Now, as the car with its fluttering white ribbons pulled up in front of the church, Lily was so glad they'd postponed their big day. As well as the moment they'd both been waiting for and dreaming of, the wedding felt, too, like a thanksgiving for her mother's recovery — and the end of the war, in Europe at least.

The leaves on the churchyard trees were bright

green against the old stone walls and the clear blue of the sky. In the porch, the kindly vicar who'd read their banns was waiting, and Beryl was hovering to adjust Lily's train and veil. The bells were ringing out — they couldn't have had those if they'd married before VE day! And as the driver opened the door of the car, the faint strains of organ music wafted from inside.

Sid helped his mother and sister out. With another quick kiss for Lily, Dora hurried inside to take her place in the front pew. Lily stood as still as she could while Beryl primped her dress and veil. The photographer stood patiently by, waiting to take the official photographs.

'They're all in there!' announced Beryl, squinting as she made sure Lily's locket was centred above the horseshoe neckline. 'Gladys and Bill and the twins, Jean Crosbie, and your mum's other friends from the WI and the WVS and the Red Cross. And quite a few from Marlows have given up their dinner hour to come.'

'There's someone else in there too, I hope! How's Jim?' asked Lily.

'Oh, him! I had to stop my Les pouring brandy down him!' Beryl rolled her eyes at her husband's interpretation of the best man's duties. 'I told him, Lily doesn't want him paralytic!'

'Oh no — was Jim that nervous?'

'No, it was only Les, any excuse for a quick one! Jim's fine. Or he will be when you get in there!' Beryl stood back, happy with the locket now, and her tone was more serious. 'You look a knockout, Lily. I've never seen a better bride, and I've seen a few.' She blinked and swallowed — gosh, if even Beryl was moved, Lily might have to believe her! Quickly, though, Beryl recovered. 'Now, how do I look? Is my hat at the right angle?'

The hat was a small straw saucer tipped to one side, which didn't distract the eye quite enough from the revealing frilled neckline of Beryl's dress. Lily was amused to see the vicar's eyes were out like his own organ stops.

'It's perfect,' said Lily.

Beryl gave her a swift hug and a peck on the cheek, then disappeared into the church, calling back, 'Good luck!'

The photographer moved forward. Sid crooked his elbow and Lily took his arm, smiling for the camera. The shutter clicked once, twice, then the photographer stepped away, checking his film. The vicar inclined his head.

'Ready?' he asked.

'Ready, Sis?' repeated Sid.

The organ music had stopped. There was a pause, then Lily heard the first four thrilling notes of the bridal march.

She took a deep breath. The butterflies fluttered their wings one last time, then settled.

'Ready,' she said.

* * *

'Aye aye, here they come!' Les had been craning to see the door.

'And you've got the ring?' asked Jim.

'No,' retorted Les, 'since you last asked me five seconds ago, I've nipped out and pawned it! Now, on your feet!'

Les nudged Jim to his feet and they took their places

in front of the altar.

Jim pulled down his cuffs and smoothed his dark hair. He straightened his shoulders and stood up to his full six-foot height. He tried to steady his breathing. It wasn't nerves, it was simply excitement and disbelief that he and Lily were here at last. Was he allowed to turn around? He wasn't sure, but he couldn't resist. He turned and looked over his shoulder.

The aisle seemed a mile long — what must it look like to Lily? But here she was now, as slim as a reed on Sid's arm, in a dress of lace which showed off her small waist and long legs. Jim saw the fond smiles and admiring looks of their guests as she passed, and her beaming smile back. In a whisper of fabric, she came to a halt beside him. She handed her bouquet — of lilies, of course — to Sid, who passed it to Dora in the front pew. Lily was wearing the locket Jim had given her one Christmas, he noticed — her 'something old', perhaps. Above it, her cheeks were pink, her eyes bright, her mouth smiling. What a pity he'd have to wait until the vicar gave him permission before he could kiss her.

'You look beautiful,' he mouthed, and then: 'I love you.'

Lily just had time to mouth back, 'You too,' before the vicar began intoning:

'Dearly beloved, we are gathered here in the sight of God and in the face of this congregation to join together this man and this woman in holy matrimony . . .'

2

Sid stood up and chinked his knife on his glass. Gradually the hubbub in the small function room subsided. For a brief moment all that could be heard was summer birdsong and the drone of bees through the French windows which stood open to the hotel garden.

The small reception at the White Lion had been Sid's idea, and he was generously paying. He'd told Lily he wanted to spare their mum the worry of catering so she could relax and enjoy the day.

Dora had still made the wedding cake though, with pooled rations from friends and neighbours. Anything else would have been a travesty. She'd fed it with Sid's naval rum and, thanks to donated coupons and a lot of shoe leather, she'd even found a rare-as-hen's-teeth box of icing sugar. Now the cake had been cut and everyone had a piece in front of them, along with a glass of champagne. Marlows had its own wedding traditions for staff who got married, and the bottles had been generously donated by the owner, Mr Marlow himself.

'Right,' Sid began, 'I'm here today in what they call *loco parentis* —'

This prompted a 'Get you!' from Les and catcalls from Bill, a naval pal of Sid's, now married to Lily's friend Gladys.

Undeterred, Sid carried on.

'For the ignorant among you, that means 'in place of a parent'. Now, our dad can't be here today, sadly, and nor can our big brother Reg, because he's still doing his bit out in North Africa.'

Seated between them, Lily glanced up at her brother, then past Jim to her mum. She hadn't expected Sid's speech to start off so soberly.

He continued:

'Reg would have fought me for the honour of giving Lily away, I know — but only 'cos we couldn't get Jim to stump up any money for her!'

There was laughter in the room — and from Lily. Jokes and insults — that was more like it!

Sid's speech quickly moved on, citing incidents from Lily's childhood which had her blushing and hiding her head in her hands, while Jim patted his pockets and pretended to look for a receipt so he could take her back. But as Sid wound up, his tone became more serious again.

'Before we left home this morning, me and Lily were talking about how much has changed in the last few years, and how much she's changed. And of course she has — on the surface. I keep calling her my kid sister but in truth she's a beautiful young woman, never more beautiful than today, now she's Jim's wife. But the thing is, folks, underneath, the essentials haven't changed and they never will. Lily will always be the same bright spark that lights up a room, interested in everything and everyone, lively, generous, someone we're all proud to know. In Jim she's met a bloke who's her true match. He's a gentle brake on some of her wilder ideas, a sounding board and a massive support to her. I know he loves everything about her, and will always look after her — if she'll let him! Ladies and gentlemen, I give you — the bride and groom!'

Everyone rose to their feet and raised their glasses.

Lily looked up at Sid and mouthed a thank you. Then she met Jim's eyes and they stole another quick kiss before he got to his feet to reply.

'I'm not sure how to follow that,' he began. 'Sid's stolen a lot of my lines!' As everyone shouted 'Shame!' he quietened them with a gesture and went on. 'I just want to say I'm the happiest man alive, so proud that Lily agreed to marry me in the first place and so looking forward to our life together.'

Lily sat back and let Jim's words wash over her — his thanks to Dora, to Sid, to Beryl and to their friends for their presents and their presence there in the room. She was in such a bubble of happiness she felt it could never be broken. The formal part of the day might be coming to an end, and it had been wonderful, but the really important part, the part that had been most difficult for them to postpone, when she and Jim could finally be alone together, was still to come.

★ ★ ★

'What do you mean, you don't know? Where's he taking you?'

'I don't know where the honeymoon is, and I don't want to!' In the bedroom with its patterned carpet and luxurious drapes that the hotel had loaned them as a changing room, Lily let Beryl undo the tiny covered buttons at the back of her dress and stepped carefully out of it. 'Isn't it meant to be a surprise?'

'Well, I envy you, wherever it is!' Beryl mourned. 'Me and Les and Bobby won't be having a holiday.' She placed Lily's dress on a padded hanger. Three-year-old Bobby was being looked after by a neighbour today, so Beryl could concentrate on Lily. 'But it's an ill wind. I've never been so busy, all these demob-happy fellers being marched up the aisle by the girls who've been waiting for them!'

Down in the foyer, Dora was having a similar conversation with Gladys. Les had disappeared on some mysterious task: Bill and Sid had gone into the garden for a smoke and, no doubt, some war-talk. There was still a lot of it about.

'I hope we can have a little break once Bill's demobbed,' Gladys said, resting a hand on the pram handle and gently rocking it. Bill would be returning to Portsmouth later that day to await his demob papers.

'It'd be lovely for the twins,' smiled Dora. Joy and Victor were a year old now. 'And they've been good as gold today. Not a peep in the church!'

'They have, haven't they?' Gladys smiled lovingly at her children, asleep and tucked end to end in the big pram — they still just about fitted. Dora looked at her with affection. Gladys, an orphan, had been plump, shy and mousy when she and Lily had first met at Marlows — chalk and cheese, but fast friends all the same. Marriage and motherhood had given Gladys a new confidence, Dora reflected, and she'd matured into a nice-looking girl.

They turned as Lily and Beryl came down the stairs to join them. Seeing Lily's going away dress, leaf-green with little white flowers, Gladys let out a gasp of admiration that was almost pride.

'Oh Lily! Don't you look a picture!' she cried. 'What a beautiful dress!'

'Only thirty bob, plus the coupons of course!' said Beryl in approval. 'Lovely, isn't it, for the money? She did well.'

12

But Lily wasn't bothered about bargains.

'Where's my husband?' she demanded, looking around. 'Has he abandoned me already?'

'We haven't seen him,' said Dora. 'Unless he's outside, with Sid and —'

Her voice was drowned out by a terrific roar from the front of the hotel, and the unmistakable rattle of tin cans.

'What the . . . ?' Lily moved through the glass doors and out onto the steps. There was Jim astride a motorbike, the sidecar daubed with 'Just Married', and tin cans on strings trailing from the back bumper.

Sid, Les and Bill stood to one side, grinning.

'Your carriage awaits, Cinders,' said Sid, as Jim hopped off the bike and bounded up the steps.

'I borrowed it,' he said, taking her hands. 'Do you trust me to get us safely away from here?'

Lily looked up into his deep brown eyes. She'd trust him with her life, of course she would.

'I trust you to get us to the moon and back,' she said.

'That may take a little longer than we've got,' smiled Jim. 'But come with me anyway.'

★ ★ ★

An hour and a half later, the bike was roaring under an archway into the stable yard of another hotel. Jim brought it to a shuddering stop on the cobbles and jumped off.

Lily looked around. The early evening sun glowed on rosy old brick; the hotel had mullioned windows and a thatched roof. Jim ran his fingers through his own thatch of hair as he removed his helmet and opened the sidecar door for Lily to step out. Cramped, windblown, laughing, she shook her hair out of her eyes — she'd almost lost her hat before they'd gone fifty yards and had held it on her lap the rest of the way. A shower of confetti — a mix of dried flowers and little hole-punch circles she'd squirrelled away at work — fell from the folds of her dress. It was a miracle it hadn't been scattered to the four winds.

'Where are we?' she asked, looking around in wonderment. There'd been no clues on the road: the signposts had been removed during the war and were still missing. It had been beautiful, though, once they'd left Hinton behind: the verges thick with cow parsley that reminded her of the lace of her wedding dress; skylarks soaring into the sky from their nests in the hayfields.

'Stratford,' said Jim. 'On Avon,' he added, as if she might think they were in Stratford in the East End of London.

'Shakespeare!' said Lily.

'Right!' said Jim. 'And because Hitler, in his one redeeming feature, was such an admirer of the great man, he left Stratford completely untouched in the war.'

Lily sagged against Jim, loving him so much she could hardly bear it. Almost anywhere else there'd have been reminders — barbed wire on the beaches, 'Danger: Unexploded Bomb' signs, pitted pavements, broken buildings and potholed roads. Here, they could pretend the war had never happened.

'Let's go in,' she said.

In a trance, she went through the ritual of booking in. She signed her name for the first time as Mrs Lily Goodridge, and followed the porter upstairs, listening as he explained that the bathroom was down the corridor, taking in the four-poster bed with its heavy tapestry drapes in their room. Finally the porter left them and they were on their own.

'Well,' said Jim. 'What now? Do you want to go out and explore, or . . .'

Lily reached up and took his kind, thoughtful, much-loved face in her hands.

'There'll be plenty of time for that tomorrow,' she said.

'Really? You're sure? You're ready?' Jim asked gently.

'I've never been more ready,' Lily replied.

★ ★ ★

It was funny sitting opposite Jim at breakfast next morning in the panelled dining room, trying to be serious and sober in front of the other guests when all she wanted to do was smile and smile and sing out with happiness. Her hand shook as she poured their tea and watched him reach for the toast, knowing where their hands had been before, and the thrills of pleasure they'd brought each other.

Dutifully, they kept their conversation neutral. Jim showed her the guidebook: Shakespeare's birthplace and his tomb in Holy Trinity church were on the 'must-see' list, he said. But as he did, he touched her foot under the table, then hooked his leg around hers and pressed them together. It was all Lily could do not to leap up and drag him upstairs again.

Finally, the other guests, who'd been rather earlier down to breakfast than Lily and Jim, left the room. Lily burst into helpless laughter.

'Do you think they guessed?' she asked. 'That we're on our honeymoon?'

'Oh I doubt it,' said Jim sarcastically. 'Not when we might as well have a giant illuminated arrow over our heads.'

'Oh, well, I don't care!' A shaft of sunlight through the tiny panes of the window shone on Lily's hair, giving her a golden halo. 'They must have been newlyweds themselves once, even that stiff military-looking chap and his wispy wife.'

'Yes, that'll be us in a few years' time,' warned Jim in a doomy voice.

'We will never be like that!' insisted Lily. 'They barely spoke a word to each other!'

'No, that's true,' said Jim, downing the dregs of his tea. 'You'll still be rattling on like you always do while I sit quiet. But with any luck I'll have gone deaf!'

Lily snatched up Jim's guidebook.

'Are there any solicitors advertising in here?' she demanded. 'Because if you carry on like this, I might be filing for divorce before the day's out!'

★ ★ ★

Back in Hinton, Lily's mum had been late down to breakfast too.

'Ten to eight when I woke up!' Dora marvelled to Sid as they sat over their final cups of tea.

'It's hard work, being mother of the bride.' Sid put the lid back on the bramble jam that Dora had made last autumn when the WI had had an allocation of sugar. 'It was a big day for you. In some ways, it was your day as much as Lily's.'

'Didn't she look lovely though?'

16

'She did.'

'I can't wait to see the photographs,' Dora sighed. 'I wonder how they're getting on?'

'I'm sure they're fine,' smiled Sid. 'And not thinking about us at all.'

'No, well, that's as it should be.' Dora stood up. 'I'd better clear these crocks away.'

'I'll give you a hand, then I must be off. No peace for the wicked!'

Sid was at the Admiralty in London. He was always discreet about what he did there, and dismissive of any suggestion it was anything more than clerking, but that extra stripe on his sleeve hadn't gone unnoticed yesterday, nor his throwaway remark that he'd been asked to stay on in his post for the time being. Selected to stay on, more like, Dora had thought proudly.

'I know, love. Duty calls.'

'I'll be up to see you again as soon as I can, Mum.' Sid stood up and automatically checked his tie in the mirror, then pinched the creases in his trousers. He'd always been particular about his appearance: five years in uniform had only enhanced it.

Half an hour later, after Sid, supplied with sandwiches and a piece of wedding cake for the journey, had been waved off at the door, Dora shook herself into action.

Though it was Sunday, there were still things to do. The dog, Buddy, had to be walked, the leftover wedding cake cut up and taken round to neighbours and friends; the spot of gravy that had got onto the skirt of her suit needed attention. Lily and Jim's double bed would be arriving next day: there was Lily's old single bed to strip and the new sheets to iron, the ones that

17

Sam had kindly sent as a gift.

Dora smiled ruefully. Sam, a Canadian corporal, was responsible for the dog too, a spaniel he'd adopted and who'd been his parting gift. Dora had got to know Sam when he'd been stationed nearby but he'd had to ask for a compassionate discharge to go home to his sick wife, Grace.

Life, thought Dora — it was all beginnings and endings, war or no war. That would never change.

3

'I don't want to leave,' said Lily, pretending to pout as they packed their things. 'Can't we stay here for ever?'

They'd had two blissful days. They'd fed the swans the crusts saved from breakfast, then taken a rowing boat out on the river, floating down past, and through, the willows that veiled the banks. They'd ticked off the sights, Jim quoting 'Shall I compare thee to a summer's day?' in the knot garden of Shakespeare's birthplace and making Lily blush. And then there'd been the nights.

Jim waved a pair of socks at her as he put them in the suitcase.

'You just want to get out of doing my washing! Too used to the high life — you'll want a maid to do them, I suppose! Now come on, I've got to get the bike back!'

Lily smiled happily.

'All right then,' she conceded. 'We'll go. As long as we take this feeling back with us.'

Jim came round the bed and took her in his arms.

'Of course we will. In fact, it's only going to get better.'

'How can it?'

'Well,' said Jim, 'we've got to try out that new bed at home, haven't we?'

* * *

And when they got back, Jim was right, as usual, and the happy feeling persisted. Some things were still the

19

same — Jim had been lodging at Dora's for the last four years, after all, though now they shared a bedroom. For Lily, though, there were some changes to get used to, and enjoy, like the unaccustomed weight of the wedding band on her finger, and the feel of her two rings nestled together. 'Welcome to the club!' teased Gladys and Beryl when Lily proudly showed off her new ration book and identity card in her married name.

The first day back at work — Lily as first sales on Childrenswear and Jim as first sales on Furniture and also deputy supervisor on the first floor, they were the centre of attention. Everyone who hadn't been able to be there wanted to hear about the wedding and crowded round in the canteen to see the photographs once they were developed. Lily felt a thrill of pride when she collected her first wage packet in the name of Mrs L. Goodridge, though she was still addressed as 'Miss Collins' on the shop floor. Cedric Marlow, the owner, liked the old ways.

Lily felt some of her old ways, though, ought to change in keeping with her new status. She'd always helped her mum around the house, but now she felt she should do more.

'But you're out all day,' Dora protested when Lily suggested they should have a rota for shopping and cooking the evening meal.

'Other women manage, women with children as well,' replied Lily firmly. 'And I've got to learn. Jim and I will have our own home someday. I can't let him starve.'

At the table, Jim said nothing, busy working through the crossword in the local paper. He'd experienced Lily's cooking before, the sunken cake and the soggy

20

pastry, but he thought it prudent to keep quiet. 'Looking forward to it,' he said loyally.

With pride one night, Lily produced her first effort — macaroni cheese. Even though she'd sliced a tomato on top and put it under the grill for a few minutes, like the picture in the recipe, it still looked like a lumpy eiderdown on which someone had had an unfortunate accident. And when it came to taste . . .

'Very nice,' said Jim, chewing manfully.

Lily pulled a face.

'Your tastebuds must be working better than mine,' she said. 'It tastes like chewing gum in glue to me.'

'It's not easy making anything tasty with that powdered cheese.' Dora took a sip of water, perhaps to help her mouthful down. 'And the tomato's a nice touch, love.'

'You don't have to finish it, Mum, honestly.' Lily pushed her own plate away. 'I'm beginning to feel as if I've swallowed a piano.'

But Jim doggedly ploughed on, bless him, and even had a small second helping. Luckily Dora always kept a tin of bicarbonate of soda in the house.

★ ★ ★

Gradually, the new Mr and Mrs Goodridge settled into married life and their usual routines resumed. Jim returned to tending his precious veg in the yard on Sunday afternoons, and Lily often popped round to see Gladys.

'Well I voted for Mr Churchill and I don't mind anyone knowing,' Gladys declared as she poured their tea one Sunday towards the end of July. With so many men still awaiting demob overseas, and others still fighting the Japanese, the election results had been delayed so that their votes could be counted. Now they'd finally been announced. 'I feel sorry for him, poor man, leading us through the war and that's all the thanks he gets! Chucked on the scrap heap!'

Lily wasn't quite old enough to vote, but Jim, having put his cross in Labour's box, was cock-a-hoop at their landslide win.

'Mr Churchill's so old, though, isn't he?' said Lily. 'And . . . well, people want to move on from the war. Forget about it. I know I do.'

'Well, I can't do that till my Bill's home for good.' Gladys gave a sigh that came from somewhere deep inside. 'I haven't seen him since your wedding. He was hoping then he'd be demobbed within days.'

Gladys did seem low. She seemed to have forgotten that during the war she hadn't seen Bill for months, even years, at a time.

'You're tired, that's all,' soothed Lily. 'Tired of doing it all on your own.'

As well as the twins, Gladys had the burden of looking after her gran, who spent a lot of time in bed, but only because the older woman liked it that way. Florrie Jessop had taken Gladys in when her parents had been killed in the Coventry Blitz. It had seemed like an act of kindness at the time, but she led Gladys a proper dance, expecting her to chase around after her every whim. With the twins now walking, or rather staggering about and getting into everything, Gladys was often run ragged.

Lily led her friend to the comfiest chair and plumped up the cushion.

'You sit down for five minutes while the twins have their nap. I'll bring down your gran's dinner tray.'

'Would you? Thanks, Lily.' Gladys flopped into the chair. 'You're a godsend!'

Lily went out into the small hall. She had her foot on the first stair when behind her, she heard a key in the lock. Turning, she saw the door open and a familiar shape framed against the sun in the street outside. It was Bill — but not a Bill she'd seen before — a Bill with a smart new haircut and a snazzy demob suit!

He put his finger to his lips and Lily, getting his gist, pointed towards the back room. She then mimed that the twins were asleep and that she was on her way up to Gran. Bill gave her a thumbs up and tiptoed down the hall. Halfway up the stairs, Lily heard Gladys's shriek of delight and could imagine the rapturous reception Bill was getting.

To give Gladys and Bill some privacy, Lily lingered in Florrie's stuffy bedroom longer than she might have wanted, while the older woman droned on about her supposed aches and pains. She tidied the bedclothes and bedside chest with its sticky bottles of liniment, grubby handkerchiefs and well-thumbed copies of *Woman's Weekly* that Dora passed on. Lily was reading Florrie a serial about a Victorian governess from the *People's Friend* when the old woman finally dozed off. Lily crept downstairs. She had enough experience of married life herself now to know she didn't want to walk in on them, but surely Gladys and Bill's reunion would be over by now?

It was. When Lily knocked and ventured in, Bill, his braces down and tie loosened, was extracting something from the inside pocket of the suit jacket that was flung over a chair. He handed it to Gladys, who looked at what she was holding, puzzled.

'Tickets? Train tickets?'

'For a week's holiday,' Bill announced with thinly disguised pride. 'You, me, and the nippers. In Weston.'

'Oh, Bill!' Gladys was transformed from the worn-out drudge of before. All it needed was a glass slipper for a real Cinderella moment. Lily's heart sang with happiness for her friend, but the idea of Weston did make her smile.

'Weston?' she grinned. 'You are a case, Bill! You've just come home from six months there!'

Bill had been posted to HMS *Birnbeck*, a shore base in Weston-super-Mare for the last few months of the war.

'Which is how I've had plenty of time to get to know the place!' Bill retaliated with a grin of his own. 'It's ideal for the twins. Miles of sand, donkey rides, amusements, fishing in rock pools . . . I've found us a tip-top guest house, and booked that as well. A nice landlady, she'll provide a cot and all. Sea View, it's called.'

'When the tide's in!' smiled Gladys.

She'd visited Bill in Weston and had barely seen the sea, or so she'd said. But nothing was going to throw Bill off course. He was a sailor after all.

'Exactly!' he declared. 'We don't want pounding waves and cross-currents knocking Joy and Victor off their little legs, do we?'

Lily could see Gladys was welling up. It didn't take much.

'Oh Bill . . . You are lovely. So thoughtful.' Lily smiled fondly at them as Gladys spoke for every serviceman's wife — well, she hoped it was every one — 'It's so good to have you home!'

★ ★ ★

'Safe journey! Don't forget to send us a postcard!' shouted Lily from the platform as the train pulled out.

'Blimey!' Jim flinched away. 'I should think they'd have heard that if they were in Weston already.'

They'd come to the station to see their friends off. Now Joy and Victor had their noses pressed to the glass of the third-class compartment while Gladys waved, and Bill gave a thumbs up.

Lily tucked her arm through Jim's as the train shrank to a speck in the distance.

'I do hope they have a good time,' she said. 'Goodness knows, they deserve it!'

It would have been hard for the little family not to enjoy themselves, for Weston was everything Bill had promised. The sun even shone — some of the time — and it was a bit breezy, but at least it was dry. They did everything Bill had promised, too — they bought buckets and spades for Joy and Victor, even if the children were more interested in knocking mud pies and sandcastles over than building them. They dangled the twins' little feet in the water when the tide came in over the rippled sand. They took a boat out round the bay, Gladys squealing when they hit the slightest swell, Bill delighted to be on the water again and confidently leaping out to secure the rope when they came in to the jetty. Now, with Joy toddling and Victor on Bill's shoulders, they were dawdling along the prom — dawdling being the only progress possible, since apart from Joy's tottering steps, it was August bank holiday and Weston was jam-packed with trippers.

'It's a hard life, isn't it?' said Bill as they leaned on the rail overlooking the beach. Below them people had set up deckchairs and windbreaks on the portion of sand not still covered in barbed wire and 'Keep Out' notices. 'When the biggest decision of the day is shall I have kippers or use my bacon ration for breakfast!'

'And a wafer or a cornet come three o'clock,' smiled Gladys, a slave to her sweet tooth. Sugar was still rationed, of course, but at least ice cream was back on sale.

'Care for a photograph, sir?' said a voice behind them. 'You, the missus and the little 'uns?'

A photographer, not much more than a lad, in blazer and flannels, was beaming at them, his camera on a strap round his neck.

'What do you say, Gladys?' asked Bill.

'Ooh, yes please! Just give me a minute to run a comb through my hair and put a bit of lipstick on, can you?'

'Go on,' chided the photographer. 'You're as pretty as a picture as you are, isn't she, sir?'

He may have been young, but he had all the patter.

Gladys combed her hair and touched up her lipstick. She retied the bow in Joy's hair and straightened the bib top on Victor's shorts. Bill transferred his son from his shoulders to his arms so the photographer could fit them all in.

'Righto!' he called. 'Hold still, now! Watch the birdie! Say cheese!'

Gladys and Bill smiled obligingly, Joy beamed and Victor looked slightly suspicious, as he often did with anything new.

The photographer took three shots in quick succession, checked his camera, declared himself satisfied and presented Bill with a card.

'Ready for you tomorrow, sir. The booth's further

along the prom here, towards the big hotel.'

'Thanks,' said Bill. 'We'll come and take a look.'

'No obligation to buy, sir, but I'm sure you won't want to miss the chance of a lovely keepsake for the family and a nice memento of your trip. Happy days, eh?'

And off he bowled to accost a gaggle of girls who were sitting on the railings further along, licking ice creams and shrieking happily as the wind lifted their skirts.

★ ★ ★

'Oh, doesn't Bill look happy!' Lily exclaimed when Gladys showed her the photographs. 'I mean, you all do, but it looks as if you're all on a ship, with that railing and the horizon behind, and the breeze in your hair! Bill's in his element!'

'He was,' said Gladys. She was happy herself, despite the huge pile of washing they'd brought back which she was now sorting through. 'I think he'd have stayed there for ever. But we're home now, back to reality, and he's got to find a job. Did Jim manage to ask at Marlows for him?'

This was partly why Lily had come round.

'I'm sorry, Gladys,' she said reluctantly. 'There's nothing going, I'm afraid. Jim asked Mr Simmonds especially.'

Mr Simmonds was the senior supervisor at the store, overseeing all floors. He was married to Miss Frobisher, Lily's boss on Childrenswear.

Gladys wrinkled her nose as she added a stained nappy to the terry-towelling pile.

'No, well, I knew it was a long shot, and anyway . . . I

loved my job on Toys, but I can't really see my Bill doing shop work, kow-towing to customers all day, can you?'

Lily considered. She wasn't sure where she could see Bill, now she thought about it. Not in a shop or an office. In fact, not in a nine to five job at all. He was a Londoner by birth and had worked on boats all his life — first on lighters and then on pleasure cruisers on the Thames. The Navy had been the obvious service for him in the war and he'd done well, serving as a Wireless Operator at sea for over three years.

But those days were over. The war was properly over, too, even in the Far East. While Gladys and Bill had been away, the Americans had dropped two massive atomic bombs and the Japanese had finally surrendered.

'He'll find something,' Gladys went on. 'He's so willing and cheerful and easy-going. It won't be long before somebody snaps him up.'

Lily hoped she was right. She'd thought it best not to repeat what Mr Simmonds had actually said, and which Jim had known for himself. The local Labour Exchange was bursting at the seams with demobbed servicemen whose old jobs didn't exist any more or had been taken by stand-ins during the war, some of whom were being kept on. And with costs high and restrictions still biting, it wasn't as if businesses were keen to take on extra employees. Former staff had been applying to Marlows in their droves, and only a few had been re-hired.

As for Bill, his past experience was hardly relevant in their landlocked Midland town. Hinton was about as far from the sea as you could get — or any water, apart from the canal and the duck pond in the park. Oh well, as Gladys said, hopefully something would turn up.

4

'Miss Collins!'

Lily was clipping price tickets to boys' shorts with the fiddly little metal fasteners when Miss Frobisher approached. She was in one of her summer-weight outfits, a pearl-grey suit and an oyster-coloured blouse with a bow at the neck. When Lily had started at Marlows, the uniform code had been strict — a black or navy dress or skirt and white blouse. As clothes rationing had taken hold, though, Mr Marlow's strictures had had to be relaxed, but Miss Frobisher always kept to a palette of fairly sober colours — for work, anyway. In her early thirties, tall and slim, with swept-up honey blonde hair and an enviable figure, she could have worn a potato sack and looked good, anyhow.

Lily straightened up and smoothed down her own outfit — a pale blue blouse and grey skirt. Miss Frobisher had been at a management meeting.

'Yes, Miss Frobisher?'

'I have some news.' Miss Frobisher always got straight to the point. 'I've known this was coming, but Miss Thomas has formally handed in her notice.'

'Oh! That's a shame!'

With Miss Temple, Miss Thomas was one of the department's part-time salesladies, or salesgirls as they were called, rather ridiculously as both women had come out of retirement to help out during the war. It was no surprise that Miss Thomas, the older of the two, was keen to return to an easier life.

'Yes. But it leaves us — well, me — in something of

a quandary.'

'Yes?'

'Just because the war's over, the store's not going to be able to return to full staffing.'

Lily knew that pre-war, there'd been six staff on Childrenswear, three of them full-time.

'With rationing and coupons still the order of the day,' Miss Frobisher went on, 'the profits simply aren't there. Apparently, I'm supposed to manage with one full-time and one part-time member of staff, plus the junior, from now on.'

'I see . . . Well, we'll cope.'

Although, thought Lily, she couldn't work any more hours than she already did — or any harder.

Miss Frobisher straightened her wedding and engagement rings — she and Mr Simmonds were not long married themselves, though Miss Frobisher had a six-year-old son from a previous relationship. When she spoke again, she sounded uncomfortable.

'The thing is — it seems Nancy Broad has been taken on again.'

Lily looked blank.

'Miss Broad,' Miss Frobisher explained, 'was first sales on the department until just before you started. When she left to go into the Auxiliary Territorial Service.'

Now Lily really did see. If the department was to have only one full-time and one part-time salesgirl, and she and this Nancy person were at the same level . . .

'So I'll have to move?' she asked, trying to keep the dismay out of her voice.

Lily had worked on other departments — from the minute she'd begun as a junior, Miss Frobisher had been keen for her to progress. For experience, Lily had been sent off to Shoes, to Schoolwear and, last year, to Small Leather Goods on the ground floor. But of them all, she loved Childrenswear the best.

She'd spent four years learning all there was to know about overlocking and smocking, about boys' cap sizes and babies' romper suits. Marlows had dozens of departments, but Lily couldn't think of anywhere she'd rather be, or where she'd do so well or feel so at home. In Miss Frobisher she had a boss who was firm but fair, whom she liked and respected. Let alone the fact that Jim's department, Furniture and Household, was right next door, another plus.

'Not necessarily.' Miss Frobisher tried to sound reassuring. 'I pointed out to Mr Marlow that I have my first-floor supervisor duties as well. If I'm going to perform those to his satisfaction, then an extra body on Childrenswear is very necessary!'

There was a snag with this argument, and Lily realised it straight away.

'But not another full-time first sales wage. Not both me and Nancy. Another part-timer, or another junior apart from Molly, maybe . . .'

'I know.' Miss Frobisher lowered her voice. She was trying to sound reassuring. 'Initially, while Miss Broad settles in again, Mr Marlow has said I can keep both of you. That gives us a few weeks. In that time, I'll have the chance to make a better case. I'll talk it through with Mr Simmonds. Perhaps if he fights my corner with Mr Marlow . . .' She made a wry face. 'You know how it is. It might have been women who kept this country going throughout the war, but a man's word still carries more weight!'

'Well, that's nice, isn't it!'

Jim had had to go and visit a manufacturer of Utility furniture, so Lily had sought dinnertime refuge with Beryl, whose little bridal shop was tucked into one of Marlows' former window spaces. Beryl had been packing up a wedding dress and veil for collection, but Lily's news stopped her in her tracks.

'The hours and the effort you've put into that department!' Beryl went on. 'Running it by yourself when Miss Frobisher swanned off on her honeymoon, nearly getting yourself killed by being there after hours when that bomb dropped — and now you've got to move over for this . . . what's her name?'

'Nancy,' said Lily glumly. 'Nancy Broad.'

'Well, shabby, that's what I call it!' said Beryl indignantly.

'Nothing's going to happen straight away,' said Lily, clutching at straws. 'Miss Frobisher has argued to keep us both, in the beginning. And she hopes she can persuade Mr Marlow to keep us both there permanently.'

'Huh! I should think so too! Why should you be the one to move, when she left Marlows in the lurch to go and swank about in uniform!'

Lily said nothing. There was something Beryl didn't understand, and couldn't have done.

Even before she'd turned eighteen, and certainly once she had, Lily had thought of joining up. She'd felt guilty about staying home in Hinton; she wanted to do her bit for her country. But she'd been too late. At the ATS recruiting office she'd been told it wasn't worth them training her with the end of the war

33

expected within months. Lily had come to accept it, but there was still the tiniest niggle of regret. When she and Jim had children and they asked, 'What did you do in the war, Mummy?' was she only going to be able to say that she'd stood on a shop floor selling children's interlock vests? Now Nancy was going to come back, full of her exciting life in uniform, and rub it in. There was nothing for it, Lily thought. She'd better start practising a smile that didn't look too much like gritted teeth.

★ ★ ★

Of course, it would be on Nancy's first day that the bus was late. Lily wouldn't have minded, but she'd given up her usual walk to work with Jim to catch it because she especially wanted to be early. But the bus had barely got halfway into town when it juddered to a halt in a queue of traffic. Lily fidgeted and fretted for five minutes that seemed like hours, then couldn't bear it any longer. She pushed her way down the aisle and jumped off, hurrying along the pavement. Further along she saw the cause of the problem: the road ahead was blocked off by makeshift barriers with the sign: 'DANGER' attached. People were muttering about a ruptured gas main.

It wasn't unusual: gas mains, sewers, water pipes — there'd been so little money for repairs during the war that the ancient pipework was crumbling. But the road wasn't only blocked to traffic — even pedestrians weren't allowed through, so Lily had to run three sides of a square before arriving at Marlows just in time to sign in with the timekeeper, stuff her things in her locker and dash up to her department.

When she got to the first floor, Miss Frobisher's blonde head was bent over some stock sheets with a dark head beside her. Lily squared her shoulders, pinned on the smile she'd practised and approached.

'Good morning, Miss Frobisher. And . . . Miss Broad?'

The girl looked up. She was three or four years older than Lily, not as tall and fuller in the face and figure. She had a creamy complexion with rosy cheeks and glossy dark hair held back with two tortoiseshell clips. She was neatly dressed in a manner even Mr Marlow would have approved of — a charcoal grey skirt and crisp white blouse. Lily looked on enviously — in uniform most of the time, and on ATS pay, Nancy would have had plenty of money spare to buy nice things. Lily's rummage sale blouse (distinctly off-white) and skirt (also grey, but horribly baggy in the seat) looked very limp in comparison.

Nancy held out her hand and shook Lily's.

'Pleased to meet you,' she said.

Her voice was strong and clear with barely a trace of local accent, knocked out of her in the ATS, perhaps, just as Lily's own accent had become less pronounced over the years at Marlows, at work at least. What rank had Nancy held, Lily wondered. Promoted to lance corporal or a corporal maybe, and used to giving orders. Lily hoped she wouldn't try that here.

'You too,' she replied, already feeling false.

'Miss Broad needs to get to know how we do things these days,' Miss Frobisher said. 'I've made a start with the paperwork, but can I leave you, Miss Collins, to finish off and to show her where everything is kept?'

'Of course.' Lily had made a special effort the night

35

before to make sure everything on the rails and in the glass-fronted drawers was in apple-pie order. 'A pleasure.'

Perhaps that was laying it on a bit thick, but Nancy smiled back anyway. Her eyes were almost as dark as her hair. She looked, Lily thought, like the girl on the packet of Sun Maid raisins that her mum's friend Sam sometimes included in his much-anticipated food parcels from Canada. There was something so lively and attractive about her.

Miss Frobisher went off to join Mr Marlow on his daily tour of the first floor and Lily and Nancy were left to it. Lily took a deep breath. She wanted to lay the ATS ghost to rest as soon as possible — so she might as well come straight out with it.

As she opened one glass-fronted drawer after another, showing Nancy their contents, she began.

'It must be strange coming back here after your time away. What did you do in the war exactly?'

'Oh, that!' said Nancy airily. 'I was a predictor operator.'

'A what?'

'Kerrison predictors,' Nancy explained. 'In an ack-ack battery. Named after the bloke who invented them. Kerries, we called them.'

* * *

'She had a heck of a war, Jim, and the thing was, she was so modest about it!'

Lily had relayed some of what Nancy had told her over tea that night, but when she and Jim were undressing for bed, her head was still full of the girl.

Jim took the studs out of his collar and laid them in

36

the glass pin tray on the chest of drawers.

'The predictor's a bit like a telescope, right? The operator had to get the enemy aircraft in their sights, the gubbins inside the predictor did the calculations, and the predictor operator told the gunner when to fire.'

'That's about it.' Lily peeled off her slip and stockings and hung them over the back of the chair. 'With her Marlows experience, I expected Nancy to say they'd stuck her in the stores at a training camp or something, giving out sanitary belts and socks.'

'Come on, Lily, you know the ATS girls did a whole range of stuff.'

That much had become very obvious as Lily and Nancy had chatted. Admiring, despite herself, she went on:

'As well as the drills, and all the Army ways, she had to learn all about guns and pass a special test to do what she did. They didn't let any old body at these predictor things!'

Jim's mouth twitched, but he said nothing. He folded his trousers and placed them under the mattress to keep the creases in.

'She was at nine different sites in three years!' Lily marvelled. 'Cornwall, Yarmouth, Hull, then all along the South Coast, and in London and Croydon when those awful doodlebugs and V2s were falling.'

'The ack-ack guns weren't much use against those,' Jim pointed out, getting into bed.

'That wasn't her fault! I mean, what a terrifying job — and responsible, too, actually helping to win the war!'

When Nancy had told her, and oh-so-casually, Lily had been dumbstruck. She'd almost wanted to reach out and touch her, to make sure she was real. After her disappointment at not being able to join up, Lily had 'done her bit' at home in Hinton. She'd actually done a lot, joining Dora in the WVS. She'd carded wool, made camouflage nets and helped to resettle a second wave of child evacuees from London, escaping the V1s and V2s. She knew it had been valuable work, vital even, but it had been voluntary and piece-meal. Yet here was someone whose daily and nightly efforts had actually brought down enemy planes!

'You make her sound like Boudicca,' said Jim, snuggling down. He could see what was happening: Lily had always been prone to bouts of heroine-worship. It had been the same with Miss Frobisher, and still was, to a degree. 'Nancy Broad didn't do it all single-handed, you know!'

'No, but it's quite something.' Lily slipped her nightdress over her head and picked up her hairbrush. 'And all that moving about, place to place, starting over with new people, under pressure the whole time, under attack, dirty great guns going off in your ear . . .'

'Well, she's going to find it very dull back in Hinton, then,' said Jim. 'Maybe she'll leave within the month, and the problem on Childrenswear will be solved. That'd suit you, wouldn't it?'

'I don't know now.' Lily looked at him in the mirror as she brushed her hair. She put the brush down, turned and sighed. 'If she genuinely needs a job . . . Oh, it'd be so much easier if I could hate her, and I thought I would, but I really like her, Jim!'

'Well, I'm starting to go off her,' Jim replied, 'if she's going to occupy your mind this much.' He pulled down the covers and patted her side of the bed. 'Now come here and get into bed, please, and don't bring

Nancy Broad with you!'

Lily obeyed and as she slid into Jim's embrace, Nancy was quite forgotten.

5

During the grace period that Miss Frobisher had negotiated with Mr Marlow, Lily's opinion of her new colleague didn't change. In fact, the more she found out about Nancy, the more she admired her — and the worse she felt.

'My dad was in the Territorials,' Nancy explained as they swapped the position of a three-arm and a four-arm rail. The winter stock was beginning to dribble in. It was in paltry amounts, but it was still an excuse for a change-around. 'So he went straight off in '39. But they got him at Dunkirk.'

'Oh Nancy! I'm sorry. How awful.'

'Yeah. We heard afterwards that he got off the beach . . . but the ship he was on got struck before they'd hardly left the jetty and he was drowned.'

Lily shivered at the thought. So near and yet so far.

'The worst of it was,' Nancy went on, but matter-of-factly, rather than in a way that smacked of 'poor little me', 'my mum found herself someone else — or she'd been seeing him all along, I don't know. But she married him pretty darn quick. He came to live with us and it was clear from the start he didn't want me around. So I joined up. Added a year onto my age, and it was no questions asked at that time, they were that desperate.'

Lily had told Nancy about her frustrated attempt to join the ATS and how she'd been told she was 'too late' as the war was nearly over.

'But you've come back to Hinton even so?'

'Oh, my mum and stepdad have moved away.' Nancy bent and screwed the upright more firmly into the splay-legged stand. 'They're near my sister up north now. Her and my mum always got on better. I was a daddy's girl.'

Lily knew it was often the way. Her own father had died when she was a baby, but her mother had always said that in those few short months Lily had been the apple of his eye.

'So I'm lodging with my Auntie Marge and Uncle Bert. It's good of them to take me in, 'cos we've never been close. But it's only for now, till we know what's happening here.' She looked at Lily and pulled a face. 'It's awkward isn't it, both of us the same grade, and both with a right, sort of, to the job.'

Lily swallowed uneasily. 'Maybe we should have a duel,' she said. 'Hatpins at dawn!'

They both laughed, but time was ticking on. Someone was going to have to make way.

* * *

The following Sunday, Lily had arranged to meet Gladys and the twins in the park. Everyone still called it the park, but for the last six years it had been almost entirely turned over to allotments, and that wasn't going to change in the near future. The papers and the wireless were full of grim news about rationing having to continue for many months, maybe even for years. The situation in Europe was dire, and with winter approaching, some of Britain's food stocks would have to be sent there. Things at home were going to get even tougher. Dora often said she didn't know what she'd do without the vegetables Jim grew in their backyard.

The park's duck pond, though, had been restocked with a few mallards and was still a prime destination for migrating Canada geese. Lily wondered if the birds would survive the winter, or find their way onto someone's dinner table, but for now they were a source of delight to Joy and Victor. The twins were on their walking reins, Gladys holding Victor's strap, Lily clutching Joy's, so they could haul the children back from the water's edge when they strayed too close.

'I don't know what to do,' Lily told her friend when the twins had flung the few crusts which Gladys could spare into the water. 'Shouldn't I do the noble thing and give way to her?'

'Noble? You'd be mad! Why should you?' Gladys was indignant. 'I can't understand why she's been taken back on when loads of others who had a job at Marlows before the war have been turned away! What's so special about Nancy blooming Broad anyway?'

'She's a very good worker,' Lily acknowledged.

'My Bill's a good worker, but he can't find a decent job!'

Gladys was normally so even-tempered, but if it came to defending 'her Bill' or her children, she was a lioness.

Bill had been sorely disappointed in his search for work: all he'd been offered were casual labouring jobs. There were enough of those around with the number of bomb sites that had to be cleared, but he was having to travel to where the work was. He'd just picked up a job in Birmingham — there was plenty of bomb damage there — and had left earlier that day to stay in a hostel. He'd be away the whole week.

The lack of work for him in Hinton was a big disappointment for Gladys too. Having missed their early months, she'd expected Bill would finally be at home to see his children grow up and to enjoy family life. If this was going to be the pattern from now on, Gladys would be left coping with the twins — and her grumpy gran — on her own again.

'I know, and it's such a pity for you both,' Lily sighed. 'But Nancy's had a hard time of it. She's lost both parents one way or another, and she's so nice. She mucks in, she's never tried to get one over on me, she's lovely with the customers . . .'

'Well, I think you've gone soft,' declared Gladys. 'Possession's nine tenths of the law, that's what they say, isn't it? You sit tight!'

At that point, Victor took a reckless step towards the water and both Gladys and Lily lunged to rescue him. As they gently coaxed the twins away from the pond's attractions and back to the pushchair, Lily reflected that they'd done well to have any conversation at all. It was usually impossible to get through a sentence without an interruption from the twins. Children were delightful, but they weren't half hard work.

★ ★ ★

'What was the matter with you? You were tossing and turning all night!' Jim asked as they walked to work next day. It was late September, and the mornings, though still bright, were starting to have that unmistakable nip in the air.

'I couldn't sleep,' said Lily. 'I was thinking.'

Jim tucked her arm closer through his. He had a pretty good idea what must have been bothering her.

'Go on,' he said.

'Two into one won't go,' said Lily simply. 'There's only room for one first sales on the department, and no other vacancies in the store at that level. So if I'm going to make way for Nancy, and in all conscience I feel I should — then I'm going to have to take the plunge and leave.'

Jim stopped dead.

'You'd do that?'

'There are other shops in Hinton! Marks and Spencer, . . . Boots, even, or Woolworth's . . . and the smaller ones as well.'

Lily tailed off. Now she'd said the words out loud, she knew that leaving Marlows was the last thing she wanted to do. Jim knew it too.

'They don't all sell children's clothes and that's the bulk of your experience.'

'I know that. I'll have to adapt.' Lily had recovered her resolve and started walking again to show it. 'It's not as if I haven't worked on other departments. And it wouldn't hurt me to broaden my experience.'

Jim looked at her sidelong.

'Yes, right. Say it often enough, you might even come to believe it.'

'Oh, you're not helping'! Lily flared. 'Wave your magic wand then, and create me a job at Marlows!'

They were turning the corner now, and there, like a totem, was Marlows itself, with its elegant 1920s facade, its windows — now free of the ugly bomb-proof tape — gleaming in the sun, its name picked out in black and gold.

Jim turned Lily to face him, holding her by the

elbows.

'There's a few days to go before Mr Marlow's deadline is up,' he said. 'Hang on till then. Don't do anything rash.'

'Me? Rash?' Lily laughed — their shared past held some pretty good examples of her impetuousness. Then she sobered, leaning her forehead against the rough tweed of his overcoat. 'I just want to do the right thing, Jim.'

'I know you do.' Jim lifted her head and kissed her. 'And I love you for it.'

★　　★　　★

Miss Frobisher was closeted with a rep, Miss Temple was in the stockroom, Nancy was on early dinner and Lily was counting a bag of pennies into the drawer of the till. Cash tills on every department instead of the old pneumatic tubes were at least one thing they had to show for the end of the war.

'Lily! Lily!'

Lily looked up. Jim was speeding towards her, his face alive with excitement.

'I couldn't get away before,' he gabbled, 'we had a delivery, but it's happened! The Hand of Fate has intervened!'

'What are you talking about?'

Lily closed the cash drawer and placed the little cloth bag under the counter.

'The magic wand that *you* were talking about! Miss Miller's handed in her notice!'

Miss Miller, a mature lady of fifty, worked on Small Household, which came under Jim's department.

'Really? Why?'

45

'Her husband's got a job in Scotland! So she's got to move up there with him!'

'Oh! So you're thinking . . . her husband's old job here might suit Bill?'

'No, her husband's some kind of engineer, it's nothing Bill could do! I'm thinking about you, silly!'

'Why?' Light dawned on Lily. Miss Miller was first sales grade. 'Oh, I see . . . you mean for me to take her job? But Mr Marlow would never let you and me work on the same department, being married!'

'I know that,' said Jim patiently. 'But there's no reason why Nancy can't transfer, is there?'

Lily put her hands to her cheeks.

'Oh Jim! That would be wonderful!'

She looked swiftly left and right. There was no one senior in sight and she reached up and gave him a quick kiss.

'Well!' exclaimed Jim. 'I thought it was 'don't *shoot* the messenger', but I'm not complaining!'

And so, after all Lily's agonising, a solution had appeared. Nancy had been away from Childrenswear for long enough not to feel the kind of emotional attachment that Lily had to the department: she didn't care where she worked in the store, she said, as long as she had a job.

'There's so much to learn,' she marvelled when she came back to Childrenswear, flushed and excited after a morning getting to know the Small Household stock. 'It covers everything! Teaspoons and tray cloths, trinket trays and Thermos flasks — when you can get them . . . All those prices to remember and where everything's kept . . . My head hasn't spun this much since they tested us on all the stripes and pips on Army uniforms!'

Her enthusiasm was infectious.

'You do make it sound exciting. I'm quite envious now!' Lily smiled.

'No, you're best suited where you are,' said Nancy, calming down. 'I can see that. But me, I've got used to moving around these past few years. After nearly a month on here, I was starting to get itchy feet. But I shall settle down now and be sensible. I'll have to, with your Jim looking over my shoulder — I bet he'll be cracking the whip!'

'You've no idea,' warned Lily. 'You should see what I have to put up with at home!'

* * *

Miss Miller said her goodbyes, Nancy moved department, and with Lily's position on Childrenswear secure, she and Jim were happier than ever. She was even humming 'Sentimental Journey' when she and Jim pushed the back door open one evening to find Dora sitting stock-still at the table. She'd obviously been crying.

'Mum?' Lily asked anxiously, dropping her bag on a chair. 'What it is? It's not Reg, is it, or Sid? Has something happened?'

Dora shook her head.

'It's not the boys,' she said.

Jim tactfully took himself off upstairs. Lily peeled off her coat and sat down next to her mother.

'So tell me.'

Dora reached into the pocket of her apron and pulled out a letter. She pushed it towards Lily over the faded seersucker cloth — a flimsy airmail envelope with a Canadian stamp. It was from Sam, of course.

Lily took the letter out and unfolded it.

Dear Dora

I hope you and the family are well. I'll keep this brief, if you don't mind, because it's not great news. Grace died earlier this week. Her end was peaceful, which is a blessing as she had had so many struggles in the past few years since the loss of our son, and how it affected her mentally. She was never going to be the woman she was before, so perhaps the cancer was a merciful release.

I hope you are all doing OK. I gather from the news that things are not much easier in Britain even though the war is over, and that rationing is in fact even worse. I will continue to send what help I can in the form of food parcels, as long as you are happy to receive them. I loved the photographs, by the way, that you sent of Lily and Jim's wedding — it looked a very special day for you all.

With my best wishes,
Your friend,
Sam

Lily put the letter down.

'Oh, Mum. We knew it was coming, but . . .'

'That doesn't make it any easier.' Dora finished the sentence. 'That poor woman, how she's suffered. But it's Sam I feel for, all on his own.'

'Well, yes, but he's a strong person, Mum. And to be honest, he's been on his own since he went back to Canada. It's not as if he and Grace had been living together, not for years, with her — well, having a breakdown.'

48

'I know, love, I know. But it's hard when there's nothing I can do to help him from over here.' Dora took the letter back and put it in her pocket. 'Anyway, I must pull myself together and get the tea on. Jim'll be starving.'

'Don't worry about him! Do you want me to do the tea tonight?'

As she and Jim had come through the kitchen, there'd been the smell of stew, so that meant only the potatoes to prepare.

'No, no.' Dora stood up and automatically tucked her chair back under the table. Even in distress she still liked everything neat and tidy. 'The stew's made — lentils again, I'm afraid. I've only got the dumplings to drop in. And I'd rather have something to do.'

Lily nodded. She understood.

She watched her mum go and heard the familiar noises from the kitchen, the flour bin fetched from the larder, the crock mixing bowl and the old metal scales got out. Poor Sam — and poor Mum. Dora had always stoutly maintained that she and Sam were just good friends, but Lily had a strong suspicion there could have been something more — much more — between them, if things had been different.

With a sigh, she got up, went to the sideboard and got out the worn cork-backed mats. She dealt them out on the table, then went back for the cruet. In good times or bad, life had to go on. The war had taught her that.

6

And life did go on. Dora wrote back to Sam with her condolences and so did Lily on behalf of herself and Jim. Sam thanked them in his replies and said he was doing OK, but was glad he had his little hardware business to occupy him.

Lily and Jim were occupied as well. They went back and forth to work; they went out for a drink or to the cinema with Gladys and Bill, with Dora babysitting the twins. She also babysat for Beryl and Les's little boy, Bobby, when the four of them went dancing at the Palais. They'd gone dancing during the war, but it was so different now with no fear of raids and no blackout to stumble through on the way home. Lily had some new (second-hand, but new to her) sandals with stretchy Lurex straps and they sparkled as she and Jim twirled under the glitter ball to the music of Lou Praeger and Glenn Miller.

'Are you 'In the Mood'?' Jim whispered when they flopped into bed later. Lily was, of course she was. Love, as well as life, went on.

But in the morning she groaned when the alarm went off. She'd had another disturbed night, the sounds and sensations of the evening still playing in her head.

'It's all right,' Jim whispered, pushing her hair off her face to kiss her. 'It's for me, not you. I've got to get in early to print up the *Messenger*.'

Jim edited the Marlows staff newsletter, which meant he had to find the content, write the articles, and do everything else as well, including typing it up and turning the handle of the cyclostyle machine himself.

Lily yawned as he set the alarm again, giving her another half hour in bed, but she didn't go back to sleep and got up feeling sluggish and unrefreshed.

She was still yawning when she trudged up the back stairs at Marlows to the first floor. She'd have to snap out of it before she reached the department, as she'd be in charge. Miss Frobisher had warned her that she'd be spending a lot of the morning on the telephone chasing unfulfilled orders.

But as she pushed through the double doors, Lily stopped in her tracks. The first department you came to was Jim's — and there was Nancy. She was in the same position that Lily had seen her in on Nancy's first day back, with her dark head bent over stock sheets next to Miss Frobisher's blonde one. But this time, there were two dark heads close together over the stock sheets. And the other one was Jim's.

'Morning!' said Lily brightly as she passed. Was it her imagination, or did Nancy quickly move aside to put some distance between her and Jim? And did he look rather furtive?

In the days that followed, she couldn't help feeling on edge, and found herself watching Jim's department. When Jim had to lean across Nancy to straighten something in a display, Lily stiffened. When she saw them exchange a smile behind the back of a departing customer, she felt hot anger rise inside her. When Nancy wandered over and asked if she was on early dinner so they could 'have a gossip', Lily replied tightly that she was on late dinner that day, and didn't suggest an alternative. When Jim surprised her with a

51

bunch of flowers, Lily smiled and thanked him, but wondered if they were the product of a guilty conscience. And the more she tried to tell herself there was nothing going on between Nancy and Jim, the more she became convinced that there was.

Finally she could bear it no longer.

'What do you think?' she asked Beryl one Sunday afternoon, having confessed her fears. 'Am I right to be suspicious? Or am I going crazy?'

Beryl was giving Bobby his tea: an egg with soldiers. Children got priority for fresh eggs.

'Eat it all up, then there's a treat for afters!' she told her son, before turning her attention to Lily. 'Going crazy? I think you are already,' she said tartly. 'Jim? Two-timing you? You've got two pages glued together, more like! Jim'd never do that!'

'That's what I thought, but . . . OK, maybe not two-timing as such,' Lily admitted. 'But forming a — an inappropriate attachment!' It was a phrase she'd read in the local paper, the *Hinton Chronicle*, about a man who'd murdered his wife on the basis of one she'd formed — not that Lily was planning murder, or anything like it. 'Do you think I should ask him about it?'

'If you want to give him a good laugh, yes!' Beryl took the egg pan to the sink and started to wash it. 'Honestly, Lily, listen to yourself. Jim's not the two-timing kind!'

'I didn't think so . . .' said Lily miserably. 'But Nancy's very attractive. And, to be honest, I don't feel very attractive myself at the moment.'

'Well, jealousy isn't attractive,' said Beryl wisely. She put the pan to drain, and came back towards Lily, wiping her hands. She scrutinised Lily more closely. 'But you're right. You've lost your . . . your bloom.'

52

'I know. I can see that in the mirror. And I feel . . . well, so weary all the time.'

Beryl narrowed her eyes.

'Are you sure?' she asked. 'That it's this silly worry making you tired? You couldn't be, you know . . . in the club, could you?'

Lily was so shocked she had to grope for a chair and sit down. Bobby looked up from his egg as the chair scraped over the tiles.

'Finished!' he said, smashing the empty shell with his spoon to prove it. 'What's my treat, Mum?'

Beryl produced a jelly from the larder and, to cheers from Bobby, she slopped some into a bowl.

'And as a special treat you can take it next door and eat it,' she said. 'Dad's in there. But don't you make a mess! And what do you say?'

'Thank-you-for-my-nice-tea-can-I-get-down-now,' gabbled Bobby as Beryl took off his bib and he scrambled down.

'Good lad.' Beryl opened the door that led into the back room and shooed him through.

'What have you got there, son?' Les could be heard saying before Beryl shut it again and sat down in Bobby's place.

'Well?' she asked Lily. 'Do I take it from your reaction that you could be?'

Lily nodded dumbly.

'I'm late, I knew that. But thinking about it, it's about six days now.'

Beryl gave her a knowing look.

'Let me guess. Not long married . . . I bet there's been at least one occasion when you didn't take precautions.'

Lily nodded again. There'd been at least one.

'But is this what it feels like?' she asked. 'Just sort of . . . off-colour? I thought you were sick, or felt sick anyway?'

'Not always,' said Beryl. 'You might be one of the lucky ones.'

Lucky? Lily wasn't sure if that was the word. If it was true, it was amazing, but, but . . . the timing . . .

'Oh Beryl,' she said. 'I don't know what to think!'

'Well, you'll have to get it confirmed,' said Beryl. 'And then tell Jim the happy news.'

'Yes,' said Lily, still stunned. 'But don't tell anyone else, Beryl please. Not till I've had a chance to get used to the idea myself.'

★ ★ ★

She walked back from Beryl's in a trance; it was a good job she knew every paving slab, kerb and junction on the way, and that continued petrol rationing was keeping the traffic down. All evening, Lily was lost in thought, answering her mum's questions and responding to Jim's comments automatically, not knowing if she was making any sense. Jim noticed of course, and Dora, but Lily dismissed their concerns, saying she had a headache, and took herself off to bed early.

Beryl had told her she'd be wise to wait a bit longer before asking the doctor for a test, but now Beryl had put the idea into her head, Lily didn't need it confirmed. She was pregnant. Expecting. Going to have a baby. Lying in bed, she felt her tummy — still completely flat. The idea that there might be a new life beginning to form inside her made her feel very peculiar indeed.

54

The next few days were dreadful. Lily hated lies, and she might have known that she couldn't hide it for long. One evening after work, she and Jim were at home on their own. Dora had gone out to an emergency Red Cross meeting about winter clothing for refugees, who were still arriving in droves from Europe, leaving a note to say the cottage pie simply needed putting in the oven. She hoped she'd be back, but they were to get on and eat if she was late; she'd have hers later.

Lily was watching the clock; she was hungry. That was another thing: the mind really was a very powerful influence. Now she was convinced she was pregnant, her appetite had increased: she was definitely eating for two.

Jim came in from outside where he'd been locking up Gert and Daisy, the hens. He washed his hands at the sink.

'Their bedding needs changing,' he said. 'I'll have to pinch some newspaper out of the salvage.'

Lily didn't reply. She prodded the bubbling pan of carrots with a fork.

'Oh hurry up and cook!' she admonished them, slamming the lid back on and turning the gas up.

'You're not right, are you?' Jim shook drops of water from his hands and started to dry them. 'You're not yourself, Lily. And you're very pale. Like your mum says, if you're still getting these headaches like the other night, you ought to see the doctor.'

'I'm fine!' Lily threw down the fork with a clatter. 'I wish you'd both stop checking up on me!'

Jim twitched his eyebrows in surprise.

'I wasn't trying to start a row,' he said mildly.

'I'm not rowing!' Lily snapped, then sighed. 'Look,

the nights are drawing in, it's getting to be a miserable time of year and I'm busy at work now we really are down to one first sales and one part-timer —'

'I don't understand. That's what you wanted, isn't it? Nancy gone?'

'Correct!' cried Lily, frustrated and almost in tears. 'But no, you don't understand! Oh . . . just leave me alone!'

'OK. As you wish.' Looking hurt, Jim retreated into the other room. Lily heard him turn on the wireless.

She grasped the edge of the cold china sink and braced her shoulders. She felt as if she was losing her mind. What was she doing, treating Jim like this? Was that what she wanted, to drive him into Nancy's arms — and when she was carrying his child?

Tears leaked from her eyes. It should have been the most marvellous news in the world. It shouldn't have been a secret between her and Beryl. It should have been a secret between herself and Jim — their special news, to tell everyone when it was confirmed and to see everyone's delight — surprise too, maybe, but chiefly delight. But how could Lily feel delighted when, amazing as it was, the timing was so . . . she had to admit it, so . . . wrong?

Jim's words rang in her ears. 'That's what you wanted, isn't it? Nancy gone?' Well, yes — and now, she knew, no! Not if it was for Nancy to work on Jim's department, close to him, literally, every day, while Lily could only watch from afar, while she was still there at all.

She'd tried telling herself she was being ridiculous, especially after Beryl's lecture on the subject, but she knew she was watching their every move. Much as she tried to tell herself that Jim and Nancy were colleagues — of course they had to work alongside each other, in close proximity sometimes, moving stock, setting up displays, and of course they had to confer — every fibre of her being screamed when she saw them together. She cursed herself when she remembered how she'd talked Nancy up to Jim in the early days, singing her praises — practically inviting him to like her! And now Lily was having a baby. And instead of it being the most wonderful thing in the world, all that she could think of was that she'd get big and ugly and unattractive and then it would be all exhaustion and nappies and the smell of sour milk — she'd seen it with Gladys and Beryl — and she'd be stuck at home and then it was only natural that Jim would be attracted to gay, slim, vibrant Nancy and . . . and . . .

There was a hiss as the carrots boiled over and extinguished the flame. Blinded by tears, Lily snatched off the lid, wrenched the pan off the gas, clattered the colander into the sink and tipped the pan wildly over it. A cloud of steam shot up and she only realised when she felt the hot pain that she'd splashed boiling water onto her wrist.

'Ow! Ow! Ow!' she cried.

Jim shot back into the kitchen.

'What is it?'

Lily cradled her hand, the inside of her wrist already shading pink.

'Scalded myself,' she whimpered.

Jim turned on the cold tap and shoved her wrist under it.

'Shh, shh, it's all right,' he soothed. 'Keep it under the water a good five minutes. Then we'll find some acriflavine cream to put on it — your mum's bound to have some somewhere.'

Lily sagged against him.

'I'm sorry, Jim,' she sobbed. 'I'm so, so sorry.'

'What for? My tea's not ruined — yet!'

'Oh Lord, the pie! Can you check on that before it burns too?'

'Keep that wrist under the water!' Jim did as he was told, then straightened up. 'It's fine. Five more minutes, I reckon.'

He put the carrots back in the pan with the lid on to keep warm, then, when he was satisfied Lily had cooled her injury enough, he led her to a chair.

'Now come on,' he said. 'You're not fobbing me off any longer. Tell me what's going on.'

So Lily told him.

She told him about her feelings, irrational and impossible as they were, about him and Nancy.

Jim threw back his head and laughed.

'And that's what's been the matter?' he said. 'Oh, Lily! I knew you'd been looking over my way a lot, but I thought it was because you couldn't get enough of me! Look, Nancy's a nice girl, and good at her job, but I don't see her as any more than a colleague, I never have and I never would!' Then he sobered. 'You do believe me, don't you?'

'Of course I believe you! I know it was stupid, but I couldn't help myself. Because there's something else, Jim.'

'Don't tell me, you've fallen madly in love with Lance.'

Lance was the junior on Small Household, a gangling youth of fifteen, spotty and still wet behind his sticking-out ears. But the time for joking was past.

'I'm expecting.'

'What?'

'I'm having a baby. We're having a baby.' At that moment, the latch on the back gate clicked. Lily put her finger to Jim's lips, which were parted in amazement. 'There's Mum now. Please, not a word to her. It's not confirmed, but I know, Jim. I just know.'

The back door opened and, all bustle and a blast of air, Dora was on top of them.

'Hello, both! Ooh, something smells good! I need it, it's gone that cold out there! You haven't had yours yet, have you?' Lily and Jim shook their heads dumbly. 'Good, let me get my coat off and let's eat, shall we?'

7

Before they could eat, Dora had to take a look at Lily's wrist. She bound it loosely with a bit of dry rag — acriflavine, she said sternly, was for burns, not scalds.

'It's nothing serious. Jim's first aid training helped,' she said. 'We've got the war to thank for that, anyhow!'

Lily's not-so-serious scald still gave Jim an excuse to be attentive and to bear her off upstairs early, leaving Dora with her basket of mending.

In their room, Jim took Lily in his arms. He looked at her with a mixture of disbelief, wonderment and something like awe.

'Lily, this is so … incredible. Amazing. I didn't hear wrong, did I? You're having a baby. We're having a baby?'

'You didn't hear wrong.'

'How long have you known?'

'Not long. Like I said I'm not certain. But I'm ten days overdue now.'

'And I thought we'd been careful,' smiled Jim.

'You know we haven't. Not always.'

Jim grinned, giving her a swift kiss. 'Even so. I'm stunned.'

'So was I when I realised. Still am really.'

Something in her tone, a hint of flatness, alerted him.

'Lily — is something wrong? You are pleased, aren't you? I don't know how I kept from blurting it out to your mum all evening, it's sort of bubbling away inside

60

me —' He broke off as he realised, and the realisation clouded his face even more. 'I know. It's what we were talking about before, isn't it? Marlows. You've just got where you want to be at work.'

'Yes. But . . .' she faltered. 'This changes everything.'

'It doesn't have to,' urged Jim. 'It's not going to happen for months and when it does, it's not the end of all that.'

'Oh come on, Jim! You know it is!'

'It's a temporary halt, that's all. You can go back to work, I'm not going to stop you! Your mum'd love to look after the little one, I'm sure.'

Lily smiled at him sadly. Back to work, maybe, until the next baby; all being well, she was sure they wouldn't want to stop at one. And then, once there were two to look after, could she expect her mum to do that, day in, day out, on top of the alteration work she did for Beryl to supplement her widow's pension? No one expected married women to work, let alone ones with children. If anything, Lily would only be able to work part-time, like Miss Temple, and probably have to drop down to second sales to do that. She couldn't assume whatever position she got would be on Childrenswear, either. Earlier in the year, Mr Simmonds had said that Lily's next move could be to junior buyer, and beyond that, the dizzy heights of buyer beckoned. Not now.

'You don't look convinced.' Jim lifted her chin to make her look at him. 'But it can be done. Look at Beryl! Look at Miss Frobisher!'

Lily shook her head.

'Beryl had an idea for her own business; I don't. And Miss Frobisher — that's not the same. She had to work because she was bringing up her son alone, and it was the war, anyhow. All women worked, married ones, ones with children, whatever. I have to be realistic — it's different now. My life will be different from now on.'

Dora had a phrase — she had a phrase for most things — 'better out than in'. And now Lily had admitted how mixed up she felt — a conflict that almost seemed traitorous — she did, in some obscure way, feel better.

She took Jim's hands.

'Look, Jim. Don't get me wrong. I am pleased — or I will be, I know I will be, once I've come to terms with it. I think I'm still in shock, really.'

Jim smiled the smile she loved, the one that told her she could tell him whatever she was thinking, even when the thoughts were ugly and unbecoming ones, and he'd understand.

'It's a massive thing to come to terms with,' he said. 'Even if it had been planned — which it wasn't. Far bigger for you than for me. Life-changing.'

'Yes.' Lily smiled too, a steadier, happier smile, one of relief that he understood; that they were in this together. 'But look, in the end Marlows is just a job and this is a baby. A new life. A miracle.'

Jim kissed her again.

'It is. We hadn't expected it — well, not so soon — but it'll be wonderful, Lily. We'll make it wonderful. And you are going to be a wonderful mother.'

Lily wished she felt as sure.

★ ★ ★

On their next half-day from the shop, Lily arranged to go and see Gladys.

62

'I'm going to see what I can learn from the most devoted mother I know,' she told Jim as he got into his old gardening trousers, ready to lift some potatoes. 'Apart from my mum, of course.'

They'd agreed not to say anything to Dora until they were certain beyond doubt, and Lily wasn't planning to tell Gladys either, not yet. She'd told Jim that Beryl knew — that in fact it was Beryl who'd pointed it out — but for all Beryl's big talk, she could keep a secret when she had to. They'd kept enough of hers, after all — including when she'd got pregnant well before she and Les were married.

But when Lily got to Gladys's, all was not sweetness and light.

'Kept me awake all night, they did, those two little perishers,' Florrie Jessop grumbled before Lily had even sat down. Gladys was getting the twins up from their after-dinner nap and Bill was out, job-hunting as usual. 'First one then the other — teething again! I don't feel like I've had a wink of sleep! I've got bags under my eyes you could put a week's washing in.'

'Oh dear,' said Lily pointedly. 'So Gladys had a disturbed night as well. She had to get up to them — at least you could stay in bed.'

Florrie grunted. She really was a first-class misery.

'Sorry, Lily —'

Gladys came in, carrying a wriggling Victor, while Joy toddled behind. Florrie tossed her head with an impatient 'tch!' and headed for the door.

'I'll leave you to it now you've got your friend to help you,' she said — as if she'd been helping in the first place.

Joy made for Lily and presented her with the filthy rabbit she carried everywhere. As Lily expressed delight and jiggled the rabbit on her knee, Gladys put Victor down. He immediately made for the tablecloth and started tugging at it. Gladys grabbed him and set him on the rug with a rag book, a wooden engine and, unfortunately, a tin drum. She straightened up, rubbing her back.

'My back's killing me! It was walking these two up and down all night, it's a wonder I didn't come through the floor!' Remembering herself, she apologised. 'Sorry, Lily, I haven't even said hello. Cup of tea?'

'I'll make it.'

Prising Joy's surprisingly strong fingers off her skirt, Lily stood up, and felt immediately light-headed. She'd had this feeling a couple of times lately — another early symptom, she supposed. At least she wasn't nauseous, in fact she was constantly hungry: it wouldn't be long before Dora noticed that the loaf wasn't lasting as long as usual. Lily had made an appointment at the doctor's, but she knew already what he'd confirm. Then everyone could be told.

In the kitchen doorway, she turned and looked at Gladys. Backache forgotten, she was on all fours tickling a chuckling Joy while Victor, shrieking, clambered on her back to use her as a rocking horse. Florrie could be heard from above, banging her stick on the floor in protest at the noise. A taste of things to come? It was a far cry from the sedate atmosphere of the sales floor at Marlows, that was for sure.

After they'd drunk their tea safely out of reach of the twins, Lily got down on the floor too, snatching moments of conversation with Gladys when the children allowed. Once they'd calmed down, they were both very sweet and very comical. Joy nestled into Lily's side, thumb in mouth, while she read *The Three*

Little Pigs. Victor, the clown of the pair, played peep-po from behind the rag book, before placing it over his head like a bonnet. Lily marvelled at their soft yet solid little bodies, and breathed in the scent of nappy cream and baby powder. Their hair was so silky, their skin so peachily perfect. She couldn't help smiling at the way they got frustrated when they couldn't fit the wooden block in the right slot; the way they beamed when you helped them and the resulting thud meant success. No wonder Gladys loved them so. And when they were your own . . . maybe it would be all right after all . . .

Bill came home after about an hour, and Lily didn't need to ask if he'd had any luck on his job search. His face said everything and she thought it best to make a tactful exit.

As Lily closed the back door behind her, Gladys turned to her husband. Bill had slumped in a chair.

'Nothing,' he said curtly. 'Oh, I tell a lie. Public lavatory attendant in Tipton, or street sweeper in Dudley. Take your pick.'

'Oh, Bill. Not even labouring?' Gladys knelt beside him and took his hand. One nail was black and two fingers swollen where a concrete block had dropped on it on his last labouring job.

'Sweet FA.' Their hands were joined on his thigh, and he plucked at the material of his suit — his demob suit. 'But it's not all bad news. A feller outside a pub offered me seven pounds ten for my suit. I've taken his name and address. I'll take it round later.'

'Your suit?'

'I don't need it, do I? The only place I ever go is the Labour Exchange, and I'm a bit overdressed for that. It's not like I'm going to get a position as a bank manager, is it?'

'But your demob suit — do you have to?'

Bill grimaced.

'Get real, Glad. Winter's coming and the 'leccy bill's going to go up. Christmas is coming. The kids need shoes and coats, let alone presents. You need a warm coat, and a decent one, not worn-out rummage. We need a bigger pram or a pushchair. We're running down our savings as it is.'

Gladys stretched up and kissed him.

'You're a good man, Bill. I'm lucky to have you.'

'You won't say that when we're on the streets.'

'We won't be on the streets! It's Gran's name on the rent book, for a start.'

'Yeah, your gran.' Bill couldn't help pulling a face. 'She's not cheap to feed, either, all them barley sugars.'

As Victor tried to grab Joy's rusk and Gladys went to break up the squabble, Bill sat back in the chair. He wouldn't be sorry to see the suit go. It mocked him now, the replacement for the uniform he'd worn so proudly — well, not always that proudly, to be honest. But when he thought now about how he and his shipmates had groaned at reveille, at another kit inspection or lifeboat drill . . . How he'd longed for home after months on end in the stuffy sleeping quarters he shared with five others, a break from the whining interference of the radio waves when he was trying to get a fix on a signal and the endless monotony of the grey seas when he was on watch, straining his eyes for the sight of an enemy ship . . . How he'd missed Gladys and the twins, how he'd longed to be with them. And now he was . . . he loved being with them, he loved being a family man, but wasn't his job

66

as a husband and father to provide for them? Was that too much to ask?

★ ★ ★

The following Wednesday afternoon Lily had her doctor's appointment. The sample she'd dropped in still had to come back from analysis, but the doctor made her lie down and prodded her tummy lightly, though Lily suspected that was simply for show. He surely couldn't feel anything — the baby was barely the size of a broad bean, from what a quick peek at her mum's *Home Doctor* book had told her. But when she'd rearranged her clothes, the doctor said he could already confirm what he called 'the happy news'. Smiling, because it was expected, Lily took the leaflets about free orange juice and the extra rations she'd be entitled to. This was it, then. She was going to be a mother. She and Jim were going to be parents.

'What does it feel like to be right every time?' she asked Beryl when they met in Lyons afterwards, as they'd arranged. Beryl's Brides, like all the other shops in Hinton, closed for a midweek half-day.

'Pretty good,' said Beryl smugly.

Lily poured their tea. Beryl was turning her teacake this way and that, looking for the almost invisible smear of butter.

'Due in the summer. Late June or early July. Barely a year after the wedding.'

Beryl took a bite of her teacake and made a face.

'Sawdust,' she said. And then, looking at Lily shrewdly, she asked: 'You're not sure you're ready, are you? When you thought you'd be going a lot further up the ladder at Marlows.'

Lily stared out of the window. Woolworth's was opposite, where she'd thought she might have to take a job after Nancy had come back. Now, of course, things would work out anyway: Lily would leave, and Nancy might well go back to being first sales on Childrenswear; she wouldn't be working closely with Jim any more, not that there'd been anything to be jealous of there in the first place. Very neat. Quite a silver lining, if you wanted to look at it that way.

She turned back to Beryl.

'Maybe that's why it takes nine months to grow a baby,' she said, stirring her tea with its miserly ration of sugar. 'So you have time to get used to it.'

Beryl reached over and touched her hand.

'You wouldn't . . . no, you're too sensible. Too . . . moral.'

'What?'

'Well, you know when I got pregnant with our Bobby. And I wasn't sure how Les'd take it — we weren't even together any more at that point. And I tried that silly business with the hot bath and the gin . . .'

'No! Never! Nothing like that! How could you think . . . ?'

'OK, OK! I just had to say it, that's all. I never thought you would.'

'I wouldn't dream of it.'

'Good. But you don't need to — you're married, and you've got your lovely Jim — and your mum. It was you and your mum that straightened me out, made me see sense, wasn't it, and got me back together with Les. And you and Jim were such a help when I got into a mess with the business . . .' Beryl grasped Lily's hand across the table. 'I'll be right by your side in this, Lily. I owe you such a lot.'

68

'Thanks, Beryl.' Lily couldn't help but be moved by Beryl's sincerity.

'Your mum'll be thrilled,' Beryl reassured her. 'And Gladys will be too, once she knows. She's still got plenty of baby stuff hers have outgrown that she can lend you.'

'I know. Thank you, Beryl, really.'

'Don't be daft, that's what friends are for!' Lightening the mood, Beryl issued a challenge. 'Now eat up! And the first one to find a proper currant in these so-called teacakes gets to guess if it's a girl or a boy!'

8

Another week passed, but still Lily held back from sharing the news about the baby.

'Gladys didn't say anything till she'd passed twelve weeks,' she told Jim. 'How about that? By then it'll be Christmas, Sid'll likely be home — maybe Reg and Gwenda too, they'll surely be due some home leave before their next posting.'

Reg had written to say that he and Gwenda had been offered the chance to transfer to Palestine, and were going to take it. They'd heard, they said, that things weren't too rosy for returning servicemen and women back home. Gwenda's dad owned a garage in Welshpool, and there'd been the hope, from Dora at least, that Reg, a trained mechanic, could be taken into the business, but with petrol still rationed, there simply wasn't the trade to justify an extra salary.

'Whatever you like.' Jim sounded puzzled. 'But are you sure you don't want to tell your mum on her own beforehand?'

Lily shook her head.

'Let's tell everyone together,' she said.

In her heart of hearts, she knew it was an excuse: if she said anything, her mum was bound to sense her lingering doubt. She was still buying time to get more used to the idea, to get the story straight in her head — all right, to accept the situation — so that when she and Jim did break their news, she could do it with genuine pleasure.

And over the next couple of weeks, Lily found that

70

it was working. She peered into prams when she passed young mothers, or fell into step with them, asking how old their baby was and trying to guess if it was a boy or a girl — almost impossible now they were swaddled up against the colder weather. If the baby started to cry or grizzle, she marvelled at the confident way the mothers announced, 'He's tired' or, 'She's hungry', and thrilled at the thought that she'd one day be attuned enough to tell her baby's cries apart. She smiled at toddlers as they waited at zebra crossings, and felt for them if an impatient mother dragged them across faster than their little legs could carry them. When a harassed mother yanked a small child away from a sweetshop window with a curt 'No! You've had your ration this week — and stop your blarting or I'll give you something to cry for!' it was all Lily could do not to rush over and offer up her sweet coupons instead. She placed a hand protectively over her stomach. 'I'll never speak to you like that,' she whispered, and in that moment she knew she'd not only accepted her baby, she wanted it and she loved it. Jim had said she'd be a wonderful mother, and she would be, she was determined. And she changed her mind on something else, as well.

'Let's sit Mum down on Sunday, shall we, and tell her together?' she asked Jim that night.

They were both run ragged at work: it was November by now and the run-up to Christmas had begun. As usual, Jim was in charge of masterminding the construction of the store's grotto and the arrival of Father Christmas, always a big money-spinner for the store. As the first post-war Christmas, Mr Marlow wanted the event to be bigger and better than ever, without, of course, allocating any more resources. He was notably cautious with money.

'Oh! You do want to tell her first, then?' Jim was delighted. He'd known perfectly well what had lain behind Lily's wish for a delay.

Lily nodded happily. 'The sooner she starts knitting the better!'

'That's settled then,' said Jim with satisfaction. 'Now, what do you think? A whip-and-top or a little colouring book?'

He was pondering a catalogue of 'pocket-money' toys, trying to pick one for the small gift every child would get from the grotto's Father Christmas. Lily got up to look over his shoulder, and, as she did so, felt something like a cramp.

'Ooh. I'll just . . . I think I need the privy,' she said.

She pulled her cardigan over her chest as she stepped into the cold of the yard. The blue bricks were gleaming with the rain that had fallen all afternoon; clouds scudded sullenly across the sky.

Buddy's nose poked out from his kennel.

'It's all right, Buddy. It's only me.'

Lily opened the door of the privy and turned on the torch that hung on the hook. That was as far as she got before another, fiercer cramp clenched her stomach — and another. She put out a hand to the cold, slimy wall to support herself. This didn't feel right. What was happening?

★　★　★

'How are you feeling, love?'

Lily opened her eyes at the sound of her mum's voice.

'OK. But . . . oh Mum!'

'Shh, shh, there, you have a good cry.'

Lily was tucked up in her bed, in their bed, hers and Jim's.

It was all over. After her frantic cries from outside to Jim, and after one look at her, his cries to Dora, who'd been upstairs, they'd taken her inside. Jim had gone for the doctor while her mother had held her hand as the pains continued, with the inevitable result. The doctor had come and confirmed what everyone knew. The baby, the beginnings of a baby, was no more.

'I'm so sorry, Mum,' she sobbed. 'And I hadn't even told you. We were going to do it on Sunday.'

'Don't be silly, you don't have to say sorry to me! I dare say you wanted to be sure!' Dora sat on the edge of the bed, took a handkerchief from her sleeve and dabbed away her daughter's tears. She took her hand. 'It's not unusual for this to happen, Lily. It's more common than you know, especially early on.'

'That's what the doctor said,' Lily sniffed.

'It's a bitter blow. But it doesn't mean you'll never carry a baby. Sometimes, love, it's your body cleaning itself out ready for the next time.'

'Just your body? Or does your mind have something to do with it?'

Dora pulled back to look at her.

'What on earth are you talking about?'

Lily took the handkerchief and scrubbed viciously at her eyes.

'When I first found out, Mum, I wasn't at all sure. We hadn't planned it — it was too soon, I wasn't ready. To be honest, I was horrified.'

'Oh, Lily.'

'In the last couple of weeks I was coming to accept

73

it, to look forward to it, even, to want it, but what if how I felt early on made this happen?'

'Now that's silly talk,' said Dora firmly. 'You can't will something like this. It's physical, not mental. You must put any thought like that right out of your head.'

Lily closed her eyes. She didn't know if she believed or disbelieved her mother. Right now she couldn't sort out in her confusion and distress what was grief and what was guilt.

Dora said no more, but went downstairs to make her some hot Bovril, saying she'd send Jim up. He came in quietly, opening the door a crack at first, as if he was terrified to face her.

'What are you creeping about for?' asked Lily, in a flash of her usual self.

Jim came and sat on the bed. He took her hand.

'I didn't know what to expect,' he said. 'Tears, I suppose.'

'Oh, I'm done with those.' Lily indicated the balled-up handkerchief on the counterpane. 'For now. But I expect there'll be more.'

'I expect there will.' With his other hand, Jim took off his glasses and Lily saw that his eyes, too, were wet.

'Oh, Jim!' her voice broke as she reached up to him. He bent and took her in his arms. 'I feel so empty!'

'I know. It's strange to feel so upset about something that was hardly even there.'

'And that I didn't want to be there!'

'Now that's not true, is it?'

'Yes it is — at the beginning at least —'

'Lily,' said Jim firmly, pulling away and taking her chin in his hand. 'Look at me. We both knew that the timing wasn't right. You knew it, and I knew it, deep

74

down, even when we tried to argue ourselves out of it. Now your body has told you the timing wasn't right, or something with the baby wasn't right. And you can't argue with that.'

Lily bent her head.

'We'll get over this,' said Jim, holding her close again. 'We're in it together, remember?'

Downstairs, Dora waited for the kettle to come to the boil. She'd thought there'd been something different about Lily, something in her look, something in her manner. She'd known her daughter was holding something back. Well, maybe, sad as it was, what had happened was for the best. Lily and Jim were so young. Oh, they'd have risen to the challenge, and she'd have helped them all she could. But the war had taken away so much of their freedom. They deserved to live a little, to enjoy their youth, their friends, and the work they loved — Dora was sure that had been a large part of Lily's uncertainty about a baby — before they started to think about a family of their own.

The kettle hissed and rattled on the gas. Hot drinks and warm words, that's how they'd got through the war. That's how they'd get through this, for now, anyway.

Jim came into the kitchen as she watched the spoonful of Bovril dissolve.

'I'll take that up,' he said.

Dora handed him the cup.

'She'll be all right,' she said. 'You both will.'

'Yes.'

'Not straight away, but it'll pass. And Jim —'

'Yes?'

'I gather this baby wasn't planned. So the two of you might want to try to be a bit more careful in future.'

Jim gave a slight inclination of his head and left.

Dora rinsed the spoon under the tap. Her first grandchild . . . ah well. The time would come.

★ ★ ★

Lily had a day in bed at her mother's insistence, but one day of lying there feeling miserable was enough. On the second day she got up and pottered around the house, but that too did nothing to shift the leaden cloak of wretchedness she was wrapped in. There was only one thing for it.

'What do you think you're doing?' demanded Dora when Lily came downstairs the next day dressed for work.

Lily put a pinch of tooth powder on her brush and went to the sink.

'What does it look like? I'm better being occupied, Mum. You've said so yourself, many times.'

Then she turned on the tap to drown out any more of her mother's protests.

Over the following weeks, in the pre-Christmas rush at work, there were times when Lily really did forget about the baby for maybe twenty minutes or half an hour at a time. But the leaden cloak wasn't that easy to shrug off. Wherever she went, wherever she looked, there were women with prams and push-chairs, and pregnant women too, scores of them, their swollen bellies evidence, no doubt, of joyful reunions with demobbed husbands. Lily's own body, bizarrely, tricked her sometimes into thinking she was still carrying a child — her breasts ached, and she often felt light-headed, despite the nourishing food Dora made

76

her — as nourishing as rations allowed. At night Lily still sometimes turned to Jim in tears, apologising for being weak and silly, while he reassured her that she was anything but.

Dora kept her own sorrow to herself, though she told Sam when she wrote, warning him not to refer to it in his reply. Lily had begged her not to tell Reg and Gwenda, full of the excitement of packing up for their posting to Jerusalem, looking forward to their new married quarters, and enjoying their jobs with no thought of children yet awhile. To Sid, Lily wrote in person. Years before, he'd entrusted her with his own secret and she didn't want to keep hers from him. He wrote back a lovely letter full of understanding. Sid knew about loss — his first love, Anthony, a pilot, had been killed early in the war. But, he wrote, he accepted he could only know a fraction of what she and Jim — he sensitively acknowledged that too — must be feeling. Lily cried at his letter. Sid would have been the most wonderful, indulgent uncle.

* * *

Jim had thrown himself into work, too, and there was plenty of it. Taking Mr Marlow's instructions about the festive season to heart, he'd organised something new — a special Christmas shopping evening. The store would stay open till 9 p.m. when favoured customers would be able to 'browse at your leisure and enjoy free samples and special prices' as the invitations had it. The special prices weren't that special and the free samples weren't much — a small packet of snuff for the men and doll-sized phials of perfume for the women, but it was better than nothing and, when the designated evening came around in mid-December, they seemed to have been enough of a lure. The first-floor departments — Ladies' Fashions, Suits and Coats, Model Gowns, Childrenswear, Toys, Radio and Gramophone, Clocks and Pictures, even Furniture and Household, were packed — the whole store had a buzz about it.

'Look at him!' Jim said to Lily as they snatched a couple of minutes' break from the fray. He tipped his head towards Cedric Marlow. 'It's all he can do to stop himself actually rubbing his hands!'

'Good evening, Jim!' Mr Marlow's son, Robert, had shimmied up beside them.

He was nattily turned out as usual in a navy double-breasted suit, striped shirt and spotted tie, but, Lily thought critically, his fair good looks were starting to run to seed — his face was florid and despite the war, he'd managed to put on weight.

'Evening,' Jim replied politely.

Cedric Marlow was Jim's uncle, related by marriage, so Jim was Robert's cousin, but the families had had nothing to do with each other in the past, Jim's home circumstances being much more humble. Cedric Marlow had naturally hoped that his son would succeed him at the store, but after a short and unsuccessful stint, Robert had abandoned shopkeeping for something more glamorous.

'And the new Mrs Goodridge, I believe?' Robert gave Lily an exaggerated bow.

'Thank you,' she said primly, and then pointedly: 'Is your wife here? Evelyn?'

Robert waved a casual hand towards Model Gowns.

'A chance to spend money? Wild horses wouldn't keep her away.'

Yes, thought Lily, silly question. The former Evelyn Brimble was a natural blonde with a peaches-and-cream complexion, an enviable figure and the money for a wardrobe to match. As the pampered daughter of a local bigwig, now a pampered wife, she lived a life of leisure and self-indulgence, or so Lily imagined. Well, good luck to her. Lily wouldn't have wanted Evelyn's life, for all her money and connections, especially if it meant being married to Robert, who'd talked himself into a cushy job with Evelyn's father, Sir Douglas, who owned a stockbroking firm in Birmingham.

'I want to ask you something,' Robert went on. Lily and Jim stiffened. Please, not another hole that he wanted digging out of — that had happened before! 'Who's the old biddy that Dad's talking to so enthusiastically?'

Lily looked across. Mr Marlow was in close conversation with Mrs Tunnicliffe, a customer who Lily and Jim had got to know well over the war years.

'Her name is Daphne Tunnicliffe,' said Jim evenly.

'A regular customer, like everyone else who's here,' added Lily, annoyed at Mrs Tunnicliffe being referred to as an 'old biddy'. She was only in her fifties, smart and youthful, and as well turned out as ever tonight in a camel coat with a fur-trimmed collar and cuffs.

'Oh yes? A regular gold-digger, more like, the way she's making up to Dad!' scoffed Robert. 'Don't tell me, she's a widow.'

Lily and Jim were silent: he wasn't wrong. Daphne Tunnicliffe had lost her husband, and then, sadly, her daughter, Violet, only a little older than Lily, had been killed in a bombing raid.

'I knew it!' Robert crowed. 'I can spot them a mile

79

off! In my business you get to know a fraud when you see one.'

Lily controlled herself with difficulty.

'I'd better get back to my department,' she said. 'If you'll excuse me —'

But at that moment, Mr Simmonds, Mr Marlow's second-in-command and Master of Ceremonies at events like this, tapped the microphone on the little dais which had been set up in the centre of the sales floor.

'Thank you, ladies and gentlemen — well, mostly ladies,' he began, to a ripple of laughter. 'I hope you've enjoyed the evening so far. This is simply a short hiatus in the proceedings for a few words from the store's owner, Mr Cedric Marlow.'

He stepped aside and Mr Marlow took the stage. Faces turned towards him as shoppers stopped their browsing and the tills fell silent.

'Thank you all very much for coming,' Mr Marlow began. 'This evening has been an experiment, so I hope you don't mind being guinea pigs' — some laughter — 'but one which I hope we'll be able to repeat every Christmas, now we are free of at least some restrictions and in particular the hated blackout.'

There were mutterings of assent.

'I'd like to thank you most sincerely for your valued custom throughout the difficult years of the war,' Mr Marlow continued. 'But as we look to the future, we'll be making some improvements. You'll have noticed the new cash registers on every department.' Nods and more mutterings to that. 'And as we no longer need our former air-raid shelter, it will become a 'Bargain Basement' for end-of-lines, bought-in goods, and the 'buyer's mistakes' which we occasionally experience — though naturally we have very few of those!' More laughter and murmurs of interest and approval.

Lily reached for Jim's hand — the Bargain Basement had been his idea, one that his uncle had initially dismissed.

'When materials are available,' Cedric went on, 'we'll be installing escalators' — another of Jim's schemes — 'and refreshing the outside of the store. I hope these changes will enhance your 'shopping experience', as I believe the Americans call it!' As always when he attempted a joke, Mr Marlow looked slightly embarrassed. 'For now,' he went on hurriedly, 'please simply enjoy the rest of the evening — and don't forget your free samples as you leave! Thank you.'

There was a low-level smatter of applause before shoppers drifted back to their browsing and purchasing.

Robert was still standing with Lily and Jim, his eyes fixed on his father as the older man looked towards Daphne Tunnicliffe. She came towards him smiling and laid a hand on his arm. She was obviously congratulating him. It gave Lily a warm glow to see the affection between two formerly lonely people — Cedric Marlow was a widower. But when she looked at Robert, he was consumed with more than a glow — more like a hard-burning flame.

'Excuse me,' he said curtly, and made his way over to the pair.

'He is so awful!' Lily burst out. 'So mean! How can he begrudge his dad a bit of happiness?'

'Don't ask me.' Jim shook his head. 'Maybe it helps if the only person you think about is yourself.'

81

9

Then it was Christmas. Sid didn't come home after all: the excuse to Dora was that, as a single man, he'd volunteered to work over the holiday period so that family men could have their first decent Christmas break for years with their wives and children. To Lily he wrote the truth. His friend Jerome — his particular friend, if Lily could put it like that — was another airman. An American, he was due to be posted back to the States early in January and they wanted to make the most of the time they had together.

On Christmas Day, Dora always went to church, and this year, they all went. It was the first time Lily and Jim had been back to the church where they'd got married. It looked different, rearing up with the leafless trees around it, but the bells were ringing, and inside the church was full and the welcome was warm even if the building itself wasn't. Lily was doing well, singing out 'Oh Come All Ye Faithful' with the rest, but when the Sunday school children sang 'Away in a Manger' she had to look away, up to the high vaulted ceiling and the ruby and sapphire colours of the stained-glass windows until she had herself under control again.

Back home, they opened their presents and prepared their Christmas dinner. It was still scraped together from rations and what Sam had sent from Canada, but it was nonetheless special, as the three of them toasted a year which had begun with the country still at war — and had finally seen its end. Yes, there was a world to rebuild, in every sense, but Lily looked around the table at the people she loved most in the world and despite everything she'd been through in recent weeks, she felt the stirrings of a sense of peace.

And so a page turned, and a new year began, and the January sale — another busy time. Little by little, through the month, Lily came back to life, even though sometimes she still felt as if there were two of herself: one clipping coupons and ringing up purchases, the other standing alongside, watching. Miss Temple caught the flu and Nancy came back to Childrenswear for a couple of days on loan. Now her fears about Nancy were dispelled, Lily was glad to have her there, bustling and cheerful. Beryl, who'd had to be told about the loss of the baby, said it was being pregnant that had made Lily think such silly things about Nancy and Jim in the first place — it was down to all the chemical changes happening in her body. But a wash of pure grief still came over Lily from time to time — how could it not when she hung up little smocked baby dresses, or the Chilprufe rep laid out tiny vests for Miss Frobisher to approve?

Things weren't all roses for her friends either.

Bill had got work all right, as part of a road-mending gang, but it meant travelling all around the county. The work was hard, and cold, and tiresome.

'He doesn't mind hard work, but this is back-breaking!' Gladys told Lily. It was a midweek dinnertime and they were in the cosy fug of their favourite café, Peg's Pantry. Lily had got a pass out from the store and Dora was minding the twins. 'And it's breaking him — breaking his spirit, I mean.'

'Oh Gladys . . . poor Bill.' Lily meant it. Bill

deserved better than this — both he and Gladys did. Her friend looked worn and tired with it too.

'I told you he sold his demob suit, didn't I? Well, the other day, when I took out the ashes, I only found his medals in the bin!'

'No!'

'Oh yes! Says if he'd known what was in store for him come the end of the war — he works such long hours, for the overtime, to make ends meet, he hardly sees us — he says he might as well as have . . .' Gladys shuddered. 'Oh, I can't say it!'

'Then don't.' Lily took her friend's hand.

Gladys bit her lip and went on, her voice cracking.

'I've tried to keep his spirits up, I tell him how good a husband and father he is, how I love him, how the children love him, how things have got to get better . . .' She swallowed hard and sniffed, groping in her handbag for a hankie. 'He says he'd hoped for more from a Labour Government.'

'Things will get better,' urged Lily while Gladys patted hopelessly at her tears. 'The new lot can't do everything at once.' She tried to remember what she'd heard on the wireless and read in the paper. 'But there's so much going on . . . town planning, rebuilding cities . . . creating whole new towns even. That's a lot of construction work. With all this experience that Bill's getting . . . in time, he could work up to a good job in that line.'

She wasn't even convincing herself, really, and she certainly didn't convince Gladys.

'I've tried telling him that,' her friend replied sadly. 'He just comes back at me saying it'd take years, and there's plenty more experienced men ahead of him. Even them that didn't work in the building trade before were engineers and sappers in the war, so that gives them a head-start. And it doesn't come natural to him, the work. It's not what interests him.'

There was no point asking what did interest Bill. Lily knew the answer, but Gladys provided it anyway, her voice rising again.

'I'm petrified he'll want to go back to sea! Join the Merchant Navy or something! Then where does that leave me and the twins?'

She collapsed in tears. Lily tried to comfort her, then reluctantly went to the counter to pay. She hated leaving Gladys in such a state, but she had to get back to work.

On her way back, however, she met Beryl. She was upset too, though being Beryl, her distress translated into outrage.

'You'll never guess what I've had in the post!' she began, before Lily had had time to register her surprise at Beryl leaving her shop in the middle of the day. Not wanting to miss a customer, she rarely took a midday break. But giving Lily no chance to hazard a reply, Beryl flourished a letter from her bag. 'Read this!'

Lily took it.

Dear Mrs Bulpitt,

she read.

RE: NOTICE TO QUIT: TENANCY OF UNIT 4, MARLOWS, HIGH ST, HINTON:

She got no further.
'What?' she gaped.

Beryl snatched the letter back.

'Did you know about this?'

'No!'

'Or Jim?'

'No! Of course not! Beryl, how could you think —'

Beryl held up her hands.

'OK, OK, I know you'd have said — tipped me off. I just thought with Jim being' — she crossed her first two fingers — 'like this with management —'

'I'm sure he knows nothing,' Lily insisted. 'Mr Marlow's talked openly about improvements, but not about getting rid of these little shops!'

The small shop units had been created after a bomb had taken out four of Marlows' big display windows. As well as Beryl's Brides, there were two relocated departments from within Marlows — the clock and watch mender, and the shoe repairer. The fourth, which had been the Red Cross thrift shop, had closed at the end of the war. With regret, Lily could see that the decision was logical. With the opening of the Bargain Basement there was room in the store for the two Marlows' departments to go back to their original positions. That only left Beryl. And now that plate glass was available again, Marlows naturally wanted its display windows back. It was no good saying any of that to Beryl.

'What are you going to do?' Lily asked.

'I have no idea!' Beryl stuffed the offending letter back in her bag. 'I'm not bloomin' Rockefeller, am I, or Chanel or that Christian Dior, that can run to a swanky salon on the Boulevard Whatsit or Rue Thingummyjig, let alone Hinton High Street!'

'You don't think you can afford another place?'

'Not a proper shop, with a long lease and rates and

ground rent and that!' Beryl fumed. 'It's enough trouble meeting the rent here some months, and having to give Marlows a cut of the profits!'

Robert Marlow himself had drawn up the terms of Beryl's lease and he'd driven a hard bargain, deliberately, to have a hold over her.

'I suppose you could go back to operating from home,' Lily suggested.

That was how Beryl had started her business, in a small way.

'And what's that going to look like, all my beautiful stock hanging off the picture rail in the front room? Like the business has gone bust, that's what!'

Lily sighed. Beryl was right.

'Charming, isn't it,' Beryl went on. 'Marlows were pleased enough to have me here when the place looked a wreck after that bomb, and now the war's over, it's thank you and goodbye. Well, actually, not even a thank you, just sling your hook!'

Lily left Beryl furiously dashing off to the bank. Never one to hang back, or, despite what she'd said, to give up, she was going to fix an appointment to see about a loan, not that she was very hopeful, being a woman, even one with her own business. Lily hurried back to her department. She was seven minutes late, which earned her raised eyebrows from both Miss Frobisher and from Jim, and she had no excuse to offer — she could hardly blame Gladys or Beryl. She knew what was expected in these circumstances. She apologised profusely to Miss Frobisher and foreswore her afternoon break as penance.

'You didn't know about them taking the shop units back, did you?' she asked Jim as they walked home. It was a dull, damp, late January evening, but some shop windows were still lit, and the buses had their lights on, and with blackout restrictions a thing of the past, the street lights were on too. What a difference it made!

'No, but you know Uncle Cedric,' Jim replied. 'He likes to play some cards close to his chest. It makes him feel he hasn't handed over control entirely to me and Mr Simmonds.'

Lily nodded. Peter Simmonds was getting quite jumpy about when, or if, Mr Marlow, already over seventy, would retire, and what that would mean for the store. Neither he nor Jim had entirely dismissed the possibility of Robert Marlow suddenly deciding shopkeeping was for him after all, and that would be nothing short of a disaster.

'And if you remember,' mused Jim, 'Uncle Cedric did say something at the shopping evening about refreshing the outer appearance of the store.'

'I know,' Lily agreed. 'But I thought he just meant touching up the paintwork.' Then another thought occurred to her. 'I hope Robert had nothing to do with edging Beryl out, purely out of spite!'

'Because she fought him off that time?'

'He's such a worm, I wouldn't put anything past him.'

'Well, it's no good speculating,' Jim sighed. 'But it's hard to see how we can be any practical help to Beryl either. It's not like we can lend her any money.'

'Oh, I've had enough of this!' cried Lily suddenly. 'I've had a basinful of misery lately — first us, then poor Gladys, now Beryl. Let's do something to cheer ourselves up. Jim, we need a night out!'

★ ★ ★

88

As it turned out, Lily wasn't the only one who felt in need of distraction. Next day, she found herself on the same break as Nancy, who was now back on Household.

'Quiet, isn't it, now the sale's over?' Nancy spooned up what the canteen called beef soup but which everyone knew was yesterday's thinned-down gravy. 'And everything's a bit . . . drab.'

'I was saying the same to Jim last night!' Lily chased a piece of bread — still the chewy, gritty National Loaf — around her own bowl. 'We thought we'd have a night out.' And on impulse she added, 'Why don't you join us?'

When she told Jim later, he was astonished.

'You've changed your tune!' he exclaimed. 'Not so long ago Nancy was a man-eater out to get me. Now you're best pals!'

'Well, at least you and I have each other,' said Lily. 'She's new back in town, on her own, still living with those relatives of hers, it can't be much fun. I've suggested the White Lion on Saturday.'

'Oh, have you now? The White Lion? Trying to impress her?'

'No, I just thought it would be nice to go somewhere a bit smart for a change! If you don't like the idea, we can go by ourselves,' Lily retorted. 'Me and Nancy, that is. We don't get the chance to chat now she's on a different department.'

'You are joking!' Jim retaliated. 'As if I'd give you two witches the opportunity to sit over your cauldron and cackle about me!'

'You flatter yourself! I think we'd have more to talk about than you!'

They grinned at each other. They hadn't had a

back-and-forth like this since before Lily lost the baby. Maybe at long last, things really were getting back to normal.

'What time is this coven arranged for?' Jim asked.

'Seven thirty,' said Lily. 'I take it you'll be joining us?'

'I wouldn't miss it for the world,' said Jim, adding under his breath, 'I wouldn't dare.'

★ ★ ★

'Well, here we are again,' said Lily as she and Jim climbed the shallow stone steps of the White Lion hotel on Saturday night. The last time they'd been here had been for their wedding breakfast. What a lot had happened since then! In so many ways, Lily felt she'd grown up more in six short months than in the entire six years of the war.

Jim didn't reply. He didn't need to — Lily knew he knew what she was thinking. It showed in the way he placed his hand tenderly in the small of her back as he held the door open for her and shepherded her through.

Inside the foyer was still the same — the rich royal blue carpet with its pattern of scrolls and curlicues, the mahogany reception desk, the fireplace with its shining brass fender. A wide staircase swept up to the first floor and signs pointed the way down corridors to the 'Ladies' Powder Room' and the 'Telephone Cabins' — it was that sort of place. Nancy was already there, standing by the round central table, leafing through one of the *Country Life* magazines it held along with a huge vase of bronze chrysanthemums.

'Are we late? Sorry.' Jim checked his watch.

'No, you're not late.' Nancy replaced the magazine. 'I was early. I always am when I'm nervous.'

'What's there to be nervous about?' asked Lily. 'It's only us, you only saw us two hours ago at work!'

'It's not only you, though, is it?' Nancy lowered her voice, looking furtive. 'I hope you don't mind, but I've asked someone else along. A double date, if you like.'

Lily looked at Jim, who shrugged and smiled.

'That's fine, but why didn't you say so before?'

'I didn't know before. He'd left a message for me. It was waiting when I got in, so I phoned where he's staying and —'

'A message?' Lily was intrigued. 'You dark horse, Nancy! Who is he?'

'He's — oh, shh! Here he is now!'

Lily turned to see a tall, good-looking young man push through the double doors. It — or rather, he — gave her the shock of her life.

'Frank!' cried Nancy ecstatically.

'Nancy! And don't you look even prettier than I remembered!'

10

Frank Bryant! Lily's eyes signalled panic. Jim's signalled back 'keep calm'.

Lily and Jim looked on as Nancy submitted willingly to Frank's embrace. After a foot-shuffling few minutes for them, she extricated herself and apologised.

'I'm sorry, you two, it's just that we haven't seen each other in months!' She smiled at Frank as she spoke and he smiled back, that winning smile which he knew would melt the heart of the frostiest ice maiden, and which Lily knew to be all part of his armoury of charm. 'Let me introduce you — Frank, these are two of my colleagues — Lily and Jim!'

A moment's hesitation — and the moment of truth. How would Frank handle it? He was cocky enough to brazen anything out.

But Jim spoke first.

'Oh, no introductions needed, we know each other. We're old sparring partners, aren't we, Frank?'

Bull by the horns, then, thought Lily. Well, good for Jim for taking the initiative before Frank had a chance to. And for once, Frank was dumbstruck. His easy Irish blarney had deserted him.

'Really?' cried Nancy. 'But how did you all meet?'

She hadn't taken 'sparring partners' literally, thank goodness. Risky, but clever of Jim, Lily thought with relief. Frank leapt in.

'I met Lily first, didn't I, Lily, when you came to Ward and Keppler with Miss Frobisher.'

'Of course!' Nancy exclaimed. 'The babywear manufacturers!'

'I was repping for them at the time. And then,' Frank went on smoothly, 'we all, er, met up when I was next in Hinton. It's lovely to see you again, Lily.' He shook her solemnly by the hand, and the pressure of his fingers told her that he hadn't forgotten what had passed between them. She hadn't either, how he'd charmed her and tried to kiss her — and more. And how Jim, coming in on them, had punched Frank in the mouth. She withdrew her hand as quickly as she could.

Then Frank shook hands with Jim, giving him, Lily noticed, a sly wink.

'Nancy did tell me we'd be meeting another couple — well, I can't turn up out of the blue and expect a gorgeous girl like her to be free on a Saturday night now, can I?' he smiled. His soft Irish accent and the challenge in his deep blue eyes were just the same and just as seductive. Nancy, unrecognisable from the self-possessed young woman Lily knew at work, almost simpered.

'Shall we go through?' said Jim, cutting through the flannel and indicating the way to the cocktail bar. He and Frank stood back to let the women go first and Lily heard Frank say jovially:

'Did I see Lily's wearing a wedding ring? Congratulations, Jim! When was the happy event?'

Over drinks ('I'll get these, Jim, no, I insist.') the story of how Frank and Nancy had met came out. He'd eventually been assigned to war work and had ended up in a clerking job in London.

'Our eyes met across a crowded Number 12, didn't they?' Frank said.

93

Nancy beamed. 'I got off first and you followed me off the bus.'

'Even though it was three stops short of where I needed to go. But when Cupid's arrow strikes . . .'

Frank turned meaningfully to Lily. He did talk a lot of nonsense, she thought, and wondered how many other girls he'd picked up in the same way. But Nancy didn't seem to notice — or mind.

Somehow they got through the evening but when Nancy and Lily went to the ladies' — Frank and Nancy were going on dancing — Nancy turned to her, hands clasped.

'He's a bit of a dreamboat, isn't he? So handsome!'

'He's very charming,' said Lily guardedly. 'How well do you know him?'

'Oh, not very.' Nancy adjusted the bodice of her dress and leaned forward to the mirror to touch up her lipstick. 'I was moved off to Croydon after a couple of months. I didn't expect him to write, but he did from time to time, and when I moved back here I sent him my address and phone number.' She smacked her lips together to blot them. 'I never really expected to see him again. But now he's gone back into sales and he's based in Birmingham . . . well, why not?'

'Mm-hm.' Lily took a deep breath. 'Nancy . . . can I just say . . . you won't let Frank take advantage, will you? Because he did try to get fresh with me —'

Nancy, twirling the stub of her lipstick back into its case, shrieked with laughter.

'Oh, Lily,' she said, putting it back in her bag. 'Do you think he hasn't already?'

Lily wasn't surprised.

'Fair enough. He was never one to waste time!'

Nancy snapped her handbag shut and straightened

94

the handle. Then she turned to Lily, more serious now.

'Don't they all,' she said resignedly, 'try it on? Every soldier and sailor and airman — in the ranks, or officers for that matter — that I met in the war.'

'Well,' Lily felt her cheeks colour slightly. 'I never had a chance to find out. And me and Jim agreed we'd wait till we were married, but I know how hard that was for both of us, and I know many men would have been . . . well, less understanding. Or tried to be more persuasive.'

'Oh, I learnt that very early on.' Nancy looked down at the floor. The carpet was pink in the ladies' powder room, deep and luxurious: with the shaded lights, also pink, and the gilt-framed mirrors, it was like a stage set. 'You know what some people called us girls in the ATS — 'officers' groundsheets'.'

Lily did know.

'Not very nice.'

'Well, it was true in some cases,' Nancy conceded. 'There were a few who'd only joined up with the thought of bagging a husband, an officer for preference. But it worked both ways — there were plenty of blokes who saw us as easy pickings.'

Lily gave a wry smile. She was sure that was true. Nancy smiled, remembering.

'But there were plenty of decent blokes too. Most of them, I'd say, and some happy outcomes. I went to plenty of engagements and weddings.'

She perched on the edge of the vanity unit and looked at Lily. Lily had seen that look before, on customers weighing up whether to risk an expensive purchase. Shall I? Shan't I?

Nancy made her decision.

'This will stay between you and me, all right?' she said.

'Of course,' Lily assured her.

'I won't say it wasn't tempting,' Nancy admitted. 'After small-town Hinton, after the stuffy ways at Marlows, and things not being so good for me at home . . . Life in uniform was all so new and exciting and different, and there were so many men — and all so attentive, you can imagine.'

Lily could. Nancy was such an attractive girl.

'I fell in with a crowd of girls,' said Nancy. 'A nice bunch. We went to the dances and parties together and we met these blokes, also pals, and we all met up when we could. They were sappers — engineers — stationed near us. I got very fond of one of them — Alec — and him of me: we started going around together.' She smiled again and Lily nodded encouragingly. 'He was one of the good ones. Thoughtful, you know. And bright. Very like your Jim, actually, in looks and personality.'

How interesting, Lily thought. Maybe that spark — they called it chemistry, didn't they? — that she'd sensed between Nancy and Jim hadn't been all in her imagination. Jim had reassured her, and she believed him wholeheartedly, but maybe there'd been something there, on Nancy's side at least.

'What happened?' she asked. 'With you and Alec?'

'Oh, the inevitable,' Nancy said. 'He was promoted to corporal straight out of training, and that was pretty unusual. His pals ribbed him he was in line for being made an NCO. Then he and his unit got their posting. And on his last night we went out together, just the two of us . . . And we . . . well . . . we . . . you know.' Her eyes met Lily's, looking for understanding. 'I'm not a tart, Lily. We were together. And I loved him, and he did me. You do see that, don't you?'

'Of course you're not a tart!' said Lily. 'It must have been very ... in those circumstances ... anyone would have found it hard to say no.'

'It was,' Nancy said. 'And it was lovely. He was lovely. The only bad bit was him having to go away. But he asked if I'd wait for him, we said we'd write and everything — he'd have to write first, obviously, 'cos they hadn't told them where they were being sent.'

'Go on,' Lily urged gently. 'What happened?'

Jim and Frank would wonder where they were, she thought: it was a miracle Jim hadn't come knocking on the door of the ladies' by now, but she didn't care.

'Well, a couple of weeks passed and no letter. I wasn't too worried, word was they'd been sent to the Middle East so I knew the ship'd be ages getting there.'

Lily knew this too: it had been the same with her brother Reg, and Beryl's husband Les, when he'd done his Army service in North Africa.

'And then ... well, can't you guess?'

Lily opened her hands, indicating Nancy should tell the story. She didn't want to guess; she didn't want to interrupt.

'I was late,' Nancy said flatly. 'Another week went on, and another. I felt lousy and I knew I'd been left with more than a memory.'

'Oh Nancy!' Lily was aghast. 'But ... what did you do?'

'What could I do? I carried on.'

'Didn't you tell anyone?'

'No. Not my friends, not while I was still in shock about it myself. And if I'd gone running to the MO, she'd have told the CO and it'd be Para Eleven for me.'

'Sorry?'

'Paragraph Eleven of your sign-up conditions,' Nancy explained. 'Released from service if pregnant. Well, I've told you what life was like for me at home, I wasn't going to be welcome there, not me on my own, let alone with a little stranger. So I carried on, waiting for Alec's letter with the address, so I could at least tell him, and see what he said.'

'And what did he say? He didn't — he didn't let you down?'

Despite his promises, thought Lily, maybe Nancy had never heard back from Alec at all . . . but what about the baby? What had happened to that? Had Nancy had to give it up for adoption? Or . . . There were so many questions, but Lily didn't want to ask them. It was better to let Nancy tell her own story in her own time.

'I was being trained on the Kerries by then,' Nancy went on, more slowly now, 'and it was hard to concentrate, I can tell you. Then the letter came — from one of Alec's mates. They'd got there all right, he never told me exactly where, but on their first sortie they were ambushed and well — out of the four of them, only three came back. Alec was shot by a sniper. Clean through the head.'

'Oh, Nancy!' Lily cried. 'Oh, I'm so sorry!' But now, surely, she could ask. 'But the baby? What happened to the baby?'

'I lost it,' said Nancy in a low voice. 'After I got the letter, I . . . I was all of a churn. Shock, I thought. But in the evening, after supper, I had these terrible pains and I went to the bathroom and then — well, it all came away. All gone.'

Lily put out a hand and touched Nancy's arm. It was so like her own experience — but then again, nothing like it. She'd had Beryl to confide in, her mum and Jim for comfort. Nancy had had no one, not a soul. Instinctively, tears sprang to her eyes.

'You went through that all on your own?'

Nancy blinked away her own tears at the memory. She scuffed her foot about on the carpet, making a fan shape in the pile.

'Well, I didn't have much choice. So after that . . . In truth, I don't know how Alec would have reacted when I told him. It's one thing to say he'd come back for me, but a baby he'd never met? He might have written me off; and even if he'd said he'd look after me — us — well, I didn't know him that well, only a few months. Who can say if we'd have made a go of things even if he'd got back safe? Plenty didn't, and they'd been together for longer. Were married, even.'

Lily sighed. Nancy had been through even more than she'd imagined.

'So now . . .' Nancy smiled sadly. 'I don't want to go through anything like that again, however much I like someone. I don't want that heartbreak. I daren't risk it, not yet. So I keep them at arm's length, and if they overstep the mark . . .'

Nancy took a swift step towards her and before Lily knew what was happening, her arm was pinned behind her back.

'Ow! What the —'

'They taught us self-defence in case the ack-ack battery got stormed. It's come in very handy.'

'Very! I can tell!'

'Sorry,' said Nancy, releasing her grip. 'But no

99

bones broken. And no hearts, either.' She gave herself one last glance in the mirror and picked up her handbag. 'Shall we go back and join the boys?'

With Lily flexing her arm, they moved to the door, Lily still trying to take in what she'd been told. Poor Nancy! First she'd lost her dad, and then, effectively, her mum, in the space of six months, then her boyfriend, and their baby, in the space of some six weeks. Lily realised she'd taken Nancy at face value. On the surface, she was so cheerful and outgoing — but maybe that too was part of her defences. Nancy had been through even more than Lily had known and she was flattered at being taken into her confidence.

One day, maybe, she'd tell her about her own experience of loss, but this wasn't the moment. Instead, arm in arm, they went back out to the foyer, where Frank and Jim had given up on conversation. Jim was reading the *Chronicle* and Frank was studying the hunting prints on the wall.

'What have you been doing?' Jim hissed as he put the paper aside and got up while Frank teased Nancy about the length of time she'd spent on beautifying when she was already beautiful enough. Frank kissed Lily on the cheek as they said goodbye.

'As lovely as ever,' he whispered.

Then he shook Jim by the hand, but Jim hadn't finished with him yet.

'You take good care of Nancy,' he warned. 'She's a valuable member of staff on my department, so you'll have me to answer to.'

He said it lightly, but it was his subtle way of telling Frank to keep in line. Nancy and Lily looked at each other and smiled: Lily knew Nancy could deal with

Frank perfectly well. They parted on the steps of the White Lion, Lily and Jim headed for home, Nancy and Frank for the delights of the Palais.

'So,' said Jim, as Lily put on her gloves. 'What did keep you so long in the ladies'? Swooning over lover boy's charms?'

'Hardly,' said Lily.

'So I don't need to take up boxing again? Get in practice?'

'Not on Nancy's account — she can look after herself,' said Lily. 'And certainly not on mine.'

She knew that Jim hadn't missed what Frank had whispered and in that moment, and because of everything else that had passed that evening, she loved him more than ever.

★ ★ ★

Their night out hadn't been anything like the quiet drink Lily had expected, but it jolted her and Jim out of the rut they'd fallen into, and as the days gradually lengthened, they made an effort to make more of their free time. The store's amateur dramatic group, the Marlows Players, put on two groan-worthy farces. They started going to the cinema again and they went dancing again too, though thankfully the foursome with Frank and Nancy wasn't repeated.

Nancy told Lily that Frank always got in touch when he was in the area, but she was well aware he had a girl in every store, so to speak, and bit by bit, contact began to tail off. Lily smiled to herself. She knew from experience that Frank liked a challenge, but Nancy must have proved a little bit too much of one, even for him. And when Derek from Shirts and

Ties asked Nancy out, she started walking out with him.

'Two can play at Frank's game,' she said.

It was funny, Lily thought, how fond she'd become of Nancy, and how protective of her, when she'd once seemed such a threat. It was good, though, to have a new friend in her life who was always cheerful. Predictably the bank had turned Beryl turned down flat for a loan, and Gladys's problems only seemed to multiply. Her gran was claiming she had gout in her big toe, and got the doctor round to confirm it — which he was unable to do since, as usual, there was nothing actually wrong. Florrie took to her bed even more after that, meaning even more running up and down the stairs for Gladys. At the same time, Bill ricked his back on one of the road-mending jobs and was laid up himself.

'I was round there again this morning,' Dora told Lily towards the end of March. It was a Monday evening and they were folding the washing that Dora had done on Gladys's behalf and had wheeled home in the twins' pram to iron. 'Gladys is run off her feet.'

'I wish I could see some way out of it for her,' Lily said. 'And for Beryl, come to that.'

'Short of a win on the pools, I can't see a way out for either of them,' Dora agreed. 'Misery loves company, that's for sure.'

* * *

The truth of that statement was about to become apparent in another home in Hinton — Cedric Marlow's. He was on the telephone to Daphne Tunnicliffe

102

when he heard a car crunch to a stop on the gravel drive.

The telephone was in the hall and he peered through the small leaded window beside the front door. The car was a Riley tourer, a Lynx. Cedric recognised it at once.

'I'm sorry, Daphne, I shall have to go,' he said. 'It seems I have a visitor.'

'At this hour?' She sounded astonished, as well she might. It was almost ten o'clock.

'I'd better see what it's all about. I'm sorry, I'll telephone you later in the week.'

He put the receiver down rapidly and opened the front door. There, on the step, his key poised, was his son Robert.

'You're still up then! I know you country folk retire early.'

Robert swept past him into the hall as Cedric closed the door.

'It's a good job I am! To what do I owe the pleasure?'

He almost said 'the honour'. They'd never had a good relationship, stemming from the loss of the boy's mother soon after his birth. Cedric had buried himself in work, leaving Robert's upbringing to a nanny, and then to various boarding schools, but Robert had been a rebel, managing to get himself expelled from two schools and being 'asked to leave' a third. When the war had come, Cedric had managed to get him exempted from military service through his influence locally. It wasn't something he was proud of, but by then he was feeling some guilt for the part his neglect, or at least lack of interest in his son might have played in the fact that Robert had gone so badly off the rails.

His short-lived career at Marlows had been a disaster, too. Cedric was aware of only one of the schemes that Robert had been involved in, but his timely engagement to Evelyn Brimble and the offer of a job with her father had been a godsend. Robert had emerged from the situation at the store smelling of roses, which he had a knack of doing, and Cedric had come out of it with his dignity, and the store's reputation, intact — two things which were of equal importance to him.

Robert turned to face him.

'You might as well have it straight. It's all over, Dad. The job with Sir Douglas, and my marriage to Evelyn. Gone up in smoke. The lot of it.'

11

Without saying anything, Cedric led him into the study. It was the room where he spent most of his evenings: the drawing room was too large and too formal for one person. He poured two whiskies from the crystal decanter and handed a glass to his son.

Robert gulped the drink down in one while Cedric took a careful sip. He still said nothing as Robert poured himself another, then flung himself into a leather armchair while Cedric stirred the dying fire into some sort of extended life. He sat down in the opposite chair.

'Well?'

'I don't know where to start.'

'The beginning, perhaps?'

Robert swirled his whisky around in his glass, considering, then looked up.

'OK. I'm a bad boy. You know it, I know it. I dare say you thought that marrying Evelyn and working for her dad might settle me down. Perhaps I even thought it myself. And I did love her, Dad. That much was genuine.'

Noting the 'did', Cedric experienced the sinking feeling that was never long in coming in encounters with Robert. His son went on:

'The snag is, I'm not very good at being settled. I felt confined from the minute I moved to Birmingham. Before we were married, as you know, we were holed up with her parents in that flat of theirs.'

He made it sound like a hovel: it was a mansion flat

in the smartest part of the city.

'Before Sir Douglas bought you a house.'

'Yes, all right, rub it in. I've been a kept man.'

'I was simply stating a fact.'

'Whatever. So we set up on our own, me and Evelyn. She did a bit of war work, I suppose you could call it, organising charity lunches and what have you, all the time with her mother. And I trotted off to the office every day to work for her dad.'

'Some would say you had it easy.'

'I'd say I had it dull. Good Lord, it was boring. It started off OK, basically taking clients out to lunch and sweet-talking them, but then expenses got cut and I was tied to a desk. Reams of figures every day, investors telephoning every five minutes, old biddies twittering about receiving no interest on their War Loan they'd forgotten they'd sold, or some old buffer harrumphing about the commission we'd charged . . . can you blame me for wanting a bit of excitement?'

Cedric placed his glass carefully on a silver coaster on the table at his elbow. What would Robert define as excitement? Wine? Women? Song?

'And that manifested itself how exactly?'

He knew he sounded prissy and disapproving but the more he dreaded what Robert would tell him, the more measured Cedric's responses became.

'I went to a business dinner at the Grand one night — fell in with some chaps who were in a poker school. You can guess the rest.'

So that was it! The one thing he hadn't thought of. Gambling.

'I can guess that you lost,' said Cedric drily. 'And heavily. So, what happened? You obviously didn't dare

106

come to me. You tapped Evelyn for money? Persuaded Sir Douglas to pay you more?'

Robert shook his head. 'Oh, come on, Dad, I know you're the most upstanding citizen since the Messiah, but think about it! Think about my job and what it entailed —'

A cold hand seemed to press Cedric's throat. He blinked.

'You don't mean . . . you stole it? You stole from the client accounts?'

Robert downed his second whisky and stared into his glass.

'It seemed like the best idea at the time. I was going to put it back once I had a decent win, but it never came.'

No, thought Cedric, because Robert would never have had the sense to quit while ahead, if he ever was.

'Then,' shrugged Robert, 'the old stick who ran the office spotted the missing spondoolicks and went to Sir Douglas. The evidence against me was all too conclusive. Old Dougie had me in, ranted, said I was a disgrace to the firm and the family, blah, blah, blah . . . Things hadn't been too good with Evelyn anyway, my absences in the evenings becoming harder to explain. Once the balloon went up, I was out on my ear — out of a job and ejected from the marital home as well, never to darken their doors again, etcetera, etcetera.'

Cedric stared into the fire. This was Robert all over. An act of idiocy at best, a fraud worthy of prosecution at worst, and he dismissed it as lightly as if he'd mislaid a pen or had a minor prang in the car. Not to mention the end of his marriage . . . That was a disaster enough, but the rest . . .

107

'And the missing money? Are you here for a hand-out?'

'God no, Dad! I'm not that shameless!'

Aren't you? thought Cedric. It was what Robert had expected before.

'So how are you going to pay it back?'

'I don't have to,' Robert replied airily. 'Sir Douglas is going to make up the loss himself. He seemed to think it was worth it to hush things up — and be shot of me ASAP.'

Wasn't that just typical of Robert's ability to slide out of trouble! It was good of Sir Douglas to cover the loss, very good, but at least for him it drew a line under the affair. As Robert's parent, Cedric could never draw that line. He despaired at Robert's behaviour but at the same time, all the guilt he'd felt in the past about what he might have done, or not done, to cause Robert to turn out the self-centred, feckless individual that he was reared up again and threatened to overwhelm him.

'All right,' he said, standing up. 'That's enough for tonight. We'll talk some more tomorrow. Your bed isn't aired, I'm afraid — I didn't know you were coming and these days I only have someone in to clean and cook my meals, and she's long gone home.'

To his surprise, Robert jumped to his feet.

'I'll be fine, Dad, don't worry. I had a bite to eat before I left town. I'll get my things from the car and I'll see you at breakfast, shall I?'

'Er, I suppose you will . . . if you're up,' said Cedric in surprise. He'd imagined Robert lying in bed till lunchtime, given the chance.

'Of course I'll be up, I'll be coming to the shop with you! I'm back in harness, Dad, I'm going to work for you! It's what you always wanted, isn't it? Aren't you pleased?'

★ ★ ★

Cedric didn't sleep well. First, he couldn't get off to sleep; then, as he heard the grandfather clock in the hall strike two, three and then four, he wondered if he'd slept at all. His mind skimmed restlessly from one thing to another. Robert's disgrace at Sir Douglas's firm . . . should he contact Sir Douglas? Offer to make up the lost funds from his own pocket? Or would that make things worse? And then there was Evelyn. Was the marriage really over? Robert said he had loved her — had he fallen out of love? Or she with him? For good? Or might there be a chance they could reconcile, with or without Sir Douglas's blessing? If not, there'd be the awkwardness and the gossip, of a separation and divorce . . . or could that be hushed up as well? Cedric tossed and turned. He heard his daily woman come in at seven to light the stove and get his breakfast, and was in the dining room before she'd even finished laying up. He asked her to lay another place, explaining that his son had arrived unexpectedly.

In the event, Robert came down so late that he didn't even sit at the table. He drank two cups of coffee straight off, using almost all the sugar ration, then rubbed his hands and asked when they were leaving.

Cedric realised he'd been so busy going over what Robert had told him that he hadn't given a thought to what he was going to do with him now he was here. There was no role for him at the shop — he'd have to create one, an extra floorwalker, he supposed. In the-

109

ory, since Cedric was the owner, he could do as he liked. He was the boss and Robert was the boss's son, but staff morale was important too. Blatant favouritism wouldn't go down well when people who'd had jobs there before had been turned away for reasons of economy, and those who'd worked hard during the war saw themselves held back.

And what would be the story? As well as their flat in Birmingham the Brimbles had a large house in Hinton and divided their time between the two. Even if Sir Douglas and his wife, and Evelyn, were discreet about what had gone on at the firm for their own sakes, the fact that the marriage had broken down would soon become very obvious — and common knowledge.

'I think it would be best,' said Cedric, thinking quickly, 'if you stayed at home today. I need to talk to my senior team about what role we can find for you.'

'I see.' Robert's features reassembled into sullenness. 'I'm surplus to requirements here too!'

'I didn't say that,' Cedric replied with a patience he didn't feel. 'But you can't expect to land from the skies and walk into a role that doesn't yet exist!'

With bad grace, Robert agreed.

'House arrest,' he muttered, ringing the service bell. 'I may as well have a proper breakfast then. Is there any bacon?'

★　★　★

When Peter and Eileen Simmonds — Mr Simmonds and Miss Frobisher in the store, of course — arrived at work that morning, there was a note for Peter at the timekeeper's office.

110

'A request to see Mr Marlow at ten thirty, after his tour of the store,' he said as he read it.

'And he sent it here? Must be urgent! What have you done now?' teased his wife.

'Something's brewing, for sure,' Peter replied.

The brew didn't take long to boil over. As Peter mediated in a stand-off over floor space between the buyer on Handbags and her sworn enemy, the buyer on Luggage, Sir Douglas Brimble, in all his pomp, swept into the store and made for the lifts.

'Management floor!' Peter heard him bark at the cowering lift-boy.

Peter tensed. Sir Douglas was an important customer — and an influential one. If he was displeased with some aspect of service, quality or value, he wouldn't be slow to make sure all of Hinton knew about it. And when Peter arrived outside Cedric Marlow's office for his appointment fifteen minutes later, the raised voices on the other side of the door were all too clear.

He shifted awkwardly from foot to foot as he heard the store's owner being well and truly roasted. But as the encounter went on, and Sir Douglas's fury mounted, Peter's concern and embarrassment turned to dismay. This was no simple customer complaint. This sounded like trouble with Robert.

He edged closer to the door and heard the words 'bounder' (definitely Robert) and then, to his mounting horror, 'embezzlement', 'fraud', 'prosecution', 'disrepute' and 'scandal'. As if that wasn't enough, Sir Douglas changed tack: 'Shabbiest possible treatment of my daughter', 'after all I've done for him', and, finally, 'divorce' and 'immediately'.

In all this time, Cedric Marlow had barely been

able to get a word in, and, thought Peter, what was there to say? Somehow or another, Robert had had his hand in the till; at the same time, maybe cause and effect, maybe not, his marriage to Evelyn had broken down. Finally, Sir Douglas seemed to calm a little, and Cedric could be heard placating him. Then the voices came closer — Sir Douglas was leaving. Peter moved swiftly away from the door, but before he could leave the outer office entirely, Sir Douglas swept through, almost knocking him over.

Cedric Marlow looked completely drained. He motioned Peter to come in and sank back into his chair, while Peter stood.

'I'm afraid, sir,' he began, 'I couldn't help over-hearing some of that. It didn't sound very pleasant. Can I get you anything? Some water, perhaps?'

Cedric waved the offer away.

'I'm all right. I'm glad you heard. It saves me having to go over it again. Robert turned up late last night and confessed all, so at least it wasn't the first I'd heard of it.'

'I see.'

'Look, Peter,' Cedric Marlow passed his hands over his bald head as if to order his thoughts, 'Robert's well and truly disgraced himself but Sir Douglas doesn't want a scandal any more than I do. I shall pay what are effectively Robert's debts and that side of things can be hushed up. But Evelyn wants a divorce; that will have to come out.'

'There's no shame in that these days, sir,' Peter assured him. He certainly wasn't going to judge: Eileen had been an unmarried mother — not her choice, not her fault. Her son John was now six. 'Or there's a lot less shame than there was. The war's

112

caused a lot of casualties in that area too.'

This was true enough, but Cedric Marlow wasn't of the generation to approve, whatever excuses could be made. He twitched his lips without making a reply.

'The main question is what to do with Robert now,' he said. 'He wants me to take him back into the store.'

Peter hadn't reckoned on that one, but he covered his alarm as well as he could. His job now was to support Mr Marlow.

'Ah. Well, I dare say we can find something for him to do.'

'I'll need you to take him under your wing, Peter,' urged Cedric. 'The first floor runs like clockwork with Miss Frobisher and Mr Goodridge in charge, I don't want him disrupting things there. So he'll have to shadow you on the ground floor. And when I say he shadows you, I really mean . . .'

Peter understood.

'Of course, sir. No problem. I'll do my utmost.'

He could hardly say he was looking forward to working with Robert. He wasn't — 'work' and 'Robert' didn't go in the same sentence, anyway. And on past form . . . But Cedric needn't have worried. Peter wouldn't be letting Robert Marlow out of his sight.

12

The first thing Peter Simmonds did was to call Jim into his own tiny office and tell him everything. He stressed it was in confidence, but he knew Jim would tell Lily, as Peter would tell his wife. Both knew the real reason for Robert's return must go no further. Speculation within the store about why Robert was back, and any gossip about his separation from Evelyn when that became public, was to be stamped out as quickly as possible.

When Jim told her that evening as they walked home, Lily was aghast — but not for Robert or even Evelyn's sake.

'Oh Jim! You know what this means, don't you?' she burst out, before lowering her voice. 'Robert'll be up to his old tricks again, and expect you to get him out of the mire when they go wrong!'

'He won't get the chance to get up to any tricks,' Jim assured her. 'Between us — me and Peter that is — we've got to see to that.'

'Good luck with that!' Lilly tossed her head. 'You know he's as slippery as an eel in axle grease!'

'Not this time,' swore Jim. 'He'll have to be squeaky-clean.'

★   ★   ★

At that very moment, Robert's father was laying out his terms too. He'd already explained the visitation he'd received that morning.

114

'I realise now that any hope of reconciliation with Evelyn isn't on,' he said. 'Sir Douglas made that very plain.'

'I could have told you that myself,' said Robert petulantly. They were in the study again, Robert sitting crossways in his armchair, his legs hooked over one arm. Cedric, standing, had to resist the desire to shake him. Instead, controlling himself, he carried on.

'However, I was able to get him to agree to reverse, if you like, the course of events. We agreed it would be better for everyone that way.'

'Reverse?'

'The story will be that, sadly, the stresses and strains of wartime led to a breakdown in the marriage, and therefore it was thought best by everyone that you should leave the job with Sir Douglas. That way, we salvage a little dignity all round.'

Robert sighed sulkily.

'Terrific! Not for me, if I'm to be an object of pity!'

'What, you'd rather be the villain of the piece?'

'The devil does have all the best tunes,' reflected Robert wryly. 'Still, if that's the way it has to be . . .'

'It is.'

Try to think of someone other than yourself for once, Cedric added silently.

'We'd better start looking to the future then.' Robert swung himself round on the chair and got up. 'What have you come up with for me to do? I know you think I'm useless, so giving out leaflets at the door, perhaps? Cloakroom attendant in the Gents, grovelling for a halfpenny tip?'

'You'll be Peter Simmonds' assistant on the ground floor,' said Cedric.

'Goodness!' exclaimed Robert. 'A proper position!'

115

'Just . . . do your best,' said Cedric wearily. 'For me?'

So the next day and the ones that followed, Robert swaggered into the store in a waft of cologne and cockiness. The juniors and younger salesgirls, who hadn't previously experienced the full force of the Robert Marlow effect, went all swoony when they learnt about the breakdown of his marriage and wondered if they could be the ones to help him to mend his broken heart. Robert, of course, lapped it up, and positively encouraged them. Even Nancy, who should have known better after what she'd told Lily about men who chanced their luck during the war, seemed interested.

'A cat may look at a king,' she pronounced. 'Or a future Queen.' And when Lily looked puzzled, she added: 'Princess Elizabeth and her handsome naval lieutenant!'

'What, Philip of Glucken-whatever? He's still a prince, even if he hasn't got a country!' Lily objected. 'And Robert Marlow's no king, prince, or anything else, trust me. And what about Derek? And Frank?'

Nancy wrinkled her nose. 'I haven't heard from Frank in ages, and Derek's getting a bit stifling.'

Beryl, who knew Robert of old, certainly wasn't tempted. And she didn't buy the story that they'd all been told for one moment.

'Stresses and strains of the war killed that marriage? What's so stressful about living in the lap of luxury bankrolled by Daddy?' she demanded.

Lily sighed inwardly. She couldn't tell Beryl the truth, much as she wanted to. But Beryl, as shrewd, or cynical, as ever, had guessed it for herself.

'There's been some funny business somewhere,'

she said. 'Fast cars, fast women — there'll be something. We all know what he's like.'

Beryl did know, to her cost, and she was about to have it rubbed in.

At that very moment, there was a managers' meeting taking place at Marlows and Robert, unfortunately, had to be invited along. The store's maintenance manager had delivered his update on the plate-glass situation. The order was progressing: it would be through in a few weeks — before the end of Beryl's notice period.

'Good,' said Cedric. 'The Red Cross shop has already closed, the clock mender and the shoe repairer are back in the store, so we can get on.'

'Not straight away, sir,' Peter Simmonds spoke up. 'There's the bridal shop. The owner still needs to find new premises.'

'Yes, I didn't mean —' Cedric began.

'Well, that's just too bad,' Robert interrupted. 'Once we've got the glass, we should chuck her out. We can't let one gimcrack little business hold up the whole enterprise.'

'I wouldn't call it gimcrack,' Jim intervened. 'She's worked very hard to build it up.'

'Really? Tatty old second-hand frocks?' Robert sneered. 'I know you and your missus are pally with the owner — are you sure that's not distorting your judgement?'

'That's got nothing to do with it.' Jim felt indignation flame his cheeks. 'She's been given her notice and she's entitled to take it.'

'Yes, we can't go back on an agreement,' Cedric agreed. 'She could take us to court. We'll take delivery of the glass — we don't want to lose it — and wait for, what is it? — Beryl's Brides to move out.'

Robert sulked for the rest of the meeting. When it had finished, he went straight down to Beryl's shop.

'Hello, Beryl,' he greeted her as the shop bell pinged.

Beryl, a wedding dress in her hand and a pincushion on her wrist, was immediately on her guard.

'I'm expecting a customer in ten minutes,' she said. 'For a fitting.'

Robert picked up a lacy garter and examined it.

'Make the most of it,' he said. 'You've still got nowhere to go, I gather. Pity. If only you'd taken me up on my offer when you first opened this place, you could have saved on the rent and you'd have a lot more money behind you to help you find somewhere new.'

'It's you I want behind me, Satan,' flashed Beryl. 'Now get out before I call the police!'

Robert laughed and left, but Beryl was so shaken that she could hardly pin her customer's hem straight. She ended up stabbing her finger and almost got a spot of blood on the fabric. Robert Marlow, the proverbial bad penny. Would he never be out of their lives?

* * *

Across town, Bill was having much the same thought about Gladys's gran. She'd spent almost all the winter holed up in her room, but it had hardly been out of sight, out of mind — nor had her absence made Bill's heart grow fonder. Her demands on Gladys had taxed even her granddaughter's patience, and what grieved Bill most was that with working away so much, he couldn't be around to help or to defend his wife.

'You want to tell her,' he said as they had their tea; Florrie's had already been carried upstairs on a tray. Bill had got a week's work in Hinton for once, shoring up half a row of terraced houses that had been affected by one of the mercifully few bombs the town had endured.

'Oh, Bill, not again,' sighed Gladys. 'And, please, not in front of the children.'

Victor and Joy were in their high chairs and feeding themselves, more or less, with their mince and mashed potato. They were doing a lot more for themselves altogether, notably climbing the stairs when Gladys went up to Florrie and sliding down on their bottoms, which terrified her. The stairs were steep, and the hall, which was tiled, wasn't exactly a soft landing.

'Bill,' she began. 'Now you're home for a bit, do you think you could see your way to making those little gates we talked about and fixing them at the top and bottom of the stairs? You could get hold of a bit of wood from work, couldn't you? Pay for it, I mean —'

'Give over, Glad,' Bill snapped. 'You've asked me I don't know how many times!'

'Sorry.' Gladys backed off. 'Only —'

'The cobbler's children go ill shod, is that what you were going to say? I'll do it, OK, one day when I'm not fagged out from slogging my guts out for that mini-Hitler of a foreman —'

'I know the work's hard —'

Bill threw his knife and fork onto his plate.

'It's worse than hard! When I was near freezing to death on the Arctic convoys, I never thought it'd ever look like the best time of my life, but compared to freezing to death clearing a bomb site or digging a drain in an English winter, it was a —'

119

He had to stop himself from swearing, Gladys could tell.

'— it was paradise!'

The twins had stopped eating and were looking at their father, mouths open, eyes wide.

'Is that what I was fighting for?' Bill went on, his voice rising even more. 'Why me, Glad? Look at Jim and Les, exempted or invalided out of the Army, secure in their good, safe jobs! And Sid too! He had a cushy war, let's be honest, ended up with another stripe, a job and a rank, and look at me, chucked on the scrapheap!'

'Bill, you're not!' Gladys reached for his hand. 'You're doing your very best, you're supporting a family, and we love you! Sid's got none of that, has he? There's no comparison!'

But Bill wouldn't be told. He snatched his hand away, shoved his chair back and stood up.

'I'm sorry, Glad. I've got to get out of here.'

'Where are you going?'

Bill pulled on his jacket.

'Out.'

Gladys closed her eyes as the back door banged.

'Dada shout,' said Joy.

'Never mind, soon better,' said Gladys brightly, not believing it for a moment. 'Eat up your nice tea. Carrots and all, Victor, please, or there'll be no afters!'

Bill was back within the hour to apologise: he'd only been for a walk. Gladys thanked the Lord he wasn't a drinker, though he couldn't have been even if he'd wanted to — everything he earned went on keeping them, she knew. Bill went up to bed early, but Gladys stayed downstairs. She was dead tired too, but she had the knees of Victor's dungarees to patch and the cuff of Joy's cardigan had come unravelled. You had to keep on top of these jobs.

But instead of her mending basket, she got out their photo albums. Carefully she raised the covering tissue and turned the pages of their wedding album, Bill so handsome in his sailor's uniform, Gladys on his arm, both of them radiating happiness. Then she opened their family album: the studio portrait they'd had taken when the twins were a few months old, snaps that Jim had taken on his camera — picnics in the park, the twins on a rug; a couple taken in the back-yard with Gladys holding one twin and Lily the other. Then, of course, their holiday in Weston, and the one Lily had commented on, of Bill leaning against the promenade railings, the sea behind him, looking for all the world as if he were back on the deck of a ship. 'In his element!' they'd said at the time. Would he ever be that happy and carefree again? Would they?

★ ★ ★

Over the next couple of weeks, everything that Jim and Peter had dreaded about Robert's return to the store played out. He loathed what he saw as the mundanity of the daily round at Marlows and the need to dance attendance on the customers. Peter hadn't allotted him any responsible tasks, but Robert neglected even the simple ones he'd been given. He was more likely to be found leaning on a counter to chat with a simpering salesgirl or exchanging racing tips with the commissionaire than doing any real work.

In the evenings, he was rarely to be found at home with his father. Being under his eagle eye all day — because Cedric kept a check on him as well –

was more than enough. Instead he took himself off to what he sarcastically called the fleshpots of Hinton — basically the White Lion or the cinema — or beyond. Now the domestic petrol ration had been restored to some degree, he could drive out to whatever country pub he fancied, or even go back to his club in Birmingham, where he was thought to be a bit of a card, and there was always a warm welcome. There was an even warmer welcome at a certain house in Birmingham that he knew. It was the ultimate in respectability from the outside, but you could spend the evening in the company of a willing and attractive girl for a small consideration. He didn't go back to the poker school though. Even he realised there were limits to his father's tolerance.

One night in early April there wasn't much doing. Robert hadn't felt like going far, so he'd remained in Hinton. But at the Gaumont, *They Knew Mr Knight*, a torrid potboiler about a financial scam that landed someone in jail, was a bit too close for comfort. He left the cinema at the interval and with no one to chat to except the barman in the White Lion, he left there after an hour. But when he stopped his car outside his father's house — he wasn't sure where he called 'home' these days — a taxi was standing on the drive. Robert let himself in.

'Dad?' he called.

Cedric emerged from the sitting room: at the same time, the door of the downstairs lavatory opened, and a woman he instantly recognised as Daphne Tunnicliffe came out. Robert was momentarily thrown, but he hoicked his eyebrows back from their skywards direction and recovered himself.

'I'm so sorry,' he said smoothly, 'if I'm interrupting. I can easily go back out again, it's early yet —'

'Don't be ridiculous, Robert.' His father, coming out of the study, cut in. 'There's no need for that.'

Daphne Tunnicliffe came forward. She was wearing a dress of mauve crêpe with a double strand of pearls at her neck and matching earrings.

'I was just leaving,' she smiled.

Robert wasn't letting them get away with that.

'I believe I saw you in the store at the shopping evening before Christmas,' he said.

'Yes, it was a very enjoyable evening.'

'It was, wasn't it?' said Robert smoothly. 'Sadly we weren't introduced,' he added pointedly. 'I was on my way over to speak to you both when you disappeared into the crowd.'

Cedric stepped in.

'That's easily rectified. Daphne — this is my son Robert. Robert — Mrs Tunnicliffe.'

Daphne held out her hand.

'How do you do,' she said. 'I'd heard you were back, of course.'

I bet you have, thought Robert, wondering how much detail his father had confided in her. The full story, no doubt — he would have put money on it. He smiled his most winning smile, but his words had a steely edge which neither Daphne nor Cedric could miss.

'Indeed I am!' he said. 'The Prodigal Son! Well, I'll let you say your goodbyes in private. It was so nice to meet you properly at last. If you'll excuse me . . .'

He went into the study and shut the door behind him. Going to the drinks tray, he poured himself a whisky and drank it, quietly fuming.

After a good ten minutes of low murmurings, of

123

doors opening and closing, and the taxi grinding its gears and setting off, his father came in. Robert, by this time on his second glass, started on him straight away.

'So this is what you get up to when my back's turned! A nice little affair you've got going here —'

Cedric held up his hand.

'Just one moment, Robert. May I remind you that this is my house, my home, and I can entertain any-one I like, at any time I like, in it.'

'Funny you've never invited her round when I'm in!'

Cedric never raised his voice: instead there was a firmness in it when he said:

'But you never are in, are you? Do you want me to sit here on my own every evening in the expectation that you might grace me with your presence? Because I suspect I'd have a very long wait! I did and do have a life of my own, you know. I enjoy Daphne's company very much — and I intend to continue doing so. Goodnight.'

It was rare, almost unheard of, for Cedric to get the better of Robert in a confrontation, and Robert was left stunned and furious. He'd been so wrapped up in himself, so intent on pursuing his own pleasures, he hadn't been policing what he'd suspected back before Christmas. His father had formed an attach-ment — and to a widow! If this carried on, what was that going to do to his future prospects?

124

13

Nothing more was said between father and son at breakfast next morning. Robert kept his head down and actually attended to his duties at Marlows for once, and when they took a pre-dinner sherry together in the sitting room that evening, Robert seemed in a more conciliatory mood.

'I'm sorry for my little outburst last night,' he began. 'I was simply taken aback. But I was out of order to say what I did.'

Cedric inclined his head. 'You were.'

'The thing is, with respect, Dad, you're not the most worldly of men.' Robert leaned against the mantelpiece as he said it, totally at ease, a man of the world himself, lecturing the older man. 'Since mother died so young, your horizons have been limited to that shop. I just think you should be aware that the world is full of widows on the lookout for a meal ticket.'

The hairs on the back of Cedric's neck prickled. If this was Robert's idea of an apology . . .

'I take it you're referring to Daphne?' he said coldly.

'Well, of course I am! I'm only trying to protect you, Dad! From someone who might be trying to get her hooks into you!'

Cedric gripped the stem of his sherry glass so hard it was a wonder it didn't snap.

'I didn't think after what you said last night that anything could be worse,' he said stiffly, 'but I will not have you talking about Daphne in that way. She's had a dreadful time. She lost her husband when she was relatively young, and then the daughter she doted on.'

'Yes, yes, I daresay she's spun you a sob story and you've fallen for it —'

'She's done nothing of the kind!' Cedric insisted. 'That happens to be the truth! Daphne is perfectly independently well off, and she's never asked me for anything!'

'No, well, she wouldn't, would she, not openly — but who's to say she hasn't got her eye on a second husband, and upping her wealth a bit?'

Light dawned on Cedric like a wartime searchlight. It wasn't Cedric's happiness and wellbeing that was bothering Robert at all!

'You're worried about your inheritance, that's what it is! How stupid of me.'

'Well, I think I've a right to point out —'

His words were covered by the dinner gong — the warning that their meal would be on the table in five minutes.

'Robert, you need have no worries on that score.' Cedric put down his glass and stood up. 'I have no intention whatsoever of remarrying. I've never asked Daphne's age and I wouldn't dream of it, but as I'm sure you've observed, she's a good ten if not fifteen years younger than I am. She's already suffered two bereavements and, as I would certainly be the first to die, I wouldn't want her to go through another. And whatever yours and my relationship has been, is, or might become, you are my son and I know my obligations. Trust me, you will not be left penniless.'

Robert swallowed hard. He'd heard what he wanted to hear, but somehow it had left a sour taste in his mouth that wasn't down to the stuff the wine merchant was passing off as Amontillado these days.

126

'I'm sorry, Dad. I didn't mean to —'

'I know exactly what you meant. But let's say no more about it. Shall we go through?'

Robert followed his father along the hall to the dining room, but he still felt uncomfortable. He knew he'd overstepped the mark. And even after dinner, when he'd roared off in the Riley and spent the evening in the arms of his favourite lady of the night, he didn't feel much better.

* * *

Next morning, as soon as he got to his office and his secretary had brought in the coffee tray, Cedric telephoned Daphne Tunnicliffe.

'We can't go on like this,' he said, and then, in case she thought he was ending their friendship, added quickly, 'Me and Robert, I mean. There's no getting away from it, we simply don't get along, and we never will.'

'Oh, Cedric —'

'No, it's true. He's only been here five minutes, but he's a liability, Daphne, with everything he touches. At the store, he plays up to the younger female staff — they'll do anything for him, and he knows it. He persuaded the new girl on Pipes and Tobaccos to give him a tin of a hundred cigarettes — Benson and Hedges, if you please, that we've hardly seen since before the war! — when they should have been bought and paid for. Peter Simmonds spends so much time trying to keep him out of trouble and to sort out the messes he makes that he's got his eye off the ball in other areas. Only last week Peter hadn't got the year-on-year figures for me when we had our meeting — that's

127

never happened before. I could go on —'

'Please don't.' Daphne felt awkward hearing Cedric talk about his son like this.

'—and as for outside of work, well, who knows what he gets up to!' Cedric concluded unhappily.

Privately, he'd been waiting for years for Robert to be named in a paternity suit.

It was an unusual outpouring for a man as restrained as Cedric, and Daphne's heart went out to him.

'Look, my dear,' she said. 'That may well be true, but he is still your son, your only child. He's been through a lot, never mind whose fault it was, and he's obviously feeling unsettled — there was a distinct atmosphere last night. He won't be with you for ever, he'll want a place of his own, but while he's living with you, maybe it would be best if you and I stopped seeing each other. Then you can give him the attention and the help he obviously needs.'

'No, don't you see, that's exactly what he wants!' insisted Cedric, horrified at the thought. 'He's a complete dog in a manger! He's not a bit interested in me and what I do normally!' He paused and took a breath. Daphne imagined him behind the big mahogany desk in his office at the heart of his empire. He was monarch of all he surveyed, the successful businessman — and the frustrated father. 'But you're right that I have to help him,' Cedric conceded. 'Help him to find something else do . . . somewhere else to live and someone else to work for!'

He sounded so desperate, and the situation was hardly comical, but Daphne couldn't help saying with a smile in her voice:

'Someone you don't like very much, if he's the liability you say!'

'Either that . . .' sighed Cedric, 'or somewhere well away from Hinton.'

'My husband had a cousin,' Daphne reflected. 'His son, unfortunately, was rather like Robert. They parcelled him off to Malaya in the end, to another cousin with a rubber plantation. The boy did rather well. He really took to it.'

'Have you still got this chap's address?' asked Cedric, not entirely seriously — but not entirely joking, either. They went on to talk of other things, but when Cedric put the phone down, the conversation with Daphne had calmed him, and helped him to get things into some sort of perspective. It had also given him the beginnings of an idea.

A few days later, Jim and Peter Simmonds were in Peter's office, working through the competing claims for the four display windows once the new plate glass had been fitted. Before the war, Gentlemen's Outfitting, Model Gowns, Suits and Coats and Ladies' Fashions had had a window each, but to give the new Bargain Basement a window to display its wares, four would have to go into three. Gentlemen's Outfitting needed a permanent showcase and so did Ladies' Fashions: could they persuade Model Gowns and Suits and Coats to alternate weekly in the third? As the Model Gowns buyer was a fearsome harridan whose death stare could turn a man's blood to ice, Peter wasn't looking forward to suggesting it. Then there was a tap on the door.

'Ah, hello chaps! Excellent! Two birds.'

'Good morning, Robert,' said Peter Simmonds, glancing pointedly at his watch. 'Just.'

Jim said nothing. It was eleven forty-five and the first time Robert had been seen.

'Yes, sorry, I had a lot to sort out first thing,' breezed Robert. 'And, er, early warning, I shan't be here tomorrow at all.'

'Oh yes?' said Peter calmly.

'I'm off to London,' beamed Robert. 'On a buying trip.'

Jim kept his eyes fixed on the papers in front of him. Surely Cedric Marlow hadn't authorised Robert to go off buying stock? He must have had a brainstorm! Maybe Robert read his mind, or perhaps it was the shock on Peter's face, because he added:

'Don't worry, not for this place, for myself! I've got to get my tropical kit, you see.'

'Tropical kit?' squeaked Jim, unable to contain himself.

Robert looked smug.

'Yes, sorry, boys, but I'm off to Kenya. Dad's tapped up an old contact who's got a coffee farm. I'm going to work for him.'

'Kenya . . . ? Coffee . . . ?' Peter stuttered. 'Do you . . . do you know anything about coffee?'

'Apart from drinking it, nothing!' Robert grinned. 'But I'm sure I can learn. Anyway, if you two are holed up in here, I'd better get out onto the floor. I don't want to be neglecting my duties while I've still got them!'

Peter stood up at once.

'We've finished,' he said, though they hadn't. 'I'll come with you.'

In this mood of ebullience, who knew what Robert might sanction. Last week he'd let a customer — someone they'd never seen before — cash a ten-pound cheque. It had bounced, of course.

Back on the first floor, Jim passed by Childrenswear.

'Fix yourself a pass out at dinnertime,' he hissed to Lily. 'I'll organise sandwiches from the canteen. There's news.'

★ ★ ★

There'd been a cold snap with snow in the early part of the month and the weight of it had brought down a tree in the park. The branches had swiftly been snatched up by enterprising citizens for firewood, but the trunk remained, a useful substitute for the non-existent benches. The day was chilly but dry. Jim brushed away some loose bark for Lily to sit down. Lily opened her packet of sandwiches but once Jim began to explain about Robert's move to Kenya, was too open-mouthed to eat a thing.

'You know what it is,' Jim said, opening his sandwiches and realising they were bloater paste — yuck. 'He'll be what they used to call a remittance man, sent away with an allowance on the unspoken understanding that he doesn't come back. I bet this coffee farmer won't pay Robert, or not much — my uncle will be sending him an allowance.'

Lily was still taking it in.

'Well, he can afford it, I suppose,' she said. 'But honestly, Jim, Robert Marlow is the end! Slippery as an eel is about right! He's done it again — he's slithered away from any scandal that might leak out, like these things do, about what really went on with Sir Douglas and any gossip about the divorce, he's caused daily mayhem at the store, and then — vamoosh!'

'I know.' Jim chewed thoughtfully. 'Typical of him, but he'll be a long way away, that's the main thing.'

Lily threw a bit of crust to a hopeful blackbird, who thanked her with a bob of his head before he flew off.

'The further the better. But fancy Mr Marlow knowing someone in Kenya!'

In fact, Cedric had called in a favour: the coffee farmer was an old school friend. Years ago, he'd approached Cedric: he'd set up a charity to build hospitals in remote parts of East Africa and was asking for contributions. Moved by accounts — and even worse, photographs — of amateur amputations and mothers with malarial babies, Cedric had made sizeable donations ever since.

'I should think Robert'll love it out there,' said Jim as they walked back to work. 'All that Happy Valley crowd, cocktails and polo and horse racing and what have you.'

'Can I go straight and tell Beryl?' asked Lily. 'Please, Jim. Everyone'll know soon enough, and Robert did go and see her and make those snide remarks.'

Beryl had told them about Robert's visit, how she'd managed to get rid of him, but how shaken it had left her feeling.

'Yes, go on,' said Jim. 'We've kept enough of Robert Marlow's secrets in the past.'

When Lily told her, Beryl was ecstatic.

'Hallelujah!' she cried. 'Out of our hair — and off to Africa! With any luck,' she added, 'he'll get some terrible tropical fever and die in agony!'

'Oh Beryl, you wouldn't wish that on him, surely?' Lily protested.

'No, you're right, it's too good for him,' mused Beryl. 'Better if he's eaten by a lion! Yeah, that's it! Though he'd probably give the poor creature indigestion!'

132

14

If Beryl thought she'd heard the last of the Marlow family for now, however, she was wrong. At five o'clock the following day she was tidying her stock and wondering, really, how on earth she was going to display it in the cramped front room at home in Alma Terrace. The house belonged to her mother-in-law, Ivy, who'd moved away to a housekeeping job, looking after Jim's widowed father, along with Les's sister Susan. Ivy hadn't needed to take any of her furniture with her and the front room was still full of it — a sagging horsehair sofa and a huge Victorian sideboard, not to mention a stuffed badger and several chipped china ornaments. Those weren't a huge problem — she and Les could box them up and stick them in the loft, but as for the furniture, which she daren't get rid of in case Ivy ever came back . . . Despairing, Beryl shook her head, then turned it as the shop bell pinged. She found herself face to face with Evelyn Marlow.

'Don't worry, I shan't keep you beyond closing time,' Evelyn said at once — which was considerate of her, Beryl had to concede. 'I'm waiting for my mother to finish at the hairdressers.'

'Please.' Beryl swept a hand around her little shop. 'Feel free to look around.'

Continuing her tidying, she watched Evelyn as she browsed. She was beautifully turned out as usual. At first sight, her oatmeal tweed suit didn't look anything out of the ordinary, but Beryl's practised eye could see the lapels and pockets were double top-stitched

133

and the buttons were of bone. Beryl smoothed down the skirt of her dress, glad she was wearing her better one today, the navy crêpe, and not the other one she wore for work, made by Dora out of blackout material. She adjusted her wedding and engagement rings and stole a glance at Evelyn's left hand. Ringless.

Evelyn caught her looking and said quickly, 'I'm not looking for a wedding dress, if that's what you're thinking. Nothing could be further from my mind!'

'No,' said Beryl quietly. 'I can imagine. I know who you are, Mrs Marlow.'

Evelyn gave a short yelp of a laugh.

'Ah, but I'm not, am I? I'm not Mrs Marlow any more, or I soon won't be, if I have anything to do with it. I plan to revert to my maiden name.'

That was pretty extreme. So Evelyn was that bitter, was she?

'I see. Well, I'm sorry things haven't worked out for you all the same.'

Beryl was surprised to find that she meant it. She'd always thought Evelyn a spoilt brat, indulged by her doting father, and she no doubt was, but the easier and more charmed your existence, the harder it must be when it all came crashing down. Whereas if, like Beryl, you'd had a rotten start in life, with a father who'd terrorised her and her mum, and you'd had to scrape by and work for everything you had — well, you knew from the start that life was about hard knocks, so at least you were prepared.

'Thank you.' Evelyn inclined her head in acknowledgement. 'But I don't want to talk about it. I'm sure there's been enough gossip already around here.'

But there was a wavery note in her voice and Beryl knew she was right — under the hard exterior and the bitterness, Evelyn was upset and humiliated and hurt. From the way Evelyn was talking, she hadn't wasted any time in filing for divorce.

'Sorry,' she said instead. 'I'll let you carry on.'

Evelyn took a lace wedding dress — the one Lily had worn — off the rail and held it at arm's length to inspect it.

'You've got some nice things.'

'Thank you.' That was high praise, coming from her.

'And they're all for hire, are they, not for sale?'

'That's right. That's what most people want, if they can't borrow from a friend.'

Evelyn re-hung the dress and turned to face her.

'How did you start?'

'In a small way.' Beryl smiled at the memory. 'With my own wedding and bridesmaid's dresses and leaflets through doors and a card in my front-room window.'

'Really?' Evelyn put her head on one side, listening.

'It was early in the war,' Beryl began. 'People still wanted to look like a bride, but who could afford to splash their coupons on a dress you were only going to wear once? Unless you were — if you'll excuse me — someone more in your position, who had a lovely heirloom dress they could wear, or had the money and the contacts to buy something off-coupon.' Evelyn bobbed her head in agreement. 'But as the war went on, and after the bomb here in '42, when the High Street got hit, and Marlows got damaged, it had to shut its bridal department, and the only other big store in town got wiped out entirely. So more and more women of all . . . classes, if you like, started to look to me for something to wear to get married in.

And I branched out into short length too, for those quick 48-hour-pass weddings, when there was no time to sort a big do. Smart outfits for special occasions and mother of the bride . . . you know.'

'Hm.' Evelyn had moved to another rail, and was looking at an apricot-coloured dress and edge-to-edge coat in heavy silk. 'So where do you get your things?'

'Oh, it varies,' Beryl shrugged. 'Private sales, some-times, stuff I hear about, or classifieds in the better magazines. End-of-lines, sample sales, shops that are closing down . . .' She sighed. 'I've built up all these contacts . . . so much hard work . . . It's why it's such a blooming nuisance that they're chucking me out.'

'Who are? Marlows?'

'Yes. They want this little unit back soon to use as window space again. I've been telling my customers, and I'll write to past clients. I've got a notice to put in the window, but I've been putting off doing it. As if ignoring it'll make it go away!'

Evelyn looked puzzled.

'So you're moving premises, that's all?'

'I wish!' Beryl turned down her mouth. 'I can't afford anywhere else in town; rent and rates on a proper shop'd put me out of business. I've looked at little shops further out, but there'd be no passing trade like here. And anyway . . . I don't want to be on some tatty little parade in a poor part of town stuck between a fish and chip shop and a place that mends dentures! Not when I've worked so hard . . .' She tailed off. 'I'm sorry, I don't know why I'm telling you all this.'

'Because I asked, I suppose,' said Evelyn with a hint of a smile. 'So what are you going to do?'

'I'll have to go back to trading out of my front room

136

at home. Alma Terrace.'

Evelyn's brow wrinkled.

'I don't know it, I'm afraid.'

No, you wouldn't, thought Beryl, wishing she hadn't mentioned the address. *Not your part of town by a long way.*

But Evelyn was continuing.

'There'll be even less passing trade there, surely?'

'Yes, I know. I'll have to rely on word of mouth, advertise in the local paper maybe, start leafleting again . . .' Beryl bucked herself up. 'Sorry, it's not like me to be such a moaning Minnie! At least we've got the telephone at home, and if I can get a bit more money behind me, maybe one day I'll be able to afford to buy my way back into the centre of town. A side street, anyhow.' She stopped abruptly and looked at her watch. 'Crikey, it's past closing! I ought to get home and I'm keeping you from your mum. She'll be standing out in the cold, wondering where you are!'

'Oh, don't worry about her. She'll have gone straight to the White Lion. We're meeting my father for a drink and then dinner.'

Beryl smiled to herself. Of course they were. She thought of the tin of whale meat in the larder for herself and Les.

Evelyn pulled on her gloves. 'I'd better get along, even so.'

'Right.'

Evelyn moved to the door. The bell pinged as she opened it, letting in a blast of the cold evening air. But in the doorway she hesitated. She turned and said: 'Thank you, Beryl — it is Beryl, I take it?'

Beryl's nod confirmed it.

'It's been nice talking to you,' Evelyn added. Again

there was that hint of vulnerability. 'It's taken my mind off my own problems for a bit, anyhow.'

'You're welcome,' said Beryl. It had come to something when she was a comfort to Evelyn Marlow!

'Goodbye,' said Evelyn. 'I hope you sort something out.'

'Bye,' Beryl called after her as Evelyn was swallowed up in the evening gloom.

Beryl moved to the door, turned the sign to closed and drew down the blind. On a night like this, Robert Marlow had barged through that door just as she was closing, with his offer to 'help' with her rent in return for payment in kind. What a vile man he was! Beryl and Lily had always thought he and Evelyn deserved each other, but now Beryl thought differently. No one deserved Robert Marlow with his selfish charm and the careless way he treated people. And she was glad Evelyn had got out.

★ ★ ★

News of Robert's departure spread through the store like one of the African bushfires he might soon be encountering. There were long faces among the juniors and salesgirls whose dreams of a Cinderella story (if only they knew the reality!) had been shattered, but Nancy was philosophical. Both Frank and Derek had been supplanted by Harry, who'd been lured from Woolworth's to run the Bargain Basement. He was of average height, average build and average looks — his ears stuck out like the fins on a barrage balloon — but he had a cleft in his chin like Robert Mitchum and he was unfailingly cheerful. He was a very suitable match for Nancy, Lily reckoned, and a much more likely long-term prospect, if and when Nancy decided she was ready for one.

Lily filled Gladys in as well when she went round for a cup of tea after work. She didn't know the full extent of Robert's past misdeeds in Birmingham or in Hinton, so she was simply swept away by the adventure of it all. Her view of Africa had been shaped entirely by what she'd seen at the pictures.

'Do you think it'll be like *King Solomon's Mines*?' Gladys asked breathlessly. She was peeling Bramleys to stew for the twins' tea. 'Native chiefs and witch doctors?'

'I'm not sure Africa's still quite like that,' Lily pinched a bit of apple peel and nibbled it. 'And it's not the kind of life Robert'll be leading anyway. He'll be with all the upper-crust English.' But she was tired of talking, and thinking, about Robert Marlow, so she changed the subject. 'How's Bill?'

Gladys sighed.

'Oh, Lily. He's changed.'

'Changed how?'

Gladys laid down the paring knife.

'He's not so angry about things any more, but he seems . . . I dunno, resigned, I suppose. And somehow it's worse seeing him like that. It's like he's given up hope.'

'Oh Gladys, I am sorry.'

'I hate it. I only wish there was something I could do!'

'You are doing something, by bolstering him up and being you and being the good wife and mum that you are. Bill values that, you know he does.'

'I wonder sometimes.'

'He does. And you'll find a way out of this — for all

139

of you. You're stronger and cleverer than you think you are!'

'I don't feel it.' Gladys picked up the knife again and began slicing the apples into a pan.

'You are. Look at how determined you were to find Bill's mother before the wedding. I wasn't convinced you could do it, but you dragged me off to London and we did find her.'

'Yeah, and that was a big success, wasn't it?'

Penniless, Bill's widowed mother had had to put him in a Barnardo's home while she looked for work. After Lily and Gladys had tracked her down, Bill had met up with her, but sadly, too much time had passed for him to feel anything for her.

'I don't suppose his mum could help now, could she?'

'How?' Gladys countered. 'She's got no money or anything, now she's divorced that horrible second husband and he cut her off without a penny.' This was true. Bill's mum was up north, working as a lady's companion. 'No,' Gladys concluded. 'I've got to come up with some way of getting Bill out of this state myself. Somehow.'

When Lily had gone, and Bill came home, she relayed the news about Robert Marlow to him — at least it was something different to tell him apart from the twins' sayings and doings. Shirt sleeves rolled up, Bill was washing off the day's grime from his labouring work at the kitchen sink.

'So?' he said over the noise of the running water and Gladys clattering about with plates and pans. 'What's it to us?'

Joy and Victor were playing in the other room with the door to the scullery open and the door to the hall firmly shut. Bill still hadn't made the stair gates she'd asked for, but Gladys feared bringing it up again in his present mood. She continued with her own train of thought.

'Kenya, though . . .' she mused. 'Do you think there'll be snakes?' She shuddered as she said the word. 'Ughhh. It wouldn't be for me!'

Bill held out his hand and she passed him the towel.

'Well, you're not very likely to get the chance to find out, are you?' he said — not unkindly, but flatly.

Suddenly there was a fearful clatter and a sickening thump from the hall.

'Oh my God!' cried Gladys. 'The stairs! That'll be one of the children —'

She raced into the other room, Bill following.

'But how?' he asked. Then he saw — the door to the hall stood open.

'One of them must have managed to reach the handle!'

And when they ran into the hall, sure enough, there were the children — looking at the crumpled figure of Gladys's gran lying at the foot of the stairs. One slipper had come off, her dressing gown was open, her nightie was rucked up over her knees, and her false teeth had flown out.

Victor and Joy turned their innocent little faces to their parents.

'Gan-gan,' said Victor.

'She go nigh-nighs,' Joy added sagely. She picked up Florrie's teeth and solemnly handed them to her father. Bill put them gingerly to one side and crouched down.

Gladys had already fallen to her knees beside the old woman.

'Get the doctor, Bill, quick, or an ambulance!'

But Bill had seen enough casualties in the war to know there was no point in the ambulance and the doctor would only be needed to sign the death certificate. He felt for a pulse to make sure, his own heart thumping, horribly conscious of Gladys's desperate eyes on him. Slowly he raised his head.

'I'm sorry, Gladys. She's dead.'

15

Bill yanked open the front door and looked wildly up and down the street. Seeing a neighbour's lad on his way back from the corner shop, he whistled him over.

'There's been an accident. Go for the nearest doctor — Dr Croft, isn't it? — to come here, then get yourself round to Brook Street, number 31. Tell the lady there the same, and ask if she can come and help — 31, Brook Street. Got that?'

The lad looked at him with a question in his eyes. 'All the way to Brook Street?'

'It's an emergency . . . oh, all right!' Bill fished out a pocketful of change and gave him an extravagant sixpence. 'Now go! Run!'

From behind him came the sound of Gladys keening over her grandmother's body. When he went back to the sorry scene, the children turned their uncomprehending little faces to him. Gently Bill raised his wife to her feet, led her into the back room and made her sit down. The children trailed after them.

The sixpence must have added wings to the boy's heels because the doctor arrived within twenty minutes and when Dora, Lily and Jim got there some time later, it was all over. Florrie's body had been taken away and Gladys put to bed with a mild sedative. Bill was sitting numbly in a chair while the children tugged fretfully at his trousers, whimpering. Jerkily, Bill relayed that Florrie had fallen down the stairs. Despite her own shock, Dora quickly took charge.

'First off, those children need to be in bed,' she

said. 'I'll take them up. Lily, you can help me. And we'll look in on Gladys. Jim —'

Jim knew what the next most vital job was on such occasions.

'I'll get the kettle on.'

'And I don't suppose you've had your tea, have you, Bill, with all this going on?' Dora clucked. 'Fix him a sandwich, Jim, there's a good lad. He needs something inside him.'

Within the hour, some kind of order had been restored. Gladys was fast asleep, as were the twins. Bill had eaten, and all four sat round while he recounted the evening's events. And there were more shocks to come.

'What do you mean, Dr Croft started acting a bit strange?' Dora frowned.

'He was . . . he said . . . how did he put it?' Bill thought back. 'The circumstances surrounding the death, that was it . . . they weren't clear. He had the local bobby come round.'

'What? The police? He can't think . . . ?' Jim sounded sceptical.

But Lily, the great Agatha Christie fan, knew what the police involvement meant. A suspicious death. Method, tick — a simple shove from behind. Opportunity, tick — there was only Bill and Gladys's word that they'd been together in the kitchen the whole time, and didn't husbands and wives always give each other alibis? And as for motive, well — living with Florrie Jessop would have made a saint swear, as Dora frequently put it. But to bump her off . . . ?

'He didn't believe that Florrie fell? He thinks someone pushed her?' she asked incredulously.

Bill opened his hands wide, palms up.

144

'I dunno. That, or she threw herself down, or that something else fishy was going on. He said the police had to be called, and they might want a . . .' he groped for the word '. . . a pathologist, that was it, to look into it to see exactly what injuries she had, and exactly what had caused her death.'

'As if you'd been ill treating her?' Lily's voice went up the scale even further. 'Come on, the opposite was true! I hope you told him so!'

Bill looked brokenly at them. 'I was . . . it was difficult. Gladys was in bits, the kids were round my ankles . . .'

'And PC Ruston?' Dora knew the local bobby — she often saw him on his beat when she'd been round helping Gladys. He was an older man, stolid and reliable, but more used to clipping unruly lads round the ear or hauling drunks home than attending the scene of a suspicious death. 'What did he have to say for himself?'

'Not a lot, he seemed under the sway of the doctor.'

'Oh, good grief!' Lily was truly incredulous by now. Jim stepped in.

'Look, Bill, no one in their right mind could think that you or Gladys would do anything to harm anyone. From what you've said, you called this Dr Croft because he lived nearest, right?'

'Yeah, and I wish I hadn't now!'

'But he's not Florrie's regular doctor, is he?' Jim continued. 'He doesn't know her. Maybe what he meant was, did Florrie have anything wrong with her already?' This provoked a snort from Lily, but Jim persisted. 'You know, giddy spells, blackouts, unsteady on her feet — anything that might have caused her to fall.'

Lily was shaking her head in disbelief, but Dora, with her usual good sense, had moved on to practicalities.

'So what's the upshot, Bill? You can't have a funeral without a death certificate.'

'No. There was talk of it all having to go to the coroner before we could get one. An inquest.'

Lily looked hopelessly at Jim, and then at her mother, then at Bill.

'I know,' he said. 'Like we haven't got enough to worry about already. It'll finish Gladys, this will.'

There was no more to be said. Lily and Dora tidied up the toys and folded the washing on the clothes horse, then they washed up and set out the breakfast things. Bill stepped outside 'to clear his head', he said, and Jim followed him. The night was clear and the moon was almost full; it was so bright Jim could see its seas reflected in the puddles of the yard.

'This would have to happen,' Bill sighed. 'Things haven't been great between me and Gladys anyhow, with me working all hours or working away. And she knows — God forgive me — but I couldn't stand her gran.'

'From what I know, Florrie didn't work very hard to make herself likeable.'

'There's been plenty of times I've wished her dead, I can tell you,' Bill admitted.

'I hope you didn't say that to the doctor or the police!'

'I'm not that daft. I still feel guilty, though.' Bill's open, honest face was haggard in the bright moonlight. 'Gladys had been on to me to make some kind of gate — a barrier — for the top and bottom of the stairs. To stop the kids climbing them on their own

146

and taking a tumble.'

Jim frowned. 'I don't see how that would have helped Florrie.'

'A gate at the bottom would have broken her fall, wouldn't it?' said Bill.

Jim patted him on the arm. From what he knew of Florrie Jessop's bulk, she'd have crashed straight through it, but it seemed disrespectful to say so — don't speak ill of the dead and all that.

'Look, you've had a hell of a shock. It's easy to get things out of proportion. Wait and see what happens next. But for goodness' sake, Bill, keep any thoughts like that to yourself!'

* * *

Over the next week, Dora dropped everything so she could be with Gladys while Bill went to work. He'd picked up some more work in Hinton — ironically, for the firm that was going to be making good the brickwork before the glaziers fitted the new windows at Marlows.

'How's Gladys doing?' asked Beryl. She was in her final week of trading and Bill had been sent round to take some preliminary measurements.

'She's like a corpse herself,' Bill reported wearily. 'Won't eat, tossing and turning all night and torment-ing herself. I was having a wash in the kitchen, see, with the tap running, Gladys was getting our tea, and the twins were making a bit of a racket when Florrie fell. All Gladys can keep saying is what if her gran had been banging on the bedroom floor with her stick all the while and we didn't hear, so she had to get out of bed and come down for whatever it was she wanted.'

147

Beryl clicked her tongue. 'That's a hiding to nothing, that is.'

'You try telling Glad that. Hold this end of the tape, will you?' Beryl took it, and Bill walked away, unrolling it as he went. 'We had to give full statements to the police the day after it happened. I was on tacks, I can tell you, wondering what she'd say.' He reached the far wall and squinted at the tape, then took his pencil from behind his ear and jotted a number in his notebook. 'Luckily she was so out of it she just answered yes and no to everything they asked. But it seems they want an inquest, all the same.'

Bill walked back towards Beryl, re-rolling the tape. 'Is that really necessary?'

Bill shrugged.

'They seem to think so. I reckon my first mistake was calling that Dr Croft — he was a right old misery guts. He's the one that put the poison down for us.'

'Maybe you got him in the middle of his tea,' Beryl sympathised. 'So when is this inquest?'

'Friday. Dora's having the kids.'

'Good.'

They both looked up as the shop bell tinkled. Bill took the arrival of a customer as his cue to leave.

'I've got all I need for now. See you, Beryl.'

'Yes . . . bye, Bill. Good luck on Friday.'

But Beryl sounded distracted, and no wonder. It wasn't a customer as such: it was Evelyn Marlow again. She crossed with Bill in the doorway, then advanced towards Beryl, looking serious.

'I'm glad you're not busy,' she said. 'I was hoping we could have a little chat.'

Beryl was immediately on her guard. Surely Robert, in a last thrust to wound Evelyn, hadn't told her about the pass he'd made at Beryl?

'Oh yes?' she said as calmly as she could. 'Would you like to sit down?'

'Thank you.'

When she'd first set up her shop, Beryl had borrowed a lyre-backed chair from Dora's front room. She'd polished it up and re-covered the seat in a remnant of rose brocade. She pulled it out now from the little desk-cum-counter and perched herself on her stool the other side. Evelyn sat down. She was in a different suit today — lovat green this time, with a velvet collar and cuffs. Beryl sighed. What she'd give for one of Evelyn's outfits!

Time to bite the bullet.

'What can I do for you?' she asked.

'It's more a case of what I can do for you, as they say.' At Beryl's baffled look, Evelyn went on: 'If that fellow was who I suspect — an advance party from the builders — then this couldn't be better timed. The other night, as I said, I was meeting my parents. Well, I told my father about your predicament.'

Beryl's eyes widened as she tried to remember what she'd said. The idea of Sir Douglas and Lady Brimble and their daughter discussing her little shop over their oysters and fine wine — or whatever the White Lion was serving these days — seemed incredible. But Evelyn was continuing.

'I think there's potential here, and he agrees. I'm on my own now and I want something to do. I know a lot about clothes — they've always been a passion of mine — and I've always been interested in more than just buying them for myself. My father's willing to set me up in business, a bridal and occasion wear business in fact, both for hire and, as things improve, for

149

sale as well. He'll pay for premises and so on to get me started. But' — she gave a self-deprecating laugh — 'obviously I can't be tied to a shop six days a week! So I'd like you to manage it.'

Beryl was glad she'd suggested sitting down. For a moment she couldn't think of a thing to say. Even when Evelyn prompted her, she still looked at her blankly.

'Well?'

'Um. Me . . . and you?'

'Why not?'

'I — I don't know.'

Evelyn lifted her immaculately tailored shoulders.

'There you are then. I don't see you'll get a better offer.'

Beryl hadn't expected any offer to come her way — certainly not from Evelyn. She didn't know what to think.

'It's very sudden, that's all,' she stammered. 'You've taken me by surprise. I — I'll have to think it over. Can you give me a day or so?'

'All right.' Evelyn stood up. Her smile was charming, with a hint of cunning. 'But time's running out here for you, Beryl, and from what you said before, I don't really see what other option you've got. This is a chance to stay in business without any of the worry. I'd jump at it if I were you.'

★ ★ ★

It was clear from the moment she arrived at Dora's that Beryl was agitated. Her hair was in its usual smooth waves and her make-up was fresh — she still swore by the wartime maxim that 'Beauty is a Duty' — but

150

her cardigan was buttoned up all wrong and she even refused a piece of Dora's bread pudding. She'd told Les what had happened, of course, but it was Jim and Lily that she really turned to as a sounding board for tricky business decisions. They listened as she outlined Evelyn's offer.

'Well?' she asked when she'd finished.

Lily looked to Jim to go first.

'I don't know, Beryl,' he said. 'It's not exactly a chance to 'stay in business', is it? At least, not like you are at the moment, with your own business.'

'Yes,' said Lily. 'I can't see Evelyn letting you keep your name over the door. So what happens to Beryl's Brides?'

'I did ask her when I got my senses back. She said I'd have to wind it up.'

'Oh Beryl!' Lily was shocked. 'But you've worked so hard at it!'

'I know,' Beryl sighed. 'But the trouble is, she's got a point. Wouldn't this be a better option than sticking it out on my own, scraping along working out of the front room again?'

Jim took his glasses off, looked at them and put them on again. He always did it when he had something serious to say.

'Only in some ways. You might not have so much worry, you might have a bit more security day-to-day, but you'd be an employee. You'd be giving up control.'

'And to Evelyn!' added Lily. 'Look, I know she's had a tough time, and maybe it's done her good, but has she really changed that much? Jim's right as far as it goes when he says you'd have security, but what if she gets bored after a bit and decides it's not for her? You'd be back where you started, only worse!'

Beryl put her head in her hands. 'Oh, you're not helping!'

'I'm sorry.' Lily felt for her. 'But you know what my mum'd say — you need a very long spoon to sup with the devil!'

Beryl lifted her head, agonised.

'I dunno what to do now! When I came round I thought I'd decided — I was going to say yes! And look' — she delved in her bag — 'she's already found a couple of empty shops that I'd never even thought of looking at 'cos I knew I could never afford the rent! South Street — and Park Road!'

Lily snatched up the estate agents' particulars.

'Park Road? That's dead posh! There's that nice china shop along there, and the Irish linen shop —'

'And the Tudor Rose tea rooms. Our shop'd be right opposite!'

'That's the point, Beryl, that's what I was going to say!' Jim butted in. 'See what you said? *Our* shop. Tell her you'll do it, but as well as taking a salary, you want to be a partner.'

'What?' Beryl opened her eyes wide. 'Like part-own it? But you know me and Les are flat broke — we've got no money to invest! Not the sort she'd be talking about —'

'I'm not talking about money,' said Jim patiently. 'Look what you're bringing. You're the one who'll be there every day, actually making the sales. You're providing some of the stock. You're providing the initial contacts. You're providing experience and expertise. What's she bringing? OK, the set-up costs, but apart from that? A few years of swanning around like a fashion plate?'

'He's right, Beryl!' Lily glowed with pride as she

152

always did when she was reminded how clever Jim could be, and it inspired her too. 'Remember the Marlows' sales manual? The importance of goodwill? That's what you're bringing, and it's got to be worth something! Actually, it's worth a lot, else why would Mr Marlow value it?'

'Plus' — Jim was on a roll now — 'if the bank won't look at you for a loan —'

'Because she's a woman!' Lily fumed.

'— if the bank won't look at you, tog Les up in his best suit and send him. Say it's to do up your house or something. He's got a regular job, after all, one he's had for years. They might not loan enough to go in fifty-fifty with Evelyn, but any say in how things are done would help. And if she did sell up, you'd be entitled to a cut — and a cut of the profits while you're trading!'

'Right . . .' Beryl blinked, trying to take in everything she'd been told. Lily squeezed her hand.

'It won't be the same as having your own business. But it'd be better than Evelyn having all the say in things. Don't you agree?'

'Yeah . . . of course.' Beryl's chin came up. This was the Beryl they knew, the fearless fighter. 'I'll do it! And I can't wait to see her face when I tell her!'

16

It was bright and breezy on the day of the inquest which would pronounce on Florrie Jessop's death and establish if further investigation was needed. Anyone but Gladys would have taken this for a good omen, but she was in such a state that the daffodils nodding in the flowerbed in front of the town hall might as well have been heads on spikes.

'I wish I hadn't worn these shoes, they're killing me,' she fretted to Bill. 'My feet have spread that much since I had the children — oh and bother it! I forgot to tell Dora about that bit of junket in the larder for their dinner —'

Bill let her talk. He was feeling pretty uncomfortable himself, and not just because, having sold his demob suit, he'd had to get his only other one out of pawn. It dated from before the war, when he hadn't yet put on the muscle he'd built up in years of PT in the Navy and more recently hauling barrowloads of bricks from bomb sites. But his real unease came from what the coroner might say about Florrie's death, and the guilt he couldn't shake off at how often he'd hoped and prayed it would happen.

Inside, they were shown to a largish room with a table for the coroner and rows of seats in front of it. Dr Croft was already there, and PC Ruston; they acknowledged Gladys and Bill as they took their seats. The window was slightly open at the top, letting in the fresh spring air and the sound of birds merrily cheeping in the flowering cherry tree outside. In the

154

midst of life, thought Bill. They'd no sooner sat down than the coroner came in. Everyone stood up, then sat down again, Gladys and Bill copying what everyone else did. The coroner opened the proceedings.

'Good morning.' After an indistinct murmur in reply, he addressed the room, looking at them — at Gladys and Bill in particular — like a schoolmaster over his half-moon spectacles, but his voice was kind. 'Now, for those for whom this is a first time, an inquest is an investigation into the circumstances surrounding a death — in other words, who, when, where and how it occurred. Its purpose is simply to establish the facts, not to attribute blame. It is an investigation, not a trial. I hope that's clear to everyone?' Everyone nodded, Gladys and Bill automatically, rather than because they'd actually taken it in. 'Now if I could call the first witness . . .' He looked down at his notes. 'PC Ruston, please.'

PC Ruston, solid in his blue uniform, helmet under his arm, took the stand. He explained that the deceased was a mature lady of sixty-six years, a Mrs Florrie Jessop, and that he'd been called to the address by the doctor. The deceased was lying in the hallway at the foot of the stairs. The body had not been moved.

Dr Croft himself then took the stand and explained that he had confirmed life being extinct at 5.57 p.m. There were minor bruises and abrasions to the body but the cause of death appeared to be a fracture of the cervical vertebrae — in other words, a broken neck. So far so straightforward, but at this point, the coroner told Dr Croft he could stand down, and asked for evidence from the pathologist.

Bill felt Gladys stiffen beside him and he sat up straighter. It had all been sounding hopeful: he'd thought that would be it. What was the police pathologist going to say?

Dr Croft went back to his seat and, a youngish man, evidently the pathologist, took his place. He had that sandy Scottish colouring and the high colour that often went with it. With his outdoor complexion, tweed suit and woollen tie, he looked as if he'd come straight from the grouse moor. All he needed was his shotgun and cartridge bag. He identified himself as Dr Andrew McIntyre.

'Well, Doctor,' said the coroner, 'you've performed a post-mortem on the deceased, I believe?'

'Yes, indeed, sir.'

'And your findings? Was she otherwise in good health?'

Dr McIntyre's mouth moved.

'She evidently didn't think so,' he said.

The coroner looked over his glasses again.

'Would you care to elaborate?'

'I had access to the late Mrs Jessop's medical notes,' said Dr McIntyre. 'Over the course of the past year she'd called her own doctor out to see her for suspected episodes of . . . if I may?' He pulled out a small notebook. 'Yes . . . dyspepsia, indigestion, heartburn, bloating, flatulence, headache, migraine, neuralgia, double vison, earache, sore throat, gingivitis, gout . . . shall I go on?'

The coroner was lying back in his chair, as if flattened by the tidal wave of Florrie's complaints.

'No, thank you,' he said. 'That's quite enough. So could any of those have contributed in any way to her death?'

'None of them,' said Dr McIntyre emphatically. 'Not even the heart palpitations, the breathlessness,

156

the giddy spells she complained of, or the varicose veins and the swollen ankles. I spoke to her general practitioner. Occasionally, on sufferance, at her insistence, he'd prescribe a tonic. But every single time he examined her, he could never find anything serious that was physically wrong. All her complaints were totally non-existent. Which is what my own examination proved.'

This time it was Gladys's turn to stiffen, while Bill's shoulders slumped with relief — and also resignation. He'd been right. Florrie had been faking her ailments all these years, the ones she'd had them call the doctor for, and the millions of others!

'In my professional opinion,' Dr McIntyre went on, 'and her own doctor's, Mrs Jessop could have gone on for years. Something of a miracle, as she was significantly overweight, and her doctor urged her every time he saw her to get more exercise and fresh air. But nothing ever changed.'

'I see.' The coroner had recovered slightly and was making notes.

'However,' Dr McIntyre continued, 'if there was one contributory factor in her death, I would have said it was the matter of her slippers.'

The pen slid from the coroner's fingers.

'Her slippers?'

'Her personal effects were brought to me for examination along with the body, and Mrs Jessop's own doctor told me he'd often commented on them.'

Next to him, Bill felt Gladys's breathing quicken.

'In recent years,' Dr McIntyre continued, 'we've all had to make our clothes and shoes last longer than they might, but her slippers were a disgrace. Loose, trodden down at the back, and the soles worn to a

157

shine you could skate on.'

This was too much for Gladys, who jumped to her feet.

'I told her!' she cried. 'Time and again! I tried, I really did! I went all over town! I gave up my own coupons when I found some I thought she'd like, but Gran wouldn't wear them! Said she didn't like the colour!'

The coroner made a downwards motion with his hand. Bill pulled his wife gently back into her seat and put his arm round her as she cried quietly into his shoulder.

The coroner addressed Dr McIntyre.

'Thank you, Doctor,' he said. 'Thank you to all who've given evidence.' As Dr McIntyre went back to his seat, he cleared his throat. 'It seems clear to me,' he said, 'that Mrs Jessop died as the result of a fall. She had no underlying health conditions that could have contributed to her death and her grand-daughter had evidently been a most devoted carer. I am happy to record a verdict of accidental death and for a death certificate to be issued accordingly. Thank you all.'

He stood up and everyone got to their feet; he left the room and everyone sat down.

Bill turned to Gladys. He didn't know what to say — that he was thankful that no blame had been attributed to them or sorry that her grandmother had taken her for such a ride all these years? Finally the right words came to him.

'Thank goodness that's over,' he said. 'Now let's get home.'

★ ★ ★

158

When they got there, all was quiet. The twins were safely down for their nap, and Dora was pleasantly occupied shining the kitchen tap to a mirror finish.

'It's not a comment on your housekeeping, Gladys dear,' she said quickly. 'You've had other things to think about.'

But Gladys hadn't even seemed to notice the smell of vinegar — diluted with water, Dora had also used it to scrub down the wooden draining board and the table.

'She needs a lie-down,' Bill mouthed. 'It's been quite . . . emotional.'

With that, he led a compliant, unspeaking Gladys upstairs. When he came down again, Dora had boiled the kettle and was removing the damp tea towel that had been covering a plate of sandwiches.

'Dora, you're an angel.' Bill sat down and fell on them ravenously, explaining between mouthfuls what had emerged at the inquest, and that there was no sign Florrie had ever had anything wrong with her except in her own mind.

Dora listened, nodding and tutting. She'd always said of Florrie that the cracked pot went longest to the well — not that Florrie's pot had been cracked at all.

'It's doubled the shock for Gladys, though,' Bill finished up, drawing the back of his hand across his mouth after a gulp of tea. 'And it muddles things for her, doesn't it? How do you grieve for someone who's taken you for such a fool?'

Before too long, he was about to find out.

★ ★ ★

159

Evelyn jumped back as if Beryl had poked her with a puff adder.

'You . . . you want to buy in?'

'That's right.' Beryl was enjoying Evelyn's surprise — and the feeling of having the upper hand.

'But . . . what . . . with what? How?'

'Shall we sit down?'

As before, they took their places on either side of the little desk. After her conference with Lily and Jim, Les had visited the bank on her behalf, togged up by Beryl in his best suit with a clean collar and his Hinton Grammar School tie. Well, when she said 'his' tie . . . Les hadn't actually been to Hinton Grammar obviously; he'd left his council school at fourteen like everyone else. But Beryl had spotted the tie on the floor at the last WI rummage sale and had swooped on it. You never knew when something like that would come in handy — and it had! The bank manager had beaten Les down on how much he was prepared to lend, but they'd expected that: as instructed, Les had asked for double what he was hoping for, and had been delighted to settle at two-thirds. At the end of the meeting, the bank manager had shaken his hand, admiring his 'get-up-and-go in these challenging times' and had wished him well.

Now Beryl laid her carefully prepared figures on the desk and talked them through with Evelyn. She was firm in her insistence that a part-share — and a commensurate profit-share of the takings — was her condition for joining forces with her and managing the business day-to-day. Jim had taught her the phrases and she'd been determined to bring them out.

Evelyn pursed her perfectly drawn and painted lips

160

as she thought about it. Beryl could tell she was framing an objection, so she got in first.

'I've considered it very carefully. And I think it would be only fair.'

Evelyn looked again at the figures, then held up her hands in a gesture of defeat.

'Then I have to say yes. Though I don't know what Daddy will say.'

'I'm sure he won't reduce his investment,' said Beryl smoothly. 'As he has such faith in you. And you — we — can use it to buy more and better stock.'

Excitement crept into Evelyn's eyes.

'I could go to Paris and have a scout about!'

And blow all the budget on one impossibly expensive gown, thought Beryl. She'd better stamp on that one PDQ!

'Well . . . you could go and maybe photograph some gowns in shop windows,' she hazarded. 'And perhaps we could get them copied.'

She wasn't sure such a thing was practical — or even legal — but hoped Sir Douglas would stamp on it anyway.

Evelyn looked thrilled at the prospect and smiled her most winning smile.

'I have to say I admire you, Beryl — you've got even more about you than I thought. Which bodes well for our success! I'll go to the agents and close the deal on the shop in Park Road, shall I? That's a better location than South Street.'

'Very much so!' Beryl held out her hand and Evelyn shook it warmly, then said: 'It can't all be sorted overnight, though, can it? I'll still have to pack up here for now. The work on the new windows starts next week.'

161

'Oh, no.' Evelyn frowned. 'We don't want any interruption in trade. You'll be staying right here.'

'I can't!' protested Beryl. 'I don't want to be evicted. What would that look like?'

'You won't be evicted.' Evelyn smiled a curving, cunning smile. 'All I have to do is ask Daddy to have a word with Cedric Marlow. The way things stand between them at the moment, I think you'll find you'll be allowed to stay here for as long as we need.'

A grin spread over Beryl's face, and she knew she'd been right. That was how it had been. Robert Marlow had somehow stepped out of line with Sir Douglas, and so with Evelyn, and Cedric Marlow had been caught in the backwash.

'Perfect,' she smiled.

'On that note,' Evelyn smiled back, 'I think we should toast our future.'

'Good idea.' Beryl got to her feet. 'I've got a little primus behind the curtain in the corner.'

'A primus? You mean tea?' Evelyn shrieked with laughter. 'Are you off your head? Squatting in here with the teacups? I'm talking about a place where money can be exchanged for alcohol!'

'Oh, I see!'

'Turn the sign round and shut the shop,' ordered Beryl's new partner. 'We're going to the White Lion! This calls for champagne!'

'What?'

Evelyn checked herself.

'No, no, I must learn to be businesslike. We'll go — unless, that is, you're expecting anyone for a fitting.'

'No . . . I haven't got anyone booked in till four.'

'There you are then.' Evelyn stood up. She picked

162

up her shell-shaped clutch bag with its shell-shaped clasp — Beryl had noticed the detail straight away — and tucked it under her arm. 'We're celebrating — and it's a double celebration. I've filed for divorce and the papers are all signed.'

'Oh! Well, congratulations, if that's the right word!' Beryl stood up herself.

'It certainly is,' Evelyn smiled.

'And I understand Robert's leaving the country.' Beryl fetched her jacket. 'For Kenya, I gather.'

'Yes, very convenient.' Evelyn drew on her gloves. 'Still, the further away the better. Though as Mummy says, it should really have been Botany Bay, with hard labour!'

'You're better off without him, you know,' Beryl advised as she picked up her keys. 'I know it's hard, any break-up, but you'll see it like that in time.'

'Oh, I'm starting to see it already!' Evelyn certainly did sound stronger than before. 'When I married him I was . . . how can I put it? I didn't know who I was. I was a bit like — a photograph, you know, not properly developed, and a bit blurred. But now, with the shop — with you, Beryl — I've got a purpose for the first time in my life. I can really start to see who I am and what I want to be. The picture's coming into focus.'

Beryl smiled. She'd always treat her new partner with a degree of caution — however much Evelyn tried to portray herself as the independent modern woman, she was still being bankrolled by Daddy. Her years of being spoilt and indulged were basically going to continue, as would Beryl's of making the best of things. But Beryl and Evelyn had one huge thing in common apart from their love of fashion and a feeling

163

for clothes. They both had good reason to despise a particular man, and that would always be a strong bond between them.

'Right, then,' she said. 'Champagne, here we come!'

17

The funeral was over. Despite the revelation about Florrie's robust health, and how that must have made her feel, Gladys's final gesture showed her own typical generosity. She hadn't stinted her grandmother. The hearse was a glossy black carriage drawn by black-plumed horses with muffled hooves. Inside was a mahogany coffin with brass handles and a wreath of spring flowers. On the way to the church, the undertaker in his top hat walked ahead while Bill, with Gladys leaning heavily on his arm, followed behind. There were only a dozen mourners at the short service, and that included the vicar and the verger.

Gladys wept as they stood round the freshly dug grave: Lily, standing on the other side of her from Bill, squeezed her hand. However badly Florrie had abused Gladys's good nature, she'd given her a home when she'd been orphaned, and now Gladys's only living relative was gone. Lily remembered how terrified she'd been over the scare they'd had with Dora's health before the wedding and the stomach-plunging thought that she might be without a parent. Gladys must be feeling the loss of her own parents all over again.

On Lily's other side, Jim felt for her hand. They too were mourning the loss of a life, a very young life, lost when it had barely begun. They'd talked it out long ago but they both knew that however much they'd justified it to themselves as the baby not being meant to happen, or not at that time, they'd carry the memory with them for the full duration of what should have been Lily's pregnancy.

At the wake back at the house, Bill confided in Lily and Jim.

'I've got to go away again,' he said. 'They're planning on rebuilding Coventry — brick by brick. There's as much work as I want, but I'll have to stay over there — they're putting us up in ex-Army huts. We'll be working round the clock. I'll try and get back weekends when I can, but —'

Reading his thoughts, Lily quickly reassured him.

'Don't worry, we'll look after Gladys.'

Bill frowned. 'The timing couldn't be worse for me to leave her. And she's got to go to the solicitor about the will.'

'I'll go with her,' offered Lily at once. 'Bill, we're her friends. She needs us, and we're here.'

Bill nodded, his mouth compressed with emotion.

'I knew you would be, but thanks anyway.' He looked down at the crumbs on his plate — Gladys hadn't stinted on the funeral tea, either. 'But I dunno why Florrie bothered making a will; she had nothing to leave. She only had her pension. She spent most of that calling the doctor out for nothing, and she paid her whack of the rent out of it, to give her her due.'

'You've transferred the lease to your name?' asked Jim.

'Yeah, at least that's secure. But apart from paying off all today's fandango, that's another reason why I've got to keep in regular work.'

Gladys joined them then, and they complimented her again on her arrangements. She looked pale and drawn, the shadows under her eyes emphasised by her dark dress. As they left, Lily repeated her offer to go with her to the solicitor, but when the appointment was made, she couldn't go after all. Miss Frobisher had taken a few days off, for no particular reason, it seemed, as it wasn't young John's school holidays, so Lily was in charge of the department. Dora minded the twins for Gladys and reported that, on her return from the solicitor, she'd seemed more subdued than ever.

'Bill said Florrie had no money to speak of, so maybe she's wondering how to pay off that fancy funeral.' Jim looked up from polishing his shoes and sighed. 'I'll be giving these laces a decent burial too, if I can ever get any new ones. They're on their last legs.'

Everyone had thought the end of the war would mean an end to shortages, but things were actually getting worse. Bread was rationed now, which had never happened during the war. The meat ration had been cut from one and tuppence worth to a shilling's worth a week; the bacon ration had gone down from four ounces to three, and cooking fat from two ounces to one.

'Barely enough to grease the pan!' Dora complained — and it also hit her pastry-making. Pies were endlessly topped with potato and she was reduced to making biscuits with the fat she rendered when they killed one of the chickens at the end of its laying life. Even Sam's food parcels from Canada had shrunk: the Government had ordered that any that weighed over five pounds would be knocked off the recipient's rations.

★ ★ ★

167

Not for the first time, Dora was thinking about Sam as she walked round to Gladys's one day. It was May now, with Sweet Williams, carnations and even a few early peonies outside the greengrocers — at a price. Dora smiled when she remembered the first time Sam had come to tea at the house, to meet Lily and Jim. He'd brought a bunch of pink carnations — what must they have cost him in the war!

Dora shook her head, as she always did when she was trying to get a grip on herself. Sam had been back in Canada for over two years now. It was ridiculous that she still thought about him like some silly girl mooning over a film star — and he'd been far from that, bless him! Just an ordinary-looking fellow, not tall, not short, not fat, not thin, not fair, not dark — mid-brown hair going grey in fact, like her own. But he had a big heart and such a generous smile. Dora sighed. If she thought about him long enough, she could even still feel the touch of his hand as he'd helped her up from a chair or into her coat. Sometimes, simply looking at Buddy, the dog he'd left behind, brought a lump to her throat.

'Pull yourself together, Dora Collins!' she reprimanded herself as she turned into Gladys's street. In this mood, it was a good job she'd agreed to look after the twins again today — you couldn't think about anything else with those tiny terrors around!

'So what are you up to?' Dora asked as she untied her scarf in Gladys's living room. 'Treating yourself, I hope.'

Gladys, smartly dressed in her beige duster coat over a green dress, smiled faintly. She'd asked Dora if she could cope with the twins for a full day, and Dora had readily agreed.

'Maybe,' she said. 'It's just — well, I've still got a lot

to sort out. To do with Gran.'

Dora nodded, reluctant to probe any more. There was always so much to do after a death — getting probate for the will, sending documents off here, there and everywhere, changing the name on the household bills, handing in Florrie's identity card, ration card and pension book, that sort of thing. She only hoped Gladys wasn't going to use the time to order some extravagant headstone for her grandmother — she'd paid her dues by Florrie several times over, in Dora's view.

'Well, don't forget to take some time for yourself,' she counselled. 'Do some window-shopping, have yourself a bit of dinner and sit back in the one-and nines with a bag of Pick-and-Mix. Or even the circle!'

At the word 'dinner', Joy had peeped out from her favourite place: her house under the table where she was cooking her dolly's dinner in a ration tin Bill had liberated from the navy. Victor toddled over with a balding tennis ball and Dora scooped him up.

'And what are we going to do with you, you little scamp?' she asked him. 'No, we're not playing ball, not inside. Let's build a house for Mummy with your bricks, eh?'

With a faint smile, Gladys picked up her bag.

'Thanks ever so much for this, Dora. I'll see you later,' she said.

Once in the street, she walked briskly away. Her train was in twenty minutes and she mustn't miss it.

★ ★ ★

However she'd spent it, Gladys's day out seemed to lift her spirits considerably, Dora reported that night as she doled out the tapioca pudding.

169

'What was she doing all day?' Lily asked.

'She didn't rightly say,' Dora replied. 'But it goes to show what good a bit of time to yourself can do.' She passed Jim his bowl. 'Easy on the jam, please, Jim. It's all we've got till the end of the month.'

'How would you know about time to yourself?' countered Lily, amused. 'You never have any, you're always doing things for other people!'

But Dora wasn't taking any credit.

'What nonsense! And if I do help Gladys out, it's because I enjoy it!'

Dora loved the twins — who wouldn't, with their little starfish hands, their downy soft skin and their funny lispings. But more than that, they filled the gap in her life now war work took up less of her time and Lily and Jim were wrapped up in their work, and each other. She'd never say anything, of course, and nobody knew, but sometimes she thought about the fact that she'd lost someone too, this past year — the grandchild that was not to be.

There was the clatter of the back door being opened, and a voice called:

'Only me!'

Lily, Jim and Dora looked at each other and smiled.

Beryl knew perfectly well what time they ate, but she frequently managed to call by when they were at the table, usually just in time to share their pudding ('Only a mouthful, honest!').

'Come through, Beryl,' Lily sang out. 'And bring a bowl and a spoon!'

When everyone's bowls had been scraped clean, the table cleared, and the tea leaves from earlier wetted yet again, Beryl brought out the contract which Sir Douglas's solicitors had drawn up. She wanted

Jim to have a look at it after he'd finished locking up the hens.

As Evelyn had predicted, Cedric Marlow had agreed to an extension of Beryl's notice period for as long as she and Evelyn needed, provided the builders could make a start on the other three window spaces. There was a bit of scaffolding and banging and dust as a result, but keeping the shop in any circumstances was still a lot better than operating out of Beryl's front room.

Now Beryl spread the contract out on the table and Lily pored over it.

'Wedding Belles?' she queried when she saw the proposed name of the shop.

'Evelyn's idea,' explained Beryl.

'You can't sign this,' protested Lily. 'I'm surprised the solicitors let it pass! 'Bells' doesn't have an 'e' before the 's'! All that expensive private education she must have had and Evelyn can't even spell!'

'That's what I thought,' admitted Beryl with a rue-ful grin. 'But 'belle' with an 'e' on the end is French, see. It means 'beautiful'. So it's sort of a pun.'

'A pun? In French? In Hinton?' Lily shot her a sceptical look. 'Do you think your customers will get it?'

'Maybe not all of them, not at first, anyway, but it shows what kind of customers we're aiming for,' Beryl explained. 'And they're not customers, by the way, they're clients, apparently.' Then, putting on a highfa-lutin accent, she added: 'I'm going to have to talk ever so posh.'

'You already do!'

Beryl had always cultivated a 'refined' accent — at work, anyway. Now she kept it up to say:

171

'*Thenk you so much. Do call again, med'm!*'

'Straight out of the Rank Charm School!' laughed Lily. '*Thenk you, med'm!*'

They were still chuckling when Jim came in. He and Beryl bent their heads over the paperwork and Lily went to help her mum in the kitchen.

'I'm so pleased Gladys has perked up,' she said as she wiped the pudding spoons.

'Yes, it did her good to get out,' said Dora. 'I think being in that house all day is dragging her down. It's got all the wrong associations for her now.'

Lily shrugged.

'There's not much she can do about that, is there?' Lily replied. 'It's not as if houses are going begging. No, we'll have to think of little things to keep cheering her up. Beryl says they might have a grand opening do for the shop, that'd be something.'

'And you reckon we'd be invited?' Dora laughed.

Lily wrinkled her nose.

'That's true, I suppose. Though you should be!'

Dora, with her sewing skills, did Beryl's alterations, so she'd always been a vital part of Beryl's Brides and she was going to be part of the new enterprise too. There was going to be a sewing room at the back of the shop with what Beryl promised would be a 'state-of-the-art' machine instead of Dora's old Singer that had to be dragged out of the corner of the living room when she was working. Beryl, shrewdly, had also negotiated Dora a rise in her piece rate.

Lily polished the spoon she was holding for longer than she needed. It wasn't only Gladys who was stuck in the same house. She and Jim had talked about getting a place of their own, but for now, the only one in view was a castle in the air.

'Are you drying that spoon, or polishing the plating off?'

'Sorry, Mum.' Lily knew how keen Dora was on preserving her threadbare tea towels.

Suddenly there was a smart rat-a-tat on the knocker of the front door.

'Who on earth can that be at this time of night?' Dora's face immediately set into a frown of worry.

Lily's thoughts had also flown to bad news — and to Reg and Gwenda in Palestine. Despite her brother and sister-in-law's cheery letters and snaps of themselves eating ice creams on the beach or perched on top of camels, there'd been several violent uprisings against the British presence in the country. As a result, Lily and Dora still dreaded the knock at the door and the possible sight of the telegram boy. Lily swallowed hard.

'I'll go.'

Jim had already half-risen from the table where he was still conferring with Beryl, but Lily gestured at him to sit down.

She went through to the hall and put on the light, automatically straightening her skirt and patting down her hair in the mirror by the poker-work coat pegs. Taking a deep breath, she opened the door. And there, on the doorstep with a suitcase, was . . .

'Sam?!'

'Hi, Lily.'

'But . . .' She blinked. 'Is it? It's really you?'

What a silly question. The same kind eyes, the mouth twisted in a smile, his hair still close-cropped . . . in any case, the soft Canadian accent was unmistakable.

'Of course it's me. It hasn't been that long, has it?'

173

'But — what are you doing here?'

'Gee thanks, nice to see you too! I come four thousand miles across the ocean and that's all the welcome I get?'

'Lily? Who is it?'

Dora was coming down the hall behind her.

Lily turned to see the look of amazement and, yes, delight, on her mother's face as she saw who it was.

'Sam! Oh, Sam!'

18

Led by an incredulous Dora, and with Lily following behind, Sam was hustled indoors. In the back room, Jim was on his feet, grinning widely. Working out who it was from the voices in the hall, and with unusual tact, Beryl had gathered up her things and left.

Sam dropped his suitcase and threw his hat onto a chair. He shook Jim by the hand, then, with a 'what the hell!', clasped him, then Lily, then finally Dora, in a hug.

'I can't believe I'm here!' he said.

'You can't believe it?' exclaimed Lily. 'How do you think we feel?'

'Never mind that,' said Dora. 'Sam, you must be gasping for something to drink. And have you eaten tonight?'

Sam threw back his head and laughed.

'Some things never change!' he said. 'You know what you are, Dora? A one-woman feeding station! I've eaten, thanks.'

Jim was already reaching for his jacket so he could go to the off-licence.

'What you need is a beer,' he said. 'Don't go away, I'll be back in a jiffy!'

'Oh, I'm not going anywhere,' Sam assured him.

'No, you're not,' scolded Lily. 'Not till you've told us everything!'

But Sam made them wait until Jim came back with three bottles of beer and one of lemonade — a beer each for him and Sam, and one to make a shandy for

Lily and for Dora if she wanted it. For once she did. She only touched a drink on high days and holidays, but as high days went, this one was up with the stars.

Beer in hand, Sam sat back and explained.

'You remember my pal Marvin?' The name meant nothing to Lily or Jim, but Dora remembered. She'd met him, and a few of Sam's other Army friends, when they'd bumped into them when they were out. 'Well, he stayed on here after I left, and started going out with a local girl. They got quite serious, and after he left for home, they carried on writing to each other. He was coming over to see her when he got what we call a 'Dear John' letter — you know what I mean?'

'She was breaking it off,' said Lily.

'Right. She'd met someone else. Poor Marvin, huh?' They all nodded.

'So, what was he going to do with a useless ticket to England now?' He saw light dawn in their eyes. 'Exactly! He offered it around a few of us who'd been stationed over here and I thought — why not?' He took a sip of beer. 'I hope I did the right thing?'

'Look at our faces!' said Lily, looking at her mum's. Dora was transformed. Her eyes were so bright she seemed almost illuminated from the inside. She hadn't stopped smiling since she'd first set eyes on Sam, and that alone would have made Lily smile, and Jim too. 'There's your answer!'

'But why didn't you write and tell us?' Dora asked.

'Yeah, I'm sorry about that, but there was no time,' Sam explained. 'The ship was sailing in a few days, I had to get right across the country from Alberta to Halifax, Nova Scotia —'

'And what about your shop? The ironmongers — er, your hardware store?'

Ever practical, Jim raised the point.

'My uncle's taking care of it for me. He retired last year, and he's bored out of his tiny mind. He jumped at the chance.'

'Well!' That single word from Dora was freighted with a whole cargo of disbelief, delight — and anticipation. Lily asked the key question.

'And what now? How long are you staying?'

'Six weeks. That's when the return is booked for.'

'Six weeks!'

'Don't worry, Dora, I won't impose on you here. I'll find myself some lodgings —'

Dora looked scandalised at the thought.

'No, you will not — not tonight, anyway! I'm not turning you out into the street! Not when there's Jim's old room standing empty!'

'Look, I never intended —'

'I won't hear a word against it!'

Sam gave in.

'I must say, I'm pretty beat. So, yes please. Just for tonight.'

Honour was satisfied. Lily and Dora made up the bed, Lily noting that Dora made sure to use her least-darned pillowcases, sheets and blankets. Then Dora took the eiderdown off her own bed to make sure Sam would be warm enough — the unused room was chilly on this late spring evening. Jim came up with the hot-water bottle Dora had requested, followed by Sam, who was suddenly looking tired, even though it was barely nine o'clock.

'You look all in,' said Dora kindly. 'You get your head down.'

'Thanks, Dora. I will. And I'll see you in the morning.'

They smiled at each other and, behind her mum's back, Lily smiled at Jim.

Later, in the privacy of their bedroom, she snuggled into Jim's arms.

'I'm so happy for Mum,' she said. 'Sam leaving the way he did always felt like unfinished business. Even if it's only for a visit, it's so lovely that he's here.'

Jim kissed the top of her head.

If Dora was happy, Lily was happy; and if Lily was happy, he was happy.

'I love you,' he said.

Lily turned towards him.

'What brought that on?'

'Do I need a reason?'

'Of course!'

'Because . . . because . . . why is it now?' Jim pretended to think. She couldn't see his face in the dark but she could hear the smile, and the love, in his voice. 'Oh, yes. Because you're you.'

★ ★ ★

Next morning, Jim and Lily had to leave for work before Sam was up. Beryl was waiting impatiently for them as they turned into the alley that led to the store's staff entrance.

'I can't open up till you've told me everything!' she cried, as excited as a child at the pantomime. 'Did Dora know he was coming? She never said! She's as close as an oyster, your mum! How long's he staying? Is he going to stay at yours? If so, in whose room, eh?'

She gave Lily a nod which was as good as a wink.

'Beryl!'

'Well, you're not telling me he's come over to see

178

the sights! In Hinton? What, the gasworks and the civic buildings? Give me a break!'

'He's come to see us — well, Mum, obviously, but beyond that I don't know what his plans are,' said Lily with dignity. 'He's here for six weeks, but he might be going on a tour of the Outer Hebrides in that time for all I know.'

'Well, he'd better not take your mum with him!' said Beryl in reply. 'Wedding Belles hasn't just invested in a proper sewing booth with a semi-industrial sewing machine for nothing!'

With that, she was gone. Lily knew she was only speaking in jest, but now Beryl had put the idea into her head she found herself wondering about Sam's plans — or his intentions — herself.

★ ★ ★

Back at Brook Street, Sam had just come downstairs. Dora had laid the table with a fresh cloth and set a place for him, but she had no thought of asking him anything about his intentions. It was enough for her simply to see him there, washed and shaved thanks to the jug of hot water she'd taken up and left outside his door when she'd heard him moving about. She set a plate of scrambled egg and bacon — sacrificing her own meagre ration, but he was more than welcome — in front of him. Sam looked at her.

'I'm taking the food out of your mouth,' he said. 'I can't do that.'

'Don't be silly, I've had mine!' She'd had a piece of toast with dripping, and with the excitement of Sam being there, she'd had trouble getting that down. 'Now, I've only got Camp coffee, I'm afraid — that's

179

coffee essence, you remember. Or there's tea.'

'Tea, please!' Sam rubbed his hands. 'When in Rome, as they say . . .'

Dora used fresh leaves for him, of course; they'd do without later in the week. As Sam cleared his plate ('Just what I needed!') she poured them each a cup. Then it was time for a proper catch-up to fill in some of the blanks that their letters to each other had missed out.

Dora asked gently about his wife's sad death; about his shop; more about this uncle she'd never heard him mention. Sam asked how she really felt about Reg and Gwenda being so far away, about Sid in London, and how it felt to have Lily, her youngest, married. And there was someone else on his mind, too.

'Isn't it about time I got reacquainted with Buddy?' he asked. 'He's still got his kennel out back, I take it?'

'You took the words out of my mouth,' smiled Dora. 'It's time for his walk. He's sensed something's up, though, he's been whining at the door.'

'Let's put him out of his misery.' Sam stood up. There was no need to help Dora up but he held out his hand anyway. She took it and felt the firmness of a male clasp, the slight roughness contrasting with the fine hairs she could see on the back of his hand. But he didn't hang on to her hand and she was pleased. Sam had never overstepped the mark. He recognised she wasn't the type to want it, and he wasn't the type to try it on. That was the hallmark of their relationship. It was warm and friendly and fond. But it was also respectful and it was all the more meaningful for that.

They didn't even have to set foot in the yard. Buddy must have smelt Sam through the gap between the back door and the frame where the draught whistled through, however much they tried to fill it with newspaper. As soon as Dora opened the door he leapt up like a coiled spring, his shaggy spaniel face alive with joy at seeing his old master.

'Anyone'd think we'd been mistreating him!' smiled Dora as Sam crouched down and let Buddy jump all over him and lick his face. 'You can see we haven't been, I hope!'

Sam had opened a special Post Office account in Buddy's name and arranged for monthly payments to keep him. He'd realised there wouldn't be many scraps from the table — the British were having enough trouble keeping body and soul together themselves.

Off the three of them went, just like old times, to walk in the park. Buddy allowed himself to be put on the lead, but he kept stopping and turning round as if to check it really was Sam on the other end of it. Dora knew how he felt. When Sam crooked his arm for her to link hers through, she almost had to blink away a tear. When he looked at her and smiled, she knew the next six weeks were going to be something to treasure.

Gradually, over the next few days, things sorted themselves out. Sam agreed to stay one more night in Jim's room, then insisted on moving to a small B and B on the Tipton Road. Dora went to inspect the room with him and found she knew the landlady vaguely through the WI, which reassured her that the sheets would not be too thin and Sam would be well fed at breakfast. His evening meal was optional, because he promised he'd be taking Dora, Jim and Lily out for a 'slap-up feed' at least once a week. ('I have the money, Dora, please let me spend it!') Dora smiled to herself.

He had something to learn about what constituted a slap-up feed in these hard times, but it was a kind offer, and she knew he'd be offended if they refused. She was grateful, too; their rations at home wouldn't stretch to feeding another person.

When Lily next caught up with Gladys, she was able to relay all this information, and Gladys, when she'd finished clucking about how nice it was for Dora, had something to tell Lily too.

'Sam's not the only one. We're having a holiday too,' she said. 'Well, a few days, away, anyhow.'

'Are you? Where?'

'Weston!' Gladys beamed.

'How lovely!' Lily exclaimed, but she was surprised. Florrie must have left enough money in her will to cover this treat, anyway. 'You had such a good time before!'

'I know,' smiled Gladys. 'Bill can't believe it. He's so happy!'

'You'll have a wonderful time there,' said Lily.

'Oh, we will,' said Gladys. 'I know we will.'

19

As May went on, early summer unfolded with its usual exuberance all around. In her happiness, Dora saw it with new eyes and ears. The young green of the trees seemed impossibly bright and the birds had never sounded so loud or so joyful.

With the contract signed, Wedding Belles was ready to open by mid-month — just in time, Beryl hoped, for a bumper wedding season. Soldiers were still being demobbed, returning from the Far East and other out-posts: their girlfriends would be itching to speed them up the aisle. And on the day, the grand opening was everything the new partners could have wished for.

First, there was the special opening ceremony. The Lady Mayoress cut a ribbon with a pair of Dora's dress-making scissors, sharpened to a murderous point. For the benefit of the photographer from the local paper, Sir Douglas Brimble brandished a bottle of champagne and Lady Brimble presented a bouquet to her blushing daughter — and, for appearance's sake, one which was only slightly smaller, to Beryl. Favoured customers from Beryl's Brides and mothers and daughters in the Brimbles' social circle had been invited to come for a 'private view' of the new premises and to cast their eye over the stock. The looping script under the shop's name offered 'Wedding and Occasion Wear, Mother of the Bride and Bridesmaid Outfits for Sale and for Hire' and all morning a good crowd murmured over lace and brocade, paper taffeta, crêpe and chiffon. In the end Evelyn had done a whirlwind tour of the London showrooms and wholesalers for end-of-line items and samples, and Beryl had to admit she'd come back with some beautiful finds. As Evelyn circulated making small talk, Beryl nodded at acquaintances and glowed with pride as she heard the appreciative comments about quality and finish. She was pleased to see that her own former 'as new' stock, pruned down to the very best pieces, was also meeting with approval from a new audience. Dora watched it all from the sidelines, faintly amused but also fiercely proud of Beryl's success. She was looking forward to telling Lily, Jim — and Sam, who'd been impressed with her new job — all about it.

The morning passed in a blur. When the crowd thinned, Dora quietly left too. Evelyn proclaimed herself exhausted and was borne off by her parents for a celebratory lunch. Beryl was left in charge, which was to be her role in the new business, and which suited her very well. She had a steady stream of curious customers — sorry, clients, as Evelyn insisted they must call them — all afternoon, some browsing, some hiring. It was only when she sat down to do the totting up at five thirty that she realised she hadn't eaten a thing all day, and when she worked out that they'd taken over seventy pounds' worth of future orders, she was so excited she wondered if she'd be able to eat that evening either.

As the *Hinton Chronicle* breathlessly put it next day in the headline of their article — on page three, no less:

Wedding Belles rings in a bright new future for Hinton's brides.

Beryl could not have put it better herself.

184

★ ★ ★

With the flurry of the grand opening over, Dora was acutely conscious that Sam's days in England were ticking past. She couldn't get out of her commitment to Wedding Belles, but her new working conditions, with a good overhead light and a reconditioned machine set into its own larger table, meant that her work rate was twice as efficient. To her relief, she soon found that she was only needed about three days a week. She was always finished by one o'clock, when Sam came to meet her and whisked her off to Lyons or the ABC Tearoom for lunch. She'd excused herself from the Red Cross for the six weeks of his stay — the refugees' comforts would have to be packed by other hands. She sent her apologies to the WI too: their 'Afternoon of Crafting' had been in her diary since Christmas, and she'd been looking forward to it, with its promise of lampshade-making and quilting. But those delights had paled into insignificance beside the pleasure of doing the simplest things with Sam at her side.

They did all there was to do locally — walks with Buddy, a picnic in the park if the weather was fine, the cinema if wet, but they didn't always stick to Hinton. On days when Dora had told him she'd be free of the shop, Sam would turn up waving tickets and Dora, always one for routine, had to learn to be spontaneous. He took them on days out by coach to places Dora had never been, doing things she'd never done, or dreamed of doing. They went to the Repertory Theatre in Birmingham to see *The Winslow Boy* ahead of its London run. ('That poor family! What they went through to prove the lad innocent!'). They had a long

185

day touring the Cotswolds, Dora marvelling at the honey-stone cottages ('Like a fairy tale, but those leaded windows must be the devil to clean!'). They even went, on Lily and Jim's recommendation, to Stratford-upon-Avon to walk in the memorial gardens and feed the swans, and went on the river — though unlike Lily and Jim, Dora drew the line at a rowing boat.

'You don't trust me not to tip us in, do you?' grinned Sam as they took their places on the motor-launch that would take them on an organised trip.

'I didn't propose to find out!' Dora smiled back, trying to hold on to her hat and the skirt of her dress, both of which were being teased by a stiff breeze.

'You're no fun,' Sam replied, but his look said the opposite.

Then, one afternoon in the park, as Sam threw a stick for Buddy, he mentioned another outing next day, as Dora had said she wasn't needed at the shop.

'Where to this time?' asked Dora.

She was starting to get wise to this. Spontaneous was all very well, but she needed to know how much walking was involved, or if it was a sitting-down sort of trip. Was it a day for her sensible lace-up shoes, or her better pair?

'That'd spoil the surprise!' Sam bent to retrieve the stick Buddy had dropped at his feet, so Dora was no further forward. 'Just be at the bus station at nine thirty.'

'Shoes?' said Dora.

But Sam had hurled the stick into the far distance, and was pretending to race Buddy to see who got there first. Dora shook her head in exasperated affection. The man and the dog were both as daft as each

186

other, and as . . . she pulled herself up short. She'd almost thought 'lovable'.

★ ★ ★

At the entrance to the bus station the next day, Sam intercepted her.

'Now I don't want to have to blindfold you,' he said, 'so I'm going to lead you the long way round so you don't see the destination on the front of the bus, OK? You look very nice, by the way.'

He'd seen everything she was wearing before, of course, but this was a new combination — her old blue print frock, but with the jacket of her wedding suit over it and her wedding hat with a spray of violets attached. Just to be on the safe side, she'd worn her sensible shoes.

'Thank you. But why all the cloak-and-dagger business?'

'It's a magical mystery tour,' Sam told her. 'What, you never went on one before? You have a treat in store!' He led her inside. 'Ah, ah, ah! No peeping!'

They took their seats on the bus, Sam letting her sit by the window. When everyone was on board, the driver cranked the engine into life and they set off. Dora watched the outskirts of Hinton slip past, and she realised how fast the weeks were slipping past too. 'Gather ye rosebuds,' she thought to herself, a line from a poem she'd learnt at school coming back to her.

Gradually, the view from the window of the grey and red-brick town with flashes of green turned to green with flashes of red-brick and grey, and then almost entirely to green. The bus stopped and started;

187

people got on and people got off. After the fifth stop, a crossroads, the bus made a right-hand turn, and Dora also turned, to Sam.

'I know where we're going!' she exclaimed. 'Back to your old Army base!'

'Spot on!' Sam cocked his head. 'Good old Nettleford Manor.'

Dora deliberately hadn't said the name, though she remembered it perfectly. She'd have pronounced it, like everyone in Hinton did, as 'Nettle-f'd'. But she wanted to hear him say it in his slow, soft Canadian accent, and he had — 'Neddle-ford'.

'It'll be all closed up by now, won't it?' she asked. 'Won't it make you sad to see it?'

'Sad? Why would I be? I don't think so!'

He met her eyes and Dora smiled, then looked down. As usual, it was what Sam didn't say that impressed her. No soft soap. No old flannel like 'How could it? It was out here that I first met you.' Thank goodness for that. That sort of talk belonged in the films!

The bus trundled along the lanes until it stopped with a jerk and a protest of brakes in the centre of Nettleford village. Sam helped her down the steps and Dora looked around. The village was pretty much how she remembered it from her other visit, a full three summers ago now. She hadn't known Sam at all then, but she'd known Buddy.

She'd first encountered the dog in Hinton with his previous owner, a Canadian Army major. When he'd been posted abroad, he'd left Buddy behind with his batman. Buddy had turned up on his own one day at the WVS tea bar where Dora volunteered, and she realised he must have somehow slipped his collar in the town and escaped. He'd come back to a place he remembered. She'd come out to Nettleford to return him to his new master — who turned out to be Sam.

'We have to walk from here, don't we?' she said. 'No, don't tell me! Let's see if I can remember the way.'

What a good job, she thought, she'd worn her sensible shoes. Something must have been guiding her.

It guided her steps now as she recalled the way the postmaster's wife had directed her on that original visit. Left at the church down Tanners Lane, right where the road forked . . . Just like the first time, the countryside was looking glorious again. Cow parsley frothed on the verges ('Like the head on your English beer,' said Sam, unromantically); over the hedges the corn was starting to change colour. Cabbage whites, common blues and tortoiseshell butterflies flittered from plant to plant; a skylark soared into the sky. On a hillside far away, a team of men with pitchforks were turning a first cut of hay. It was the England of picture books and calendars, of memory, of history — the image of England, Dora thought, that they'd fought the war to preserve. Both she and Sam, who was more used to wide open prairies, drank it in.

When they reached the crossroads, she hesitated.

'Straight on,' Sam prompted, and with that confirmed, it all came back to Dora. Along here, on the left, was the gateway she'd pulled Buddy into for safety when she'd heard the approach of a Jeep behind her. It had passed her, braked and reversed. Out had jumped Sam, incredulous at finding a woman he didn't know leading Buddy home on a piece of string, when he'd lost him in Hinton. After that 'The rest is history!' as Beryl had put it to Dora the other day.

189

And with a wink, 'Or do I mean chemistry?'

A couple of hundred yards later, they were at the entrance to Nettleford Manor itself. The barrier and the sentry box had gone, and the manor's metal gates had disappeared long before that, for the war effort.

'Come on!' Sam started up the drive, pitted and potholed and sprinkled with weeds.

'Can we?'

'Don't you want to see the house?'

'But the owners might be back living there.'

'After the way we knocked it around inside? Partitioned the rooms? Used their croquet lawn for target shooting and bayonet practice? Nissen huts and cabins for sleeping quarters all over the place? I doubt it! Come on, Dora, where's your sense of adventure?'

Bracing herself, she followed him up the drive between the laurel bushes. As they rounded a corner, the house came into view. It was a pale grey stone Georgian building, dignified and elegant in its time. Now its windows were boarded up and a piece of corrugated iron was nailed across the door. There was a trail of green slime down the front wall from a broken gutter. The flagpole from which the Canadian flag had fluttered was knee-deep in overgrown grasses; the flag, of course, had gone.

'Oh, Sam!' exclaimed Dora in distress. But Sam was philosophical.

'Yeah, well, I'm not surprised. Even if the house was put back to rights, from what I've read, the, er, what do you call them, the kind of gentry folk who lived in houses like this can't afford to run them now. Or' — he mimicked an English accent — 'they 'can't get the staff', don't you know.'

'What'll happen to the house, do you think?'

190

'It might become a school, or a training centre, or an institution, I guess. Or even be pulled down.'

'Oh, that would be criminal!'

'That's the reality, Dora.'

So much for her vision of the old England they'd fought to save. Though if you talked to Jim, he thought the shift from the old order to the new was a good thing, and he wasn't alone.

As they drew nearer, they became aware of the sound of voices from around the back of the house.

'Sam — there *is* someone here! Sam — wait!'

But Sam had headed off to investigate. Helplessly, Dora followed him, still not convinced they weren't trespassing.

When she rounded the corner of the house with Sam ahead of her, she saw what was happening. Three men, still in Canadian Army fatigues, were making a tour of the Nissen huts, sheds and cabins that Sam had referred to.

'It can't be —' But Sam was speeding off, approaching one of the men. 'Hey, hi there! Dennis? Dennis!'

The man looked up, shielding his eyes from the sun.

'No!' he exclaimed. 'Am I dreaming or am I dreaming? Sam? Sam Cassidy? Is that you?'

20

After the exuberant greetings were over, Dennis, who was clearly in charge, told the other two men to take an early lunch. They went off with their ration packs, then, nodding his head towards a Jeep parked under a tree, Dennis suggested that the three of them go down to the village pub. As they walked towards it, Dora could see the Jeep had the Canadian maple leaf on the bonnet and its Army number stencilled on the doors. She was baffled by the whole thing. Surely all the Canadian troops had gone home by now?

But there wasn't much chance for her or Sam to ask questions. Dennis was too busy ushering her into the front seat, while Sam perched side-on in the back on one of the little metal seats, more of a shelf really. With Dennis driving at some speed, it was all Dora could do to hang onto the frame as he swung them merrily round the lanes. The Jeep had a canvas top but no windows. She took off her hat for fear of losing it and the wind coming in from all directions lifted her hair on end.

When they arrived outside the Fox and Badger, the early hour meant the place was virtually empty. Inside the old, low-beamed pub, there were only a couple of grizzled ancients clutching tankards at the bar and talking in unintelligible mumbles, which presumably they both understood because from time to time one or the other roared with laughter, showing stumps of teeth. Dennis was obviously a familiar face, and he greeted the barmaid effusively.

'Now, Maureen, what have you got for us? Is that ham salad of yours on the menu today?'

It appeared that it was, and Dora accepted gratefully, even though the last ham salad she'd had, at the Midland Hotel in Birmingham, the day she and Sam had gone to the Rep, had been a disappointing affair of limp lettuce and a piece of pallid ham so thin it was almost transparent.

They carried their drinks to a table, Dora still trying to smooth down her hair, and Sam and Dennis fell into animated conversation.

'So you're still here?' Sam asked, though the evidence was right before his eyes. 'Frankly, pal, I thought you'd be buried on a hillside in Italy somewhere.' He looked sober. 'Ortona, maybe.'

The Battle of Ortona, Dora remembered with a wrench, had cost five hundred Canadian lives. She wondered if the Canadian major that Sam had served under had been one of them.

'I never got to Italy.' Dennis took a pull on his pint. 'I got as far as Southampton, slipped on the gangplank as we were embarking and broke my leg!'

'Trust you! A lucky break though!' grinned Sam.

Dennis grinned back.

'It sure was! They shuttled me back to Southern Command, and once I'd healed, I'd missed the boat, so to speak. It was a bad break in two places, and they signed me off unfit for active service. I spent the rest of the war behind a desk.'

'Something similar happened with your son, didn't it, Dora?' Sam, bless him, drew her tactfully into the conversation, and she explained about Sid crocking his ankle during training, which had led, after a couple of other postings, to his desk job at the Admiralty.

Dennis whistled in admiration.

'Top-level stuff! You must be very proud.'

Dora didn't have time to reply because the bar-maid, Maureen, appeared with a laden tray. Dora's mouth watered as she saw what a country ham salad consisted of. A proper thick piece of ham off the bone, with its ragged pink flesh and a good half-inch of smooth white fat was nestled against lettuce, water-cress and a sliced tomato. Maureen unburdened herself of the plates, disappeared and came back with knives and forks, mustard, salad cream, and a hunk of bread each. Even that wasn't the dreary grey National Loaf — it was made with brown flour, of course, but it was clearly home-made and looked springily fresh. There was even a tiny curl of butter for each of them.

Dennis watched her reaction with amusement.

'They live like kings out here compared to you in the cities, right?'

Dora nodded dumbly. The food looked so delicious that she hardly knew where to start. Sam and Dennis, for different reasons, were more used to this kind of fare and seemed set on finishing their drinks, but they urged Dora to begin, so she did while they carried on with their catching up.

'None of that explains what you're still doing here, and still in the Army,' Sam began. 'I thought all us Canucks were home by now. Didn't you feel the pull of the old country?'

'Well, my folks were a bit sore about it, but I wanted to stay on.' Dennis waggled his head from side to side. 'Can't you guess why?'

'You liked the people maybe?'

Sam flashed a quick smile at Dora, who tried to smile back, though her mouth was full of ham and tomato — heaven! Then it was Dennis's turn to smile.

'One person in particular. Come on, Sam, how many more clues do you need?'

'Not . . . not Kathy!'

"Reader, I married her!' Isn't that some line from one of your English novels?'

He turned to Dora, who'd managed to swallow her mouthful by now. It had been one of her favourite books when she was growing up, and her mother's too.

'Yes, *Jane Eyre*. Well, sort of.'

'There you go!' Dennis picked up his knife and fork and held them upright on either side of his plate, framing it like a picture. Sam's face was a picture, too, of amazement.

'Hang on, let me get this straight — you married Kathy?'

'Yup, she saw the error of her ways in the end!' Dennis began to eat and, following his lead, so did Sam. 'Though it never would have happened if you hadn't left the UK!' He turned to Dora. 'We held a dance at the base — when was it, Sam, Christmas '42, or early '43? Kathy was a Land Girl in the next village. A group of them came along and a crowd of us started going around together. One by one a few of the others paired off. I don't mind telling you I was pretty keen on Kathy, but she always held a torch for Sam, and he was playing hard to get!'

Dora shot a glance at Sam. Was she imagining it, or was he blushing?

'I wasn't playing anything,' he insisted. 'I only went to that dance because you guys forced me into it! I was married at the time, remember!'

While they'd waited for the drinks, Dennis had

asked after Grace and Sam had told him that she'd died.

'That never stopped most of the boys! I didn't have to worry,' he added to Dora. 'I genuinely was that rare thing, a good-looking, eligible bachelor.'

Sam snorted with laughter.

'You forgot to add modest!'

'Anyway,' Dennis continued, stacking ham, tomato and lettuce onto his fork, 'when I got stuck in England, I wrote to Kathy. She'd started going out with an airman, not one of ours, one of your boys, RAF.' This was addressed to Dora. 'Sadly, he didn't make it back from Arnhem. She wrote and told me and just before the end of the war we met up again and . . . well, you know how these things go.'

'Well, I'm very pleased for you,' said Sam.

'Yes, congratulations!' Dora added.

'Thanks,' said Dennis, adding with a wicked grin, 'but I have no illusions. Leaving aside the airman, I know I'd always have been second choice — to Sam!'

Dora smiled thinly. Sam had been clear with her from the start about his wife, but she'd never considered that he might have had other admirers before he'd met her. The thought bothered her in a way she couldn't quite put her finger on. She felt as if he'd been keeping something from her, which was ridiculous, because the subject had never come up, and from what he'd said just now, Sam had had nothing to confess anyway. Even so, the food which she'd been enjoying suddenly seemed tasteless.

She tried to hide it during the rest of the meal, but, as sensitive as ever, Sam sensed her withdrawal and steered the conversation away from the bewitching Kathy. Instead he switched tack to ask what exactly

Dennis was doing for the Army now and how long he could remain enlisted. Dora listened with half an ear as Dennis explained he'd managed to wangle himself onto the disposal side of what was called 'ordnance'.

At the start of the war, Dora had thought ordnance meant armaments. She'd learnt from Reg and Sid, though, that the definition extended to all kinds of military stores and materials, and to temporary buildings and huts and their contents — spare parts for vehicles, tyres, inflatable dinghies, stirrup pumps, buckets and tarpaulins — and sealing wax and string, for all she knew. Dennis, it seemed, was at Nettleford to check over what finally needed disposing of there. Once that was done, he admitted he wasn't sure what direction his life would take — he couldn't string things out with the Army for much longer and was expecting to be demobbed within weeks.

'It's good to be back on the old stamping ground, though,' he said. 'Especially as we've settled nearby — Kathy properly fell in love with it round here!'

And, hey presto, they were back with the marvellous Kathy again.

Dora picked up her spoon. She stirred the coffee which Dennis had ordered for them: she wasn't very partial to coffee, but at least there was plenty of milk to go with it. Outside the cretonne-curtained window, the sun went behind a cloud.

★ ★ ★

On the bus home, Dora was quiet as she watched the countryside pass by. Sam didn't fail to notice.

'You seem very absorbed,' he said. 'It's the same

197

view we saw on the way, except the other side of the road. What's up?'

'Nothing!' said Dora.

'Come on,' Sam coaxed. 'Is it because of Dennis? Look, I know he's a bit full-on. We used to call him Hurricane Dennis, but he's a decent guy underneath all his talk. You liked him, didn't you?'

'Of course I did!' And she had, really — there was nothing to dislike. Yes, he was a bit of a loudmouth, what Jim would have called a central casting Yank — but he'd made her laugh with some of his observations about the English and he'd generously paid for their lunch.

'While I'm still on Army pay I'm making the most of it!' he'd said as he scribbled his address and telephone number on the back of the bill and gave it to Sam. 'And it's not every day you run into an old pal!'

Dora couldn't argue with that and she felt mean. It must have been a real treat for Sam to meet up with someone from the old days again. If only it hadn't been for this silly niggle about Kathy, which she somehow couldn't shake off . . .

When they got back to Hinton, Sam set off with her out of the bus station, assuming he'd walk her home. Dora put her hand lightly on his arm.

'There's no need to come with me,' she said. 'It takes you right out of your way. And to be honest, I feel quite worn out. I don't think I've got much conversation left in me.'

'Fair enough, if you're sure.'

Sam was always the gentleman.

'I am, thank you.'

'OK. So tomorrow, you're working in the morning, right? Shall I call for you as usual?'

That was better.

'Please do.'

Sam swooped and kissed her on the cheek. 'Thank you for coming, Dora. It's been a lovely day.'

Dora smiled. If he was happy, she could surely be happy for him. He was on holiday, after all.

'Thank you for arranging our day out,' she said warmly. 'I'll see you tomorrow.'

★ ★ ★

But not long after Dora got to Wedding Belles next morning, Gladys sent word. She was laid low with a bilious attack and Bill was away — could Dora possibly come and take care of the twins once she'd finished work? Dora's heart sank. Just when she'd hoped for some time on her own with Sam to make up for yesterday. She'd even been thinking she might bring up the subject of Kathy, to lay the wretched woman's ghost to rest. But she couldn't let Gladys down in her hour of need. She sent word back that she'd be round as soon as she could after one o'clock, and asked Beryl if she could use the phone to call Sam at his digs and let him know their plans would have to change.

'Oh dear, a rock on the road to romance!' Beryl raised a pencilled eyebrow.

'Don't talk such nonsense,' said Dora tartly. 'And I'll thank you not to listen in, please!'

Beryl made a pretend-huffy face and swished off to attend to a customer who was hovering beside an ice-blue bridesmaid's dress.

When he came to the phone, Sam expressed disappointment and said to send Gladys his best wishes.

'What will you do?' Dora asked. 'At a loose end in

Hinton all day?'

'Oh, I think I can amuse myself,' quipped Sam. 'Maybe it's my chance to read *War and Peace* at long last!'

'You might even get through it,' Dora warned. 'These attacks of Gladys's start with a sick headache that gets worse. It can take a couple of days for her to get back on her feet.'

'Well, let me know when you're free again,' said Sam, easily. 'Like I said, I'm not going anywhere!'

21

At Gladys's, Dora found a pathetic scene. Gladys was slumped in a chair in her dressing gown with a bowl at her side. The children, still in their night things, were whining and trying to climb on her lap while she weakly tried to pacify them.

'Oh dear me,' said Dora, taking off her jacket. 'Look at the state of you!'

'I'm ever so sorry,' moaned Gladys. 'But I've been up all night and —'

'Off you go to bed,' said Dora firmly. 'Pull the curtains and try and get some rest. I'll get Joy and Victor sorted out.'

The children had perked up at once on seeing the person they called Aunty Dodo and transferred their attention to her. Gladys went to lie down as instructed, but later, even after Dora had put the children to bed, she was still as white as the sheets she was lying in. Whiter, in fact.

'Will you be all right overnight?' Dora fretted. 'I ought to nip home to explain to Lily and Jim, but I could come back and stay over . . .'

'No, no,' said Gladys weakly. 'I can't ask you to do that. The twins generally don't wake. If I can just get some decent sleep . . .'

Dora wasn't convinced, but in all honesty, she'd prefer her own bed.

'I'll come back in the morning,' she assured Gladys. 'I'm not needed at the shop.'

It wasn't strictly true: she'd had to leave a dress she

201

was halfway through altering, and there were another couple waiting. But she didn't want Gladys to worry.

When she arrived next day, she was hoping to see a bit of improvement in the patient, but there wasn't any. On the next, with Gladys still bed-bound, Dora had to send her apologies to Wedding Belles and say she'd make up the time as soon as she could. Gladys did manage a piece of dry toast and a cup of tea in the afternoon, but she was still very weak and Dora felt she really ought to have another day of rest in bed.

On her way home that night, she stopped and telephoned Sam to tell him so.

'I'm very sorry,' she said. And she was sorry — as well as conscious of the days ticking past faster than ever, and Sam's return ticket.

'Oh, don't worry about me.' Sam sounded perfectly cheerful. 'It's given me more of a chance to catch up with Dennis.'

Dora's nerve ends began to jangle.

'Oh yes?'

'Yeah, I took myself out to Nettleford again the first day Gladys went sick. I knew he'd be there, and I went round the old place with him, inside and out. My, it brought back some memories, I can tell you!'

What kind of memories, wondered Dora.

'And then last night they came over to Hinton for a night on the town!'

They?

Dora had to work hard to sound casual.

'Oh, so you've met up with Kathy again as well?'

'Yup, and do you know what, she's still exactly the same!'

How nice for her, thought Dora, conscious that her hair needed a wash and of the stain on her blouse

202

where Victor had spat out his carrots. There'd been no time for herself with running around after Gladys and two lively toddlers, much as she loved them.

'What's more, they've invited us over!'

Us? Over? Over where?

'I beg your pardon?'

'They want us to go over to their place for a meal. It's out by Nettleford, as you know, but Dennis can collect us and bring us back. They suggested tonight. What do you say?'

This was all moving too fast for Dora. Leaving aside her hair, and the fact she'd only had a cat-lick of a wash for the past few days, and that she was worn out and her back was aching from lifting the twins . . . Did she want to meet the fabulous Kathy — the woman who hadn't changed a bit and was still the lively and fatally attractive Land Girl she'd been in 1943?

'I'm sorry, Sam, I couldn't possibly.'

'Oh. But Gladys isn't expecting you till tomorrow, you're free this evening, surely?'

'Yes, I know, but . . .' Dora didn't want to admit the truth, not her exhaustion, still less her jealousy. She never lied, but . . . 'The thing is, Sam, as I said, Gladys still isn't right. I don't want to be out of town in case she needs to send for me this evening. Or in the night.'

'In the night? But you've been leaving her at night till now, haven't you? If she's that sick, has she seen a doctor?'

Dora quickly back-pedalled.

'There's no need for that. She's on the mend — I'm only trying to protect her . . . to be sure, that's all.'

'OK . . .' But Sam sounded doubtful. 'Well, as I'm at a loose end, would you mind if I went alone?'

203

What could she say? *Yes, I mind, of course I do, because Kathy might have only married Dennis as second best, and now she's seen you again, and you're a free agent, she might call time on that marriage and go back to her first love?*

'Of course not,' she said, managing to keep her voice steady. 'You must go. Please give them my apologies.'

★   ★   ★

Next day, Dora trudged round to Gladys's with her heart in her boots, but Gladys was up, dressed, and had managed to give the twins their breakfast. She was looking, if not much better, then at least a little better. That awful greenish-white pallor had gone and so had some of the dullness from her eyes.

'I'm so sorry, Dora,' she said, when Dora had got the children dressed and settled them in a circle of toys and the two of them were sitting with cups of tea. 'You've been an angel.'

'Don't mention it,' said Dora. 'I'm just glad you're feeling better. I know you get these sick headaches, love, but when it went on, I was starting to get worried. In fact I wondered if you might be expecting again.'

Gladys looked horrified, then shook her head with a laugh.

'There's no chance of that! Bill's hardly here, for one thing, when he is he's exhausted. And . . . we're very careful.'

'So what do you think brought it on this time?'

Gladys tended to get these attacks when she was worked up about something and wearing herself to a wafer — she'd had a couple around the time of Florrie's death and the coroner's court.

Gladys looked down at her cup.

'I think I was worrying about Weston. It's not long now till we go.'

'Weston? But it'll be lovely! You said Bill's so excited about it —'

'That's the problem!' cried Gladys. 'I want everything to be in place . . . to be just right for him.'

Dora was baffled.

'I don't see what can go wrong. You had such a good holiday last time. You're staying in the same boarding house, you know the lie of the land . . . I know there's a lot to get ready beforehand, the packing and that, and Bill won't be here to help, but if you forget something, you'll just have to manage without.'

Gladys smiled a wavery smile.

'I know. I'm being daft, getting worked up.'

'Yes, you are, you silly girl. Weston was all your idea, after all!'

'I know, Dora, I know it was.'

At that point Victor snatched Joy's dolly off her, Joy howled and hit him with a xylophone stick, Victor wailed, and before he could whack her back with a tin soldier, Gladys and Dora had to intervene to prevent an outbreak of World War Three.

As she walked home at dinnertime — Gladys had convinced her she could manage — Dora had to smile at herself. It was one thing to question Gladys for getting worked up about Weston. Hadn't she been getting all worked up about Kathy? Maybe, after all, she should suggest to Sam that they do get together, the four of them. Then she could see for herself if Kathy really was the threat she'd built her up into.

205

By the time she got home, she had a plan of action, and she was relieved to feel much more like herself. Fancy getting in such a stew! Kathy was married now, and happily as far as Dora knew, and before that there'd been the RAF chap she'd been involved with. Even so, Dora would rather be on her home turf: maybe Dennis and Kathy could come to Hinton and they could have a meal out together there.

But when she saw Sam the next day, and suggested it, she sensed a change in his mood.

'I'm not sure that's going to be very easy to arrange,' he said when she suggested the foursome.

Dora felt a cold chill run through her.

'Why's that?' she asked.

'Oh, I didn't mean it can't happen,' Sam said quickly. Was he covering something up? If so, what? 'But not in the next few days. I've got a bit of business to do — a few things to sort out.'

What things?

'I see. All right then, whatever you think best.' Dora covered her upset and confusion by calling the dog. 'Buddy! Come back here! Now!'

Buddy, who'd been about to introduce himself to a French poodle, looked back at her questioningly. But something in Dora's tone told him that this was one rendezvous that would have to wait. With obvious reluctance and a drooping tail, he trotted back and looked to her, and then to Sam, for the 'good boy' which should have followed. None came.

★ ★ ★

'Something's going on with Mum,' Lily told Jim.

She and Miss Frobisher were always switching

206

things around so that Childrenswear looked fresh, even if the stock was largely the same. For the summer season, they'd decided that the two plaster babies on their high plinth and the boy and girl mannequins on their lower one should be placed at opposite corners of the department so they could be seen from both the stairs and the lifts. Jim was providing the muscle to help with the move.

'Is it? What?'

Lily passed Jim the hand of the boy mannequin so he could screw it into place.

'It's her and Sam. She's only seen him once in the past week.'

'She had to spend all those days with Gladys. And now she's catching up at the shop.'

'Even so.' Lily shook her head. 'When they came back with Buddy yesterday, there was something really awkward about it. Something awkward between them. They can't have had a row, can they?'

Jim gave the plaster hand a final twist and considered the idea.

'Sam's not the type. And your mother certainly isn't.'

'No, I agree.' Lily passed Jim the mannequin's other hand. 'Oh, Mum was so happy when he first arrived! How can it all have gone wrong?'

'Ask her,' said Jim simply.

Lily rolled her eyes. Things were always so simple for men.

'She's my mother! How can I possibly ask about her love life?' She tightened the belt on the girl mannequin's summer dress.

'You think she's that keen on Sam?'

'Jim, I know your eyesight kept you out of the Army,

207

but even you must have noticed!'

Jim shrugged. 'Well, maybe she seemed a little more . . . smiley.'

Smiley? Honestly, men, thought Lily — Dora had been walking on air! But perhaps Jim had a point. Maybe somehow, she could — even should — bring up the subject of Sam with her mother.

★ ★ ★

Little did she know, but the topic was already under discussion, to Dora's extreme displeasure. Her neighbour, Jean Crosbie, had seen Dora putting out the ashes and had 'cooee'd' her over the fence. She'd bustled round before Dora could object to demand 'the latest' on Dora's Canadian beau.

'He's not my beau,' said Dora firmly, pouring tea. She'd wetted the breakfast tea leaves again. She certainly wasn't using fresh ones on Jean.

'So you say,' retorted Jean with a knowing grin.

Dora pushed her cup towards her.

'I've told you before, Jean. Sam is just a friend and if you ever thought it was anything else, then that's your mistaken assumption. Now I can't offer you any sugar I'm afraid, I'm saving it for a cake.'

'That's all right, I'm sweet enough.'

Jean had worked with Dora in the WVS during the war, and no one would have described her as sweet. In fact she was known as something of a sourpuss and was a dreadful gossip. Dora had once helped Jean through a family crisis, and had warmed to her a little at the time, but they'd never be bosom buddies.

Jean took a sip of her tea — she liked it scalding hot.

'A friend, you say?' She shook her head. 'Pull the other one, it's got bells on! That's why you've had your hair set every week he's been here, is it? Why you've been gadding off on all these days out, and letting him wine and dine you?'

'Wine and dine?' Dora rolled her eyes. 'I don't know where you get your ideas from, Jean, I really don't! Fishcakes and a pot of tea at Lyons, if you must know!'

Not that Dora had minded: Sam would have taken her somewhere smarter, and had offered to do so every time, but Dora had refused. And, they'd both admitted, simple fare was what they both preferred.

Jean made a knowing, crowing face.

'It's the thought that counts! Maybe he's saving up for the ring.'

Dora had had enough.

'He's going back to Canada soon, like he always was. And that'll be an end to it.'

As she said it, she realised it was true. For whatever reason — and she strongly suspected the reason was Kathy — Sam's visit, which had started so well, was going to end in this awful, uncomfortable and embarrassing way. Dora didn't know how to rescue things any more, and she didn't know if she should even try. She realised with a stab of pain that she felt further apart from Sam now than she had when four thousand miles of sea and land had separated them. She turned away and blinked to stop the sudden feeling of fullness in her eyes. Once Sam left, she couldn't even see the point in them writing to each other any more.

22

That evening, Lily screwed up her courage and tried to talk to her mum about Sam. But Dora had had enough of a grilling from Jean: she closed up like a clam.

'I don't think I'll be seeing so much of him now. He's got other things he wants to do before he goes home.'

Lily had known something was up, but it sounded worse than she'd thought.

'Oh. Oh dear. What things?'

Dora bent her head to her knitting bag and brought out a mass of wool. She'd unravelled an old sweater of Jim's that was past darning and washed and carded the wool. Now it needed winding.

'That's up to Sam; he wants to travel around a bit, maybe.'

'Right.' But Lily was puzzled. Wanting to see a bit more of the country than the Midlands was fair enough. It was what she'd assumed Sam might want to do, but why cram it all into his last days in England? Why hadn't he spread it out, a few days at a time, or disappeared for a week in the middle? It seemed the wrong way round somehow. 'That's a shame.'

'Not really. He must be pretty fed up of Hinton, and he's devoted quite enough of his time to me!' said Dora crisply. 'And I'd have had to put him off anyway, I've got far too much on. I got very behind at the shop what with spending all those days with Gladys. Now, are you going to help me with this wool or not?'

The discussion was clearly over and Lily turned the conversation to Gladys's holiday — they were off the next day and she'd been into the shop with the children to see if they had any sunhats for them. As former staff, she was entitled to a small discount and Lily had been happy to oblige with a cotton sun bonnet for Joy and a cap for Victor.

'She rushed off to Haberdashery to look for a little anchor or a ship's wheel she could sew on it,' she told Dora. 'She's counting the hours now till they go.'

Then she realised it was not the most tactful thing she could have said. Her mum must be counting the hours till Sam's departure too — and not in a good way.

And so the hours passed into days, the longest in Dora's life. No, that was a lie . . . she'd had worse times when her boy Reg had gone missing during the war, and before that when her husband Arthur had died suddenly and so young — but that had been a long time ago. Even the war seemed a long time ago, with the memory of how happy she'd been in the past few weeks still fresh in her mind. But, she told herself firmly, that was in the past too. She'd just have to get on with things as they were. No good crying over spilt milk, as she'd have been the first to say to someone else bemoaning their situation. Count your blessings. Laugh and the world laughs with you; weep and you weep alone. But all the little dictums which she'd found helpful in the past seemed anything but helpful now. How could anything be helpful when your heart felt like broken glass?

★ ★ ★

In Weston, however, the sun was shining and all was well. Gladys, Bill and the children had arrived safely and settled into the same boarding house where they'd stayed before and the landlady knew them.

'Look at the little poppets!' she exclaimed when she saw Bill coming downstairs with the children on their first day. 'I can't get over how much they've grown!'

Bill grinned. He refrained from saying that was what children did. Instead he said:

'Are you sure you don't mind having them for an hour or so this morning? Gladys says she spoke to you about it last night. Seems there's something she wants us to do, just the two of us.'

'I told her I'd be glad to! My husband's got a few jobs in the garden that they can help with and he can show them his pigeons. You'd like that, wouldn't you, my chicks?'

After breakfast, with Joy and Victor happily transferring the stones they'd picked out of a flower bed from one flowerpot to another, Gladys and Bill set off.

'So where are you taking me?' he asked. 'I thought it was me that knew Weston, not you!'

'That's what you think,' said Gladys with a mysterious smile. 'You don't know as much as you think you know!'

'I know we're going away from the town centre and the shops and back from the sea and the prom. These are ordinary streets, where people live.'

'Not just any old people, Bill. Us too.'

Bill stopped.

'Gladys, I think the sea air's gone to your head. We live in Hinton.'

'No, we don't,' said Gladys smugly. 'Or we won't

212

for much longer. We're going to buy a house, Bill. A house, here.'

Bill goggled at her.

'What? How? With what? Where, here? *Here*, here?'

Smiling more widely, Gladys took his hand.

'Yes. Come on. It's not much further now.'

With Bill dumbstruck, they turned right into another road, back in the direction of the sea. The houses were built of the pale local stone, semi-detached and bay-windowed. They were generally well-tended, with small front gardens, painted porches and coloured glass in the fanlights of the front doors. Halfway down, Gladys stopped outside a house which was none of that. The front square was a patch of weeds. The paint on the front door was peeling and the fanlight had been boarded over, as had the windows. There was a 'For Sale' board by the gate over which had been tacked a strip saying 'Reserved'. Gladys turned to Bill, whose eyes were out on stalks.

'When it says 'Reserved' . . . it can't be . . .'

'It is. It's for us.'

'But we can *buy* it? How?'

Gladys took a deep breath.

'Gran left some money, quite a lot actually, on an insurance policy I never knew she had. I only found out when I went to the solicitor.'

'But that was months ago! And you didn't say?'

'I couldn't! I've been cooking up this plan.' Gladys's face lit up with the triumph of her achievement. 'You were away, so it was easy. Dora had the children for a whole day. I'd had house agents down here sending me particulars on the quiet, and finally a house — this house — came up that I thought we might be able to afford. So I came down on the train, they brought me to have a look at it and . . . well, there's been lot of to-ing and fro-ing, the bank and the solicitor and letters and that, but anyway, it's settled. I know it doesn't look much —'

But Bill had pulled her close and was kissing her, right there in the street. When he finally let her go, she asked: 'You're pleased then?'

★ ★ ★

They went to a café for a sit-down: after the excitement of the revelation, or maybe the passion of Bill's kiss, Gladys's knees were trembling. The café was on the prom, overlooking the beach and the sea, but Bill hardly glanced at the view. Maybe he didn't need to, now he knew he'd be seeing it for the rest of his life. Or maybe he just couldn't take his eyes off his amazing, astonishing wife. The waitress set down their coffees and Bill released Gladys's hands long enough to take a sip.

'Go on then,' he said. 'Tell me.'

'There's no more to tell. I've left the money where it is for now, because the house will have to be in your name, so I needed to get your' — she stifled a smile — 'your approval first!'

'Well, I withhold it!' joked Bill.

'The agent agreed to reserve it for us, like you saw. I was dead lucky, it had just come on the market. I phoned the agent as soon as I got the particulars. Once I saw it, I said we'd have it then and there, even though it's — well, you could probably tell. It's a bit of a wreck inside, hence the price.'

'It's not war damage, is it?' asked Bill. 'I know Weston was bombed, quite badly, in '42, but the rest of the street looks fine, even the houses on either side. The roof looked all right and there's no scorch marks, so it can't have been an incendiary . . . is the damage at the back?'

'It's nothing like that. An old lady lived there.' Gladys tried her own coffee. It wasn't bad. 'Seven cats, according to the agent, and — you'll see — it's full of stinky old milk bottles and newspapers going back to — oh, I dunno, Queen Victoria's Jubilee, probably!'

'So it hasn't been maintained.' Now Bill understood.

'No, but I've already paid for someone — a surveyor — to check it over and the structure itself isn't that bad.'

Bill gaped again at his wife's determination — and efficiency.

'How did you even know this stuff?' he asked. 'To think to get a surveyor, I mean.'

'I do listen, you know, when you tell me about the people who come round the sites you've been working on,' Gladys chided. 'And the agent's been really helpful.'

'So what's the story?'

'There's a few slates missing off the roof at the back, some rotten floorboards and skirtings, a bit of woodworm, but no damp to speak of,' Gladys explained. 'Mostly it needs a good clear out and clean and tidy up and redecorating. And with all your experience now —'

'I can fix what needs doing!'

'That's right! We'll have to scrimp at first, and live on what savings we've got —'

Bill jumped in, grabbing her hands again.

'I'll work like stink till we move, Glad! All the overtime I can get, if you don't mind, to build up some money behind us —'

'I knew you would,' Gladys's smile held all the love, faith and trust in him she'd ever felt. 'And I don't mind, of course I don't! When we move we can live in one room for a bit, but I don't mind that either as long as we can be here. I know being by the sea is what you want.'

'Oh, Gladys.' Bill's voice cracked. 'You've done all this for me?'

'Yes, love, but — no. Well, it was you that started it, but it's for me too, and the children. It'll be a beautiful place for them to grow up. Fresh air, big skies, the beach, the sea. It's for all of us.'

'You won't miss Hinton?'

'Not really. Oh, I'll miss my friends, I'm sure, but they can come and visit, as often as they like.' She glanced out at the sea — it was miles out, but it winked at her from the horizon. 'I'm done with Hinton really, it's not like I've lived there all my life. And now we're not tied there with Gran . . .'

Bill nodded, understanding.

'It's you and me now,' Gladys went on. 'You, me and the twins. Our life. Our future.'

Bill raised his coffee cup in a toast.

'To us. And I never thought I'd say this, but God bless you, Florrie Jessop.'

Gladys chinked her cup against his with a smile.

'Yes, God bless.' As she put her cup down, she said: 'You have to admit, Bill, never mind how she was when she was alive, and I know you thought she took advantage, well, Gran's done right by me — us — in the end.'

Bill met his wife's eyes.

'She has,' he agreed.

Gladys had a point. Florrie was never going to benefit from it, so it must have been her granddaughter she'd been thinking of when she took out the insurance policy. And if he thought it was no more than Gladys deserved, he had the good sense not to say so.

★ ★ ★

On the day Gladys and Bill were due back, Lily went round straight after work, keen to hear all about Gladys's hard-earned break at the seaside. At six o'clock it was still warm, and she found Gladys in the yard, supervising the twins who were splashing about in the old zinc bath. Hugging her friend, Gladys explained they'd demanded a paddle — they'd so loved it at Weston. Lily positioned herself far enough away not to get her work shoes ruined, and looked at Gladys expectantly.

'I got your postcard but, go on, tell me, how was your holiday?' she asked.

What Gladys told her was the last thing she'd expected to hear.

'A stick of rock would have done!' she exclaimed when Gladys had explained about their move. 'But if you'd brought one, you could have knocked me down with it!'

'You can have as much rock as you like when you come on your holidays,' Gladys beamed. 'We're going to let out rooms! B and B!'

Lily gaped.

'What? Are you? How big is this place? It must be a mansion!'

'Oh, it's not that big, but when Bill saw inside, it

217

was his idea.' Lily nodded in interest and encouragement, and Gladys went on. 'Once we've made it a bit habitable for us, Bill's going to get a job back on the water, well, that was the whole idea, to get him back to the work he loves.'

Lily smiled: she'd heard enough about it since Bill had been demobbed.

'There's steamer trips over to Wales, you see,' Gladys explained, rescuing an enamel beaker that had gone over the side of the bath and giving it back to Joy. 'Or trips round the bay on smaller boats ... he'll easily pick something up. And in his spare time he'll carry on doing up the house.'

'So how's this B and B going to work? Is it a mansion?'

Gladys looked pleased with herself, and why not?

'The front room can be the guests' lounge, and for their breakfasts and that, and we'll have the ground floor back as our bedroom. There's a back kitchen with just about enough room for a little table where me and Bill and the children can eat. And upstairs, apart from the twins' room, there'll be two that we can let out. Oh and there's a bathroom!'

'Gladys! You've got it all planned! But for you to have organised buying a house in the first place, all by yourself ...' A penny dropped with a clunk. 'No wonder you were getting those headaches!'

Gladys put her hands over her face.

'Sometimes I just wanted to take my brain out and wash it! The house agent kept writing me letters, and the bank and the insurance company and the solicitor. I had to keep sending papers off to prove I was the rightful ... what did they call it ... legatee or something. And what with trying to keep it all a secret . . .'

'Yes, OK,' said Lily. 'And I can see you wanted to surprise Bill, but why didn't you tell us? We wouldn't have let on.'

Gladys made a regretful face.

'Yes, I'm sorry about that. I'd have loved to, believe me, but I didn't want to in case it didn't work out. There's a lot that can go wrong when you're trying to buy a house.'

Lily laughed. 'I'll take your word for it! I don't suppose I'm ever likely to know.'

'Ah, but that's the other thing.' Gladys's face was anything but regretful now — it was triumphant. 'How would you and Jim feel about taking on our house — here?'

'What? But —'

'Not to buy,' Gladys added quickly, 'it's only rented, but . . .'

'I didn't mean that . . . I meant, a house? A whole house? Me and Jim?'

It had seemed such an impossible dream. A fantasy, even.

'I can at least suggest it to the landlord,' Gladys went on. 'I'm sure he'd rather have someone on recommendation than any old Tom, Dick or Harry. And I'll give you a good reference!'

'Oh Gladys . . . it'd be wonderful!'

'I'd love it to go to you two. Just think, your first home together!'

Like the wartime decoding machines which, they were beginning to learn, had been such a breakthrough for the Allies, Lily's brain was whirring and clicking at about a million revolutions a second.

'I'll have to talk to Jim.'

'I know. But it's exciting, isn't it?'

'Yes, it is. Very.' Lily jumped up and hugged her friend. 'Oh Gladys, thank you!'

23

As Lily walked home, her mind was still whirring away. She found Jim in the backyard, cutting lettuce and pulling up radishes — Lily was making corned beef patties for tea. That was ambitious enough for her: she'd boil some extra potatoes, but hoped a bit of salad on the side would do for veg.

She kept her voice down: her mum was in the kitchen with the door open.

'Gladys has come up with a bit of a surprise,' she began.

Jim's eyes grew very large behind his glasses as he listened, his brow at first creasing in disbelief. Then, as Lily reached the second part of Gladys's scheme, his disbelief grew before his face cracked into a huge grin.

Throwing down his knife, he grabbed her in a hug and whirled her round, lifting her clean off the ground. Smiling down into her face, he looked to Lily as if he'd won the pools, the Christmas Club raffle and the Boys' Brigade tombola all in one day.

'But can we afford it?' Lily asked, tucking her blouse back in when he finally put her down. She stupidly hadn't asked Gladys the rent. 'A whole house?'

'If Gladys and Bill have afforded it with her not working and two children to feed, I'm sure we can!' Jim enthused. 'Think of it, Lily, we'll smarten it up a bit, I'll get some veg going in the yard like we have here, we can take the chickens —'

'Hey, steady on,' Lily put her fingers to his lips.

221

'Look, Jim, I know it's a wonderful chance for us and I'd love a place of our own. You know I would. But there is one big problem. What about Mum?'

'What about her? She'll be thrilled for us!'

'Will she?' Lily drew him down to sit next to her on the side of the raised veg bed and lowered her voice even further. 'Reg and Gwenda may never come home — they seem to love it abroad. Sid's got this wild idea to join Jerome in America if he can, and if that's not possible he's not going to come back to Hinton, he'll stay in London. I — we — are all Mum's got.'

'But we'll only be around the corner! OK, not quite, but not far!'

'I know that,' sighed Lily. 'But it's not just us leaving. Gladys and Bill and the children are like family to her and they'll be gone too. She'll be all on her own.'

'Your mum helping with the twins was always going to tail off,' Jim said reasonably. 'I don't know much about kids, but surely once they can walk and talk and, well, wipe their own bottoms, they're not so demanding?'

Lily's mouth twisted in a half-smile.

'That's true, I suppose. But that's not all. It just seems so cruel for us to go right at the moment. From the way she was talking the other night, I'm not sure Mum'll even have Sam's letters to look forward to.'

Jim was a very considered thinker, which was admirable — and could also be highly irritating, or could be to the more impatient Lily, anyway. He did that thing he always did when he was considering something: he took his glasses off, looked at them and put them back on again.

'I'm sorry, Lily, but if you think like that, we'll never

move out. This is a God-given opportunity. You know how little there is about.'

Lily sighed. It was true. Every week, out of interest, they looked in the *Chronicle*'s 'Accommodation Vacant' column. They'd even been, on the quiet, to see a couple of places for rent — a damp basement flat in the centre of town and a bedsitting room at the top of a ramshackle Victorian semi on the fringes. Both were entirely unsuitable and for what they were, ludicrously overpriced. The agent showing them round had been sniffy when they declined to proceed, and said they were lucky even to get a viewing. Two million homes had been destroyed in the war: some people were so desperate for a roof over their heads that they'd pay upfront, sight unseen.

'OK,' she said. 'We'll tell her.'

When she'd cooked the tea and they were sitting at the table, Jim gave Lily one of his meaningful looks. Haltingly, she outlined Gladys's offer, and Dora reacted just as Jim had said she would.

'Well, of course you must go for it!'

'Are you sure, Mum?' Lily asked. 'I feel bad about leaving you all on your own.'

'Dear Lord, you make me sound about eighty! I'm not that decrepit!' smiled Dora. 'You don't want to be living in one room here all your lives, do you?'

'No, but —'

'It's not that we're not grateful to you for having us,' Jim put in. 'You've given us the very best start to married life we could have had.'

'Well, that's very nice to hear. Thank you, Jim.' Dora smiled again. 'But you're taking your life in your hands, aren't you, relying on Lily's cooking?'

'Mum!'

223

Jim grinned.

'Don't worry, Dora, I know where to come if she doesn't feed me properly!'

Lily jabbed at him with her fork but she had to admit the patties hadn't been a great success — they'd fallen apart in the pan, so they were basically mush with burnt bits. In trying to stick them together she'd forgotten to check the potatoes were simmering, so they were frankly a bit underdone. Thank goodness she'd had the sense not to do cooked veg as well. Even she couldn't ruin a bit of salad!

When Lily and Jim had gone off to take Buddy for his evening walk, Dora took the kitchen chair outside and sat in the last rays of the sun where it fell in the corner of the yard. The idea of them moving out had come as a shock, but she was pleased with the way she'd been able to sound happy for them, and she was. It was always going to happen some day, she'd known that — but it would still be a wrench to see them go. For all that she had her work at Wedding Belles, she'd miss the energy they brought into the house, with their tales of goings-on at Marlows, their light young voices, their interests that were so different from hers. They kept her on her toes; they kept her, she often thought, young. But she mustn't be selfish.

Nothing stays the way it is for ever, she thought, even her friendship with Sam. Oh, she hadn't expected anything dramatic from his visit. Drama wasn't his style — or hers — which was why this mysterious disappearing act of his — it had been days now — was so odd.

So what had she hoped for? Dora forced herself to think about it. An intensification of their friendship. A strengthening of the bond between them — yes, she'd put it that strongly — of the bond between them, or the bond she'd thought was between them. The thought that he might start to sign his letters 'Affectionately, Sam' instead of 'Your friend, Sam.' And that, when time and money permitted, he might want to come over and see her again. Foolish dreams, she knew that now.

Life moved on for other people, for Evelyn and Beryl with their business, for Gladys and Bill with a new life in Weston, for Lily and Jim with the prospect of a home of their own. But they were all young; it was only right. She must derive her pleasure from seeing them blossom. She'd had her time.

★ ★ ★

Next day was Wednesday and half-day at Marlows.

Lily, in her oldest cotton frock, was sweeping the yard while she waited for her mum, who was upstairs getting ready. They were due to go to Dora's cousin Ida, swapping a few eggs for all the gooseberries they could pick from the bottom of her garden. Lily hated gooseberries — the nasty scratchy bushes and the sour, pippy fruit, but they were free, effectively, and that made them desirable.

She heard footsteps down the entry, then the click of the latch on the back gate. She looked up and there, suddenly, closing the gate behind him, was Sam. Lily propped the broom against the wall of the privy.

Sam smiled as he came towards her.

'Well, hello.'

'Hello.'

She hadn't intended to sound quite so frosty, but

who did he think he was, turning up like this out of the blue after so many days away?

'Is your mother home?'

'She is.'

'You're mad with me.' Sam corrected himself: 'I mean, you're angry. I should maybe have expected that.'

Lily spread her hands in a gesture of helplessness.

'It's not so much angry, Sam, as . . . confused. Baffled, in fact, about why you'd suddenly vanish and leave Mum in the lurch like that!'

'Is that what you thought?'

'What else could we think?'

Sam gave a despairing groan.

'What's she said?'

'Nothing!' Lily replied. 'You know her, she's not going to talk about her private life. But it's obvious you've hurt her feelings.'

Sam looked pleadingly at her.

'Oh, Lily, I'm so sorry. I've handled this all wrong. I wouldn't hurt Dora for the world.'

'But you have,' Lily protested. 'How could you not, with your disappearing act? You're just not the same as she thought you were! That any of us thought you were!'

'I had things to fix.' Again, Sam translated to make his meaning clear. 'To arrange. Things that I wanted to surprise her with, that's all.'

Lily took hold of the broom again. Sam stepped back as if she was going to hit him with it, but instead, Lily started sweeping, more vigorously than before.

'I just don't understand — any of it. Mind your feet, please,' she said briskly.

What could Sam, a visitor in the country, have had

to arrange?

Sam skipped nimbly out of the way as she pushed the broom with its little heap of dust and cinders towards the ashcan.

'No, well, maybe when I've explained myself to your mother, you will,' he said. He caught her arm. 'Will you tell her I'm here? Please, Lily.'

But there was no need. Dora appeared in the doorway to the kitchen, also in her oldest dress. She was carrying a pair of stout gloves for the gooseberry picking and a wicker basket containing the eggs. She nearly dropped them when she saw who it was.

'Sam!'

Sam stepped away from Lily and smiled sheepishly. 'Dora. I've just been getting a ticking off from your daughter.' Dora looked to Lily, a reproving look, but Sam forestalled her. 'No more than I deserved. I don't know if you're free this afternoon, but I'd like the chance to explain myself, if you'll give it to me.'

Dora looked to Lily again. Lily knew what she had to do.

'Give me the eggs, Mum, and the gloves. I'll go for the gooseberries on my own. You'd better hear what Sam's got to say.'

★ ★ ★

They went to the park, to the little rustic shelter, not much more than a hut, where they'd often sat in the past. By a miracle, today there was no one else there — not the old tramp who sometimes slept there, nor the usual gang of lads carving their initials, and worse, into the boards.

Sam waited for Dora to sit down first, and she sat

227

primly on the seat against the back wall. Sam hesitated, then instead of sitting easily beside her, chose a place at right angles, on the bench down the side. Dora pulled the skirt of her dress over her knees.

'Dora,' said Sam gently. 'Look at me. I'm sorry. I'm really sorry for going off like I did.'

'Oh yes?'

Dora pleated the fabric of her dress between her fingers. She couldn't bring herself to look at him — if he was going to tell her what she thought he was, that he'd decided he had to be with Kathy, she was terrified she might cry.

'OK,' said Sam, 'you don't want to look at me. Fair enough. I've treated you badly. First, I have to apologise, Dora, most sincerely. I never meant it to be like this.'

'No, I'm sure you didn't,' Dora replied evenly, speaking to the beaten earth floor of the hut. She'd rehearsed what she'd say often enough, not sure if she'd get the chance to say it, or if it would have to be put in a letter. 'But we have to face it. Meeting up again seemed to start off all right, but things have changed for you, obviously, and that's just how it is. I wish you well, Sam, but I don't imagine we'll be seeing each other again.'

'What?' She sensed Sam almost start up from the bench. 'No, no, you don't understand — you can't be writing me off?'

Dora raised her head and looked him in the eyes for the first time.

'What do you expect?' she demanded. 'I'll be honest, Sam, I thought we had a firm friendship.' She swallowed hard — if she didn't say it now, she never would. 'A fond friendship, a real bond, an understanding. But it's clearly not the case, your affections are elsewhere —'

This time Sam really did move. He dropped to the ground in front of her and grabbed her hands.

'What? My affections elsewhere? Where elsewhere? No, no, no, no, no! Don't say that! How can you think . . . that's not it at all! My affections are all for you! I'm crazy about you, Dora! I . . . if you'll have me, I want you to be my wife!'

24

Dora was speechless. Not only was it not what she'd expected, she'd expected the opposite — for Sam to say that meeting Kathy again had made him realise that he'd been a fool to turn her down in the first place. Or now that Sam had turned up again, she'd realised he was her one true love . . . How absurd that seemed now, like the plot of some tear-jerking film! But it didn't make what he'd said seem any more real. That too seemed like something she might only know as someone else's story — things like this didn't happen to her, Dora Collins!

But maybe they did . . . maybe it was real? Sam was kneeling in front of her, holding her hands and looking up at her, expectant and hopeful. Dora's throat was dry. It was real: he was waiting for a reply. Her heart was thumping so hard and so fast she was surprised the ducks on the pond hadn't heard it and taken flight; she went hot and then cold. Sam spoke again.

'I'm sorry, is that such a surprise to you?'

Dora still couldn't speak, but she managed to nod.

'I guess it's too soon for you to give me an answer, then.'

She looked at him wonderingly, then shook her head.

'Is that a no?' Sam sounded worried, no, more than worried, alarmed. 'It's no to the question?'

'No,' she stammered. 'No, it's not, but . . .'

'Oh Dora!' His face lit up. 'You mean you'd consider it? Really? Oh, I — may I?'

Without waiting for an answer, he moved to sit beside her, put his arm around her shoulders and turned her towards him. When she didn't resist or pull away, just looked at him dumbstruck, he bent his head and kissed her gently on the lips, then pulled back as if he'd gone too far. Dora put out a hand and laid it against his cheek. When she found her voice again, there'd be a lot of talking to do, but for now, she simply wanted to savour the overwhelming sense of relief. More than that — of peace.

★ ★ ★

As they talked, they walked and walked, Sam gripping her hand tightly and occasionally bringing it to his lips. Round the duck pond, past the allotments, back to the pond. Past the trenches that had been dug against bombing raids and were being filled in again for flowerbeds and the netted stretch of grass that the council were reseeding, finally trying to bring the park back to what it had been before the war. A new start, a new life — and Dora couldn't believe that she was being offered one as well. She'd given Sam her answer — it was yes, in principle, but there were big questions — huge questions — that she had to ask. She wanted — oh, how she wanted — to give herself up entirely to this new Dora, the heroine of her own romance, but his answers could change everything — again.

'The thing is, Sam,' she faltered, 'I have to ask . . . are you expecting me to move to Canada? Because —'

Sam burst out laughing.

'Are you serious? Come on, Dora, I know you bet-

231

ter than that! You told me when we went to Birmingham it was the furthest you'd been for twenty years!'

'So . . .'

'I'll come here, of course!'

He made it sound so easy, as if Canada was a bus ride away. Dora stopped in her tracks.

'What? You'd do that for me?'

'In a heartbeat! I have to go back for a while, I need to arrange the sale of the shop, and pack up the house . . . but then that's it for me. There's nothing and no one in Alberta, Canada, to keep me, whereas here, you have your job, your friends and your family — Lily and Jim, anyway.'

Even if he said it was no sacrifice, Dora could hardly take in the enormity of what Sam was intending — and for her.

'But . . . if — when you come over here, what are you going to do?' she asked. 'For work, I mean? Will you be able to work here?'

'Oh, Dora.' Sam stopped walking and Dora stopped too. 'This is what I've been looking into, this is what took the time! The immigration side in itself is no big deal, I knew that. We Canadians don't even have separate citizenship from Britain.'

Of course, Dora realised, all the people of the Commonwealth counted as British citizens, though she'd never really thought about it before — there'd been no need!

'But I didn't want to ask you to marry me and then find out that I couldn't keep us,' Sam continued. 'As if I was going to live off you! That's why I couldn't say anything before — I had to go for an interview with your Ministries of This, That and the Other, and the Canadian High Commission. I had to go to London.'

'London!'

To Dora, it might as well have been Mars. No wonder Sam had needed time to fix things up! She couldn't believe she'd got things so wrong.

They started walking again, Sam still explaining himself.

'Then, when I was sure I could get a work permit, I still wasn't quite sure how I could support us.' Sam looked triumphant. 'And that's where Dennis came in.'

Dora almost stumbled — and almost burst out laughing. Again, how wrong could she have been! The meal at Dennis and Kathy's she'd ducked out of . . . when she'd been imagining a tryst between Sam and Kathy over the washing up, Sam had remained at the table, fixing up some work, somehow, with Dennis. But—

'What work's he got to offer?' she asked. 'I thought he was about to be demobbed and was looking for work himself?'

'You don't have to look for work if you set up your own business,' said Sam, smugly.

'So you're going to work for him?'

'Not for him, *with* him.' Sam glanced at his watch. 'Look, there's a lot more to tell you yet. Shall we go and get something to drink?'

'I think that might be a very good idea,' said Dora.

★ ★ ★

Dora wouldn't usually be seen in a pub, and certainly not in the daytime, but this wasn't a usual kind of day; in fact it was turning into the most unusual day of Dora's life. Fifteen minutes later, she found herself sitting in a pub garden, nursing a ginger beer. Sam raised his half pint glass to her with a wry look.

'It should be champagne, I know, but there'll be time for that when we tell Lily and Jim.'

'I don't know what we're telling them yet!' Dora was recovering her usual forthrightness. 'My answer's still conditional, you know!'

Sam roared with laughter.

'My, now we see the real you! Is it too late for me to change my mind?' He took a sip of his drink, both of them knowing he didn't mean a word of it. 'OK. So here's the thing. Apart from getting myself the right papers, this is what I've been sorting out. How Dennis and I are going to become partners.'

'Go on.' Dora was intrigued.

'Like I say, the last thing I wanted was to land over here with no means of support. I had to find some way to support myself' — he reached for her hand again — 'to support us.'

He'd seen how Dora had lived during the war, but on this visit Sam had been shocked to see her still scrimping and saving, hoarding string, making soup from vegetable peelings, and — he noticed these things — having to wear a lot of the same clothes he remembered from 1943. He didn't intend them to live off the black market, but even within the restrictions, he was determined she should have a more comfortable life than the one she was living at the moment — a life without worry about money, a life with more leisure and less hard work. He wanted to look after her: she deserved it.

Dora was smiling at him, waiting. He carried on.

'You know the work Dennis has been doing, overseeing the disposal of all this ex-Canadian gear? Well, he's got to know some of your guys from the Ministry of Defence. The amount of stuff we left behind is nothing compared with what your guys have got to get rid of, or what the Yanks left here, for that matter. There's all sorts of things being sold off, re-used, taken down or taken apart.'

So far, that much made sense.

'The smart thing is working out what to do with it all. Well, through his contacts, Dennis knows what's going spare. And our plan is to buy up a lot of timber — invasion barges, Nissen huts, what you will, and re-purpose them into things that people want.'

'And what do people want?'

'Sheds.'

'Sheds?' Dora stared in disbelief.

'And not just garden sheds. You know during the war a lot of people started keeping chickens, like you? Making a henhouse out of bits of scrap the way Jim did? Well, now people want better housing for the birds they keep at home — and there's farmers looking to raise them on a bigger scale too.'

'Really?'

'Oh yes.' Sam took a swig of his drink. 'You're going to see a lot more chickens on British dinner tables in future. And all those chickens are going to need housing.'

'I suppose so . . .'

'There's more. You remember the panic at the start of the war when you Brits were sure you were going to be invaded? All the dogs and cats that were put down? Well, people want to be dog owners again. And dogs need —'

'Kennels!' exclaimed Dora.

'Clever girl!'

It sounded feasible enough. But, her practical side fully reasserting itself now, Dora needed to feel sure.

'So has Dennis got experience of this kind of thing?'

Sam put down his glass.

'Of course, you don't know! His folks have a timber yard back in Canada. He knows all there is to know about wood. And with my hardware background, I know all there is to know about nuts and bolts and netting and hinges and nails and screws.'

'Right . . .'

'I sense a reservation here.'

He could read her like a book, one with very tiny print.

'Only a small one.' And it wasn't that working with Dennis might bring Sam into contact with Kathy — that fear had long gone. Dora had only met Dennis once, but Sam had said himself that he was a bit of a big mouth. She hoped Dennis hadn't lured Sam into this scheme with a lot of blather.

'You do trust Dennis, do you? I mean he's a bit —'

'Flash? Cocky? I knew deep down you hadn't taken to him!'

'No, no,' Dora backtracked. 'It's not fair of me to judge, I hardly know him. I just want to know, is he reliable? He's not going to let you down? Run out on you?'

'Dora,' Sam reassured her, 'it's all an act. Underneath the chat, he's an honest-to-God good guy. When you get to know him better, you'll see. And he's been working his socks off for us already. He's picked up a contract from your Ministry of Defence — big old wooden ammo crates, 50,000 of them! We've got to break them down and use what we can to make smaller ones — for the army of occupation in Europe. And

236

any timber that's split, or not up to par, or not the right size, we get to use, or sell on!'

The idea that someone at the Ministry of Defence thought Dennis was reliable enough to make goods for the British Army was all the reassurance Dora needed.

'Well. If the Ministry of Defence trust him, who am I to say different?' she smiled.

Sam seized her hand across the table.

'Me and Dennis are the perfect partnership. He'll go out and cut the deals, bring in the business, talk the talk, walk the walk. That's not me, you know that! I know what I'm good at: I can run things day-to-day — steady the ship, if you like. And before you ask, I'll be doing the accounts.'

For someone who'd always had to worry about money, that in itself was very reassuring to Dora.

'And if you — or Lily and Jim — want to see it,' Sam continued, 'we've got a business plan. While I've been on long-distance calls and trips to London, Dennis has been talking to the bank and found us some premises on the road between here and Nettleford, so it's halfway for each of us to travel. So — any more questions?'

'Just one,' said Dora. 'The long-distance calls home? Were they about your shop?'

'Ah! That's the other thing! My Uncle Chad has loved every minute. He was bored out of his tiny mind, retired, and dreading me coming back. He wants to take it over and run it with his son, who's going to live in my apartment above. So I'll be free of the place without having to put it on the open market!'

'You have had a lot to arrange!'

Sam gripped her hand and Dora didn't take it away.

Drinking in a pub in the daytime! A man holding her hand across the table! Whatever next!

'I wish I could have told you. Maybe I should have — I didn't realise it would take so long or be so complicated. Do you forgive me?'

A shaft of sunlight fell across them, illuminating the sticky tabletop, the curling beer mats, the chip on Sam's glass. With Sam across the table from her, his eyes shining brightly, his face so honest and hopeful, it looked to Dora like paradise.

'Would I be here if I didn't?'

'True.' Sam squeezed her hand. 'Shall I ask you again? Do you think you might be able to give an unconditional answer now?'

Dora smiled. She wasn't sure her answer had ever been conditional — in truth, she might even have considered going to Canada if that had been the only way not to lose him.

'It's yes. Yes, Sam, I would love to be your wife.'

Sam leaned across the table and kissed her, the same gentle pressure as before. So that was what came next, thought Dora, being kissed in public as well! At her age! If Jean Crosbie could see her now . . . !

Sam sat back and raised his glass.

'You've made me the happiest man alive. To the future, Dora. To us.'

★ ★ ★

Dora asked Sam to leave her to walk home alone, saying she needed some time to get her head straight. He understood at once. But before they parted, he drew her into a quiet alleyway and took her in his arms, properly, for the first time. Then he

238

kissed her gently once more. Only then did he let her go.

Dora wasn't sure how she got home: she didn't register a single thing she passed, not the shops, the houses, the roads or the pavements. As she turned into Brook Street, a neighbour crossing the road raised his hat and said, 'Good afternoon'. Dora looked at him as if he'd materialised out of a manhole.

So much had happened to her in the space of a few hours that she couldn't process it — and how she'd begin to tell Lily and Jim she had no idea. Down the entry, touching the cold bricks as she went, hoping to bring herself back to earth . . . Through the back gate, the latch warm from the sun . . . Into the yard, past the bobbing heads of the hens . . .

Dora glanced up at Lily and Jim's window at the back of the house. The curtains were drawn. It could be simply to stop the sun fading the eiderdown and the rug, but in the kitchen, there was a basket of gooseberries on the table, and Jim's old gardening shoes kicked off by the back door. Dora smiled to herself. They were doing what any sensible young couple would do on their afternoon off — they'd gone to bed. She felt a shiver run through her and had to grip the table. One day, possibly quite soon, she and Sam would be a couple too, not a young couple, but a couple all the same, with all that entailed. The thought was both terrifying and exhilarating. But didn't they say 'you're as young as you feel'? And Dora felt seventeen again.

25

Once she'd taken off her jacket, Dora took a deep, steadying breath. She ran the tap and splashed her face with cold water. Patting it dry, she looked at her reflection in the small mirror over the sink that Jim used for shaving, and was amazed to see that she still looked the same — or did she? Wasn't 'feeling seventeen' actually showing in her face? Surely the frown lines on her forehead had disappeared? And the crow's feet too? The lines round her mouth were still there, of course, but that was only because she couldn't stop smiling. She hung up the towel. That was quite enough! She was home now, and she'd have to be Dora Collins again, not the giddy girl of the past couple of hours.

Dora realised she hadn't given a thought to their tea: it would have to be something quick. What a pity those eggs had gone to Ida — egg on toast would have done. It would still have to. She took down the tin of dried egg and began to mix it up with water — if she used the last of the butter that might make scrambled egg taste a bit less foul. By the time Lily and Jim came down, still slightly pink, the table was laid and everything was standing ready. Jim sat down with the paper, but Lily came straight through into the kitchen.

'Well?' she asked. 'What did Sam have to say for himself?'

Now the moment had come, Dora was lost for words. She turned away and covered her confusion by filling the water jug.

240

'Cut some bread, will you, love?' she managed.

Lily went to the bread crock, took out the loaf and put it on the bread board with a thump. Out of the corner of her eye, Dora saw her brandish the bread knife as she spoke.

'If he hasn't given you a decent explanation of why he disappeared, or if he's done even more to hurt you this afternoon, or said something to hurt you, I swear he won't be leaving this country alive! How could he treat you like that?'

Dora put the water jug down carefully on the draining board — very carefully, as her hands were shaking. She turned to face her daughter.

'He hasn't done anything to hurt me. He never meant to.'

'That's what he said to me! But he did, didn't he? Don't deny it, Mum! You haven't let him off?'

'He's asked me to marry him, Lily.'

Lily dropped the knife with a clatter.

'What? No!'

Dora laughed — she felt like laughing all the time now.

'Thank you very much! Is it so unlikely?'

'Well, yes! I mean no, but —' Lily turned and called through the doorway into the living room. 'Jim! Come here! You have to hear this!' Then she turned back to her mother, the words tripping each other up in her amazement. 'Is that why he was behaving so oddly? He was plucking up courage?' Then another thought struck her. 'Hang on — does that mean you're going to Canada with him? And we were worried about moving round the corner! Oh, my Lord, Mum! What did you say?'

It was a most peculiar meal, and not just because

dried egg, however kindly you treated it, was always pretty rubbery. No one had a thought for what they were eating anyway — Dora had no appetite and Lily and Jim were too busy quizzing her about the whys and wherefores, and learning about Dennis and the proposed business, and invasion barges and ammunition boxes and sheds and chicken houses, and the sale of Sam's shop back home and his visit to London to sort out the mechanics of living and working in Britain . . .

When all the questions had been asked, and answered as well as Dora could — inevitably they asked things she hadn't thought of — Lily and Jim washed up while Dora was told to 'sit down quietly after all this excitement!' They pulled the door behind them so she couldn't hear what they were saying.

She understood that they wanted some time to themselves — the news must have been almost as much of a shock to them as it had been to her. But she'd seen in their faces and known from the excited hugs and tears and congratulations — once she'd confirmed she wouldn't be moving an inch from Brook Street — that they were thrilled for her.

✶ ✶ ✶

Calmer next day, despite having been far too worked up to sleep, Dora went into Wedding Belles as usual. In her quiet, unassuming way she told Beryl that she might be needing a bit of time off in due course.

'Oh Dora, why? You're not ill, I hope?' Beryl peered at her. 'You don't look it, you look very well!'

'I'm not ill.'

'You're never going on holiday?' There were no cus-

242

tomers, so Beryl could drop her shop voice. 'I know what it is, all these days out you've had with your fancy man. Given you a taste for adventure, has it?'

'No, it won't be a holiday exactly,' Dora replied. 'More of . . . a honeymoon.'

She had the satisfaction of seeing Beryl's carefully made-up features reassemble themselves into a mask of shock as she groped behind her for the edge of the little desk.

'Never! You and . . . you and Sam? Getting married?'

'Well, I haven't had anyone else on the go, I can assure you.'

'Oh, Dora!' Beryl leapt up and hugged her. 'Oh, that's wonderful!' Despite her wisecracks and her endless teasing about Sam, Beryl had liked what she saw when she'd met him on the days he called for Dora. Then light dawned — or rather, didn't. Her face darkened. 'Hold on — he's not whisking you off to Canada, is he?'

Dora reassured her. 'Don't you know me at all? Sam does! He's moving over here, bless him.'

'Well, thank goodness for that!' exclaimed Beryl. 'This place wouldn't be the same without you! Hinton wouldn't be the same without you!'

'What nonsense!' said Dora smartly. 'No one's indispensable. You'd soon find someone else to do what I do!'

'I don't think so!' Beryl went on, unusually serious for her. 'You're the beating heart of this place, Dora, and the beating heart of Hinton, too, you and your family.' She hugged Dora again, tears in her eyes. 'Oh, come here! It couldn't happen to a nicer person. Oh, you so deserve this!' Then, pulling away, she sniffed.

'Oh, look, what you've done, my mascara's run now!'

When Dora finished at dinnertime, Sam was waiting outside.

'Hello,' she said shyly.

'Hello, Dora. How are you?'

'Do you really need to ask?'

Sam beamed happily.

'Just checking you hadn't had second thoughts.'

'Second, and third, and fourth,' Dora smiled. 'I hardly slept a wink. But they don't change a thing. They only made me realise how very lucky I am.'

'I'll fight you for that honour,' said Sam as they walked away.

* * *

The next few weeks were full of activity. Sam changed his ticket so he could stay on a bit longer, though he'd have to go back to Canada in due course to finalise the sale of the shop and to pack up his things in the flat above it.

'Will you want to bring much over?'

They were walking back to Wedding Belles after sandwiches in the park: it was high wedding season and Dora was having to work a full day.

She wondered where she'd put them if he planned to bring a lot of possessions, and what they might be. Clothes and personal things, and a few mementos, perhaps . . .

'I was thinking about that,' Sam mused. 'Just a few . . . heirlooms, you'd call them, I guess. My great aunt's collection of Toby jugs . . . oh, and the stuffed moose's head that my dad shot.'

Dora almost stumbled. She swallowed hard.

'A . . . a moose's head?' she said faintly 'How . . . unusual. And Toby jugs? How many?'

'Oh, only about thirty.' Sam waved an airy hand. 'I don't care for them much myself, but they'll be worth something someday, or so I've been told.'

'I see.'

Dora went quiet. There was nowhere downstairs for these relics: when Lily and Jim moved out, their room would have to be turned into some kind of museum — or mausoleum. But Sam was giving up his life for her; she could hardly make a fuss about a few bits of china, or even — she shuddered — a moose's head. That'd be enormous! It'd be a struggle even to get it through the door!

'Well,' she said bravely, 'I'm sure we can find a place for them.'

'Great!' Sam beamed. 'They'll be a little reminder of home.' Dora gave him a guilty smile.

Sam kissed her on the cheek as they parted outside the shop's plate-glass window with its two mannequins dressed in taffeta and lace. He was meeting Dennis to go over some figures.

'I'll see you later,' he said, and Dora felt the usual deep rush of happiness and, yes, relief at the thought.

Dora Collins was a resourceful woman, calm, sensible, practical, but as she hung up her jacket, she knew that though she'd urged Jim and Lily to move out well before Sam had declared his intentions, in her heart of hearts she'd dreaded it. She'd never lived on her own. First she'd lived with her parents, then with Arthur, and even when Arthur had died, she'd had the children with her. Now, thanks to Sam, she still wouldn't be on her own, cooking and eating a solitary meal, keeping the wireless on for company, knowing that everything in the house would always be as she'd left it because there was no one else to dent a cushion or leave a cup or plate on the draining board. Oh, she could have taken a lodger, but it would never have been the same as having someone — Sam — who chose to be there because he wanted to be with her — so much so that he was coming four thousand miles to prove it. Honestly, what were a few ornaments and — perish the thought — even a moose's head — to set against that?

* * *

About half an hour later, Dora was doing a fine repair by hand in her little back room when she heard the shop bell tinkle and Beryl's voice as she moved forwards with her usual greeting.

'Good afternoon, madam . . .'

There was an indistinct murmur in response and a minute later, Beryl poked her head round the half-open door.

'It's someone asking for you,' she said.

Dora lifted her head.

'Who?'

Beryl looked indignant.

'Do you mind, I'm not that nosy, I didn't ask! But it's not a client. I've never seen her before.'

Dora laid aside the dress she was working on and stood up.

'I can't think who it can be —' she began. 'Oh, unless it's Mrs Russell from the WVS. She said she'd drop in one day with some envelopes for me to address.'

'Didn't look like WVS to me,' shrugged Beryl. 'And

she wasn't carrying anything.'

'Yes, all right, Miss Marple,' scolded Dora as she moved to the door. 'You can put your deerstalker away now.'

Beryl stood aside to let her through.

'Look, it's almost cup of tea time anyway,' she said. 'If it's private, and you don't want me earwigging, have a proper break for once and nip over the Tudor Rose.'

'I don't need to go out, I'm sure it won't take long,' said Dora.

She stepped into the shop, then stopped as a young woman advanced towards her, holding out her hands. She was a blonde, a dyed blonde, and boldly dressed in a splashily printed frock and a bright green jacket.

'Dora?' she said. 'Oh, I'm so glad to meet you at last! I'm Kathy!'

26

Dora wished she'd had a bit of warning — she might have washed her hair, or put on something a bit better than her old flannel skirt and blouse! Still, there was nothing for it: at least she had her navy jacket and hat. Asking Kathy to wait, she ran a comb through her hair and swiftly applied a touch of lipstick. Even so, when they were seated at a table in the Tudor Rose, she felt like a sparrow next to a parakeet, and as Kathy began chattering away, the resemblance became even more marked.

'Honest,' Kathy began as Dora poured their tea, 'I've been dying to meet you! Sam never stops talking about you! I was so sorry you couldn't come over to ours that night but I was dreading it all the same! The way Sam raves about your cooking! I made a plum tart for afters and I was so glad you wasn't there, because the plums were sour and the pastry was half raw in the middle! You'll have to give me some lessons!'

She had a strong London accent and the way she spoke in exclamation marks left Dora blinking as they flashed in front of her. She pushed Kathy's cup towards her. Had she really thought this girl — for that's what she was, barely out of her twenties — was a serious threat?

Kathy had ordered a plate of cakes and Dora watched as she took a huge bite of an éclair. Her teeth were rather large and ersatz cream oozed down her chin. Laughing, she wiped it away and scrubbed at a blob that had fallen on her dress, its shiny rayon straining over her full figure.

Kathy took a sip of tea and her red lipstick left an imprint on the cup. She pushed a lock of brassy hair out of her eye and smiled. Dora smiled back broadly, and smiled even more inside. She'd seen at first glance Kathy wasn't Sam's type at all. If there'd ever been any romantic attraction, she knew for sure now it would have been all one-sided. Why had she fixated on what Dennis had said and not believed Sam's assurances? What an idiot she'd been!

'I don't know what Sam's been telling you, but it's all nonsense,' she said. 'I'm a reasonable plain cook, that's all. But not everyone's got the knack, especially with pastry. I've tried to teach my daughter as best I can, but she still produces some horrors!'

Kathy laughed a pealing laugh.

'Thank God it's not just me!' she cried. 'Good job Dennis can get a decent meal at the base, or he has been able to up to now!' She leaned forward and gripped Dora's hands. 'But this business he's setting up with Sam, it's going to be good, isn't it? And I'm so relieved Sam's part of it. I reckon they'll be a great team. They sort of — go together, like two jigsaw pieces, don't you think?'

'That's more or less what Sam said to me,' agreed Dora, glad that the frenzied gabble seemed to be calming down a little. Luckily the Tudor Rose wasn't busy, people preferring to be outdoors on this fine day. 'He'll keep Dennis on the straight and narrow. Steady the ship, was how he put it.'

'Exactly! His steadiness, that's what I always liked about Sam.' Kathy smiled a wide smile and a girlish dimple appeared in each cheek. 'He was always a bit different from the others, that bit older and wiser. I used to pour out all my troubles to him and he used to listen, bless him.'

'He's a good listener,' Dora agreed. 'What sort of troubles did you have, if you don't mind me asking?'

Kathy rolled her big, blue, doll-like eyes.

'Oh, you know, silly things, how the girl I shared a room with snored, dreadful problems with mice where we were billeted, the landlady that didn't give me my rations . . .'

Dora felt a wash of sympathy. Those poor girls, sent miles from home in the first dark days of the war: it must have been so strange for them. At the same time she smiled to herself. All the intimate chats in dark corners of dance halls and pub inglenooks that she'd imagined between Sam and Kathy, and they'd been about mice infestations and snoring!

'And Sam helped?'

'He's so practical, isn't he?' said Kathy. She'd demolished the éclair and her mouth was full of fairy cake. 'He told me to sew a few pebbles or even buttons in the collar of the girl's pyjamas so she couldn't sleep on her back, and he brought me some mouse-traps from their stores. And when he heard about the landlady, he made me insist on a new billet.' She wetted her finger to pick up crumbs from her plate. 'It was like talking to my dad, really, God rest him.'

'Oh, you lost your dad, did you?'

'Yeah, and my mum, in the Blitz. Our street disappeared overnight, more or less.' Kathy snapped her fingers. 'Pff! Just like that. I'd left home by then, and my brothers were away fighting.' She paused briefly, then sighed. 'But you've got to get on with it, haven't you?'

Dora's heart went out to her. She and Kathy were as different as chalk and cheese, in age, in looks, and in talkativeness too. But she was a good soul with no side to her, Dora could see that, and she could also see that Kathy and Dennis were made for each other. Their surface brashness hid a deeper insecurity. Future foursomes — and she was sure there'd be some — held no fear for her. And, if Sam could stand in for Kathy's dad, maybe, somehow, here was someone else she could mother.

★ ★ ★

Dora was looking forward to telling Sam about her surprise visitor, but she might have known Kathy would have got there first. When he met Dora from work at the end of the day, it seemed Kathy had bowled straight back to the pub where Sam and Dennis had been poring over the small print in the Ministry's contract.

'Gushing like a geyser,' he smiled. 'You're going to teach her to cook and bake, I gather.'

'Am I?' said Dora, astonished.

'Well, yeah! She said Dennis can look forward to — how did she put it? Feather-light cakes and melt-in-the-mouth pastry in future.'

'That's your fault,' teased Dora. 'Singing my praises. How embarrassing!'

'Well, you're never going to do it for yourself,' replied Sam, unabashed. 'But look, I'm sorry if she took you by surprise. I wasn't expecting her to turn up with Dennis, but she did, with the sole aim of hunting you down. Dennis had told her where you worked, see. There was no chance to warn you.'

'Not to worry,' Dora smiled. 'I'm glad I've met her. And I liked her. She . . . she wasn't at all what I expected.'

'No?'

'I don't know about a Land Girl, I'd call her more a force of nature!'

Sam laughed.

'You can say that all right. She's quite something, isn't she?'

Not so long ago, that phrase coming from Sam's lips would have struck fear into Dora's heart. Now she heard it differently.

'Oh yes! She could talk the leg off an iron pot, as we say around here.'

'And how!' Sam agreed. 'She's a nice enough girl, but boy, she never lets up! To be honest, a lot of the time when she'd single me out to talk to, I used to sit there and let it wash over me.'

Dora thought that was probably a good tactic. Sam tucked her arm through his.

'You know what I like about you, Dora?' he said. 'Among many things?'

Dora shook her head.

'Ah, you see! That just proves it. You don't say anything unless you've got something to say. You're comfortable with silence. Not many women are.'

Dora said nothing in reply, but her smile said it all.

27

Things were moving along for Gladys too. Now their future in Weston-super-Mare was all mapped out, there was no stopping her. She couldn't wait to move and harried the estate agent and the solicitor almost daily.

'It's the squeaky wheel that gets the oil,' she told Dora firmly. Dora tried to suppress a smile. Perhaps there was more of Florrie Jessop in Gladys than anyone had ever suspected, though at least in Gladys the family trait of sheer doggedness came out in a productive way.

Bill, too, was transformed.

'Goes off to work whistling!' Gladys reported to Lily when they next met up. It made Lily think of the dwarfs in Walt Disney's *Snow White* picture that she'd seen as a child, though even then the cheerful willingness with which Snow White had assumed the role of housekeeper for the little tribe had left her cold.

She'd soon have a home of her own to look after, though, so she'd have to shape up. Gladys's landlord had been duly impressed by Lily and Jim's wage slips and a glowing reference from Mr Simmonds, and they'd been promised the tenancy of Number 5 April Street once Gladys and Bill had a moving date.

'It's a pretty address, April Street, but a bit of a strange one,' Sam observed as he listened to Lily's excited chatter about the house when he came round for tea. 'Sits between March Road and May Terrace by any chance?' Sam was spending a lot more time at

253

Dora's now ('Getting his feet under the table — literally!' as Jim joked) but nobody minded, least of all Dora.

Lily explained that the street was named after the daughter of a Victorian bigwig and benefactor, and lay between Ernest and Henry Streets, named after his sons.

When they'd eaten, and Lily and Jim had taken Buddy for his evening walk, Dora asked Sam if he'd take a look in the room they'd soon be vacating and measure up for some shelves.

'Sure, but why?' he asked. 'Are you thinking of opening up a library?'

'No, they'll be for your Toby jugs, of course,' said Dora.

'What Toby jugs?'

Dora frowned.

'The ones you're bringing from Canada. Your old aunt's — your heirlooms.'

Sam's face creased.

'Dora, you never bought that story? I wasn't serious!'

'What? Weren't you? You sounded it!'

'Oh my Lord!'

Sam laughed till he had to hold his sides, while Dora put her hands on her hips.

'And the moose's head? I suppose that was a big fib as well!' But she couldn't help laughing herself — and at herself, for taking him at his word.

'Come here!' said Sam, offering her a hug. 'If you're going to be that easy to wind up, I'm going to enjoy this marriage even more than I thought I would!'

★ ★ ★

Soon everything was falling into place. Sam would go back to Canada, but planned to return in September, when he and Dora would have a quiet ceremony at her local church. Gladys and Bill would be leaving Hinton within weeks for their new life in Weston, which meant Lily and Jim could move too. Yes, Dora would have to spend a short while living on her own, but Lily and Jim were a stone's throw away, and anyway, as she said, she'd have plenty to keep her occupied with her own wedding to plan.

'I feel so boring!' Beryl complained when Lily called by the shop one day. 'Nothing's changing for me!'

'Haven't you had enough change already?' Lily laughed. 'A new shop, a new partner, a new business . . . how much more do you want? How's the shop doing, by the way? You've been open a good few weeks now.'

'Has it only been weeks? It feels like forever!' Beryl said wryly. 'But in a good way!' She leaned in closer to whisper to Lily, though there were no customers to overhear. 'Profits are forty per cent above what we expected.' She leaned out again to say: 'And before you ask if that's just initial interest, I thought the same, but the order book's full right through to the autumn.'

Lily seized her hands.

'Oh Beryl, I'm so happy for you! And you haven't fallen out with Evelyn yet?'

'I hardly see her,' said Beryl. 'Which suits me fine. But when she does come in, actually, we get on quite well.' She grinned conspiratorially. 'And the best of it is, she's got a spy in the camp in Kenya! Her parents have got friends out there.'

'Have they?' Lily was agog. 'So have you heard what Robert's up to — as if I can't guess!'

'Well, he hasn't got eaten by a lion — yet,' said Beryl with some regret. 'But he's already run up a load of debts — horse racing, apparently — that I suppose his dad'll have to bail him out of.'

'Oh, he hasn't!' exclaimed Lily. 'No wonder Mr Marlow keeps banging on about margins and profits!'

'There's more.' Beryl couldn't keep the satisfaction out of her voice. 'There's talk Robert's carrying on with some other posh bloke's wife — oh, and he's learning to fly! Some crackpot idea about taking tourists on . . . what do they call it over there . . . on safari, that's it.'

Lily shook her head.

'He'll never change, will he?' she said. 'That'll be another five-minute wonder. He never sticks to anything for long.'

'No, you're right,' Beryl agreed. 'All hat and no cap, that one! It'll be hot-air balloons next, or rocket trips to the moon.'

'Poor Mr Marlow.'

'Oh, well, at least he's got that nice woman for company,' said Beryl. 'Mrs Tunnicliffe. She came in the other day, actually.'

'Did she? She wasn't looking for something special for herself, was she?' asked Lily hopefully.

'What? No, of course not!'

'Oh.' Disappointed, Lily wrinkled her nose. 'I'm still hoping she and Mr Marlow might make a go of it. Marry, I mean.'

'Well, you never know,' said Beryl sagely. 'Look at your mum and Sam! Never too late, is what I say.'

'Maybe. So what did Mrs Tunnicliffe want?'

'Oh,' Beryl replied. 'That, yes. She was with a friend

256

of hers who was looking for a bridesmaid's dress for her daughter.'

'A bridesmaid's dress . . .' Lily smiled. 'Funny, isn't it?'

'What is?'

'That sort of completes the circle. It was Violet Tunnicliffe who gave me her old bridesmaid's dress to wear to your wedding, and her mother who was adamant I should keep it after Violet died. And it was that, with your wedding dress, that you used to start your business!'

'Yes . . . I was going to tell you,' said Beryl hesitantly. 'That dress . . . the cornflower blue . . . it's beautiful, but it's been so popular and had so much wear, so much letting up and down and taking in and out, and been cleaned that many times . . .'

'What?'

'I'm thinking of asking your mum to cut it down and use the good material to make a short dress for a flower girl. Would you mind?'

Lily didn't even have to think about it.

'No,' she said. 'You must. I think that's a lovely idea. We all have to move on, Beryl, and one way or another, we all have. You, me, Gladys, even Mum.'

'Even Robert Marlow,' said Beryl. 'Thank our lucky stars!'

★ ★ ★

Before Sam left, there had to be a party. It was Sid's idea — in fact, he insisted.

'You've let this man waltz back into our lives,' he protested. 'He's going to marry our mum and I've never even met him!'

257

But he was smiling as he said it, and lighting a cigarette at the same time, Lily could tell, even down the crackly phone line. She knew their mother had written to him, and Sam had added a couple of pages of his own. If Sid hadn't felt their happiness seep out from the minute he opened the envelope, well, he wasn't the sensitive and good-hearted fellow Lily thought he was.

'We have vetted him properly, haven't we, Jim?' she replied. 'And made sure his intentions are honourable.'

They were crammed in the phone box by the chip shop and Sid was on the phone at his digs. Lily heard her favourite brother exhale and could imagine him blowing the smoke rings he'd perfected. That was when he announced that he intended on paying a visit to Hinton the weekend before Sam was due to leave.

'And if that's not reason enough for a celebration in itself, I don't know what is!' he said.

This was true: they hadn't seen him since the wedding, and Sid reminded them of that, too.

'It'll be your first anniversary, so there's that to celebrate as well as Mum's engagement,' he added. 'Oh, and Gladys and Bill's move — Bill dropped me a line, full of it.'

'It'd be nice to give them a proper send-off,' Lily agreed. 'And Sam too, though that's only temporary, of course. All right, let's fix something up! How do you want to do this, Sid? Jim and I can organise it, but are we having it at home, or shall I book a room in a pub or —'

'Sis, I think you've forgotten who you're talking to! I'm one of the unsung heroes, I'll have you know, the backroom boys who won us the war!' Jim, craning to share the receiver, hitched up his eyebrows when he heard this, but Sid had never been shy of a spot of exaggeration. 'I think,' Sid carried on with dignity, 'you can trust me to organise a bit of a bunfight a hundred miles up the road!'

'Well, if you're sure . . .'

Sid clicked his tongue against his teeth.

'Tell Mum it's on, then sit back and leave it to me.'

Sid might have called it 'a bit of a bunfight', but Dora knew better.

'Well, I hope he's not going to go mad,' she clucked. She and Lily were taking down the curtains in Lily and Jim's room for washing. 'A small family meal, that's all we need, I'll be embarrassed enough at that, if Sidney goes and makes one of his speeches! And there's no need for him to book anywhere. I'd be happy to have it here.'

Lily looked down from the chair she was standing on to unhook the curtains.

'I know you would, Mum, but it's your party, he doesn't want you doing all the work!'

Dora gave in.

'All right, but if he goes and insists on the White Lion again, then let him book a table on a Sunday dinnertime, or an evening — we don't need a big fancy do, just you and Jim, me and Sam, and Sidney. I'm very fond of Gladys and Bill, but he can see them separately to say goodbye, and we can too.'

Lily smiled. She knew Sid wasn't about to settle for that.

Sure enough, a letter duly arrived.

All booked! it began.

259

Right, this is the drill: we're back at the jolly old White Lion, Sunday the sixteenth of June at twelve noon in the same private room as before. All food and drink is laid on, courtesy of yours truly — and no arguments, please, Mum. I want you — and Sam — to enjoy the day, without worrying about whether the rations'll stretch and will half a roll of Izal last in the privy all afternoon! Because you may find that there are a few more well-wishers there than you think! (Yes, I'm in charge of the guest list too!) See you on the sixteenth. Toodle-pip!

Dora was dumbfounded.

'But I wrote and told him what I'd said to you . . . did you know what Sid was up to?' she demanded of Lily.

'Not a clue,' said Lily truthfully. 'But you can hardly say no when he's kindly set it all up, can you? Now, what are you going to wear?'

In secret, Lily was impressed with her brother.

'No wonder they kept him on at the Admiralty,' she mused to Jim as they walked to work. 'But I wonder what his plans are now, really?'

'He might stay in the services forever, Reg and Gwenda seem to want to,' said Jim, pulling her to a stop as a van careered round the corner of the road they were about to cross. 'Anyway, you can ask him when you see him. If you live to see him!'

28

The day of the party drew nearer. Sam presented Dora with a small diamond cluster, and Dora took off the wedding ring she'd worn for almost thirty years to put it on. The next day, she made a special trip to the churchyard where the children's father was buried.

IN LOVING MEMORY OF ARTHUR COLLINS

said the headstone.

DEVOTED HUSBAND AND FATHER, DEPARTED THIS LIFE 27TH MARCH 1927, NEVER FORGOTTEN.

Dora knelt and arranged the flowers she'd brought with her in the little vase at the headstone's base.

'And you never will be, love,' she said softly. 'But I know you'll understand. I've waited a long time for this, but Sam's a good man, just like you. I know he'll look after me, just like you did. And I know you'd want that for me. And the children.'

She stayed a while by the grave, with the smell of cut grass and the pigeons murmuring soothingly in the swaying evergreens. Before she left she pressed her fingertips to her lips and held them against the rough stone.

'Night night, love,' she said.

★ ★ ★

With that done, Dora felt free to begin to think about what Sid would keep calling her engagement party, and even to look forward to it.

On Lily's insistence, she put in some extra hours at the shop on her own behalf, to run herself up a dress of dusty pink crêpe. It was a copy of a model gown in one of the fashion magazines that Evelyn arranged artistically on the sales desk, pretty much her sole contribution to the running of the business — which kept everyone happy.

Lily, meanwhile, badgered the salesgirls on Dress Fabrics in Marlows for something for herself till they came up with a suitable remnant — deep blue with a pattern that looked like feather fans or, to Lily's eye, seashells — very appropriate for a reunion with a naval brother. Dora made it up in a style Lily liked — short-sleeved, square-necked and button-through. When she modelled it for Jim on the night before the party, she found he liked that style too: there were no fiddly fastenings, so Lily could slide out of it quickly. It was their anniversary weekend, after all.

Next day, at twelve noon exactly, Lily and Jim, Dora and Sam arrived at the White Lion. Never thinking he'd need one, Sam hadn't brought a suit with him to England, but Dennis knew someone who, like Bill, had decided to sell his demob suit, so Sam was nattily attired in a grey pinstripe with a cream shirt and a maroon spotted tie; Jim was in his best work suit. In the little function room, the doors were open to the garden once again and Sid, in his naval uniform, was there to greet them, tall, straight-backed, blond hair slicked smooth. Maybe Lily was biased, but if anyone was like the dashing Prince Philip of Greece and

Denmark, whose engagement to Princess Elizabeth was surely imminent, it was Sid!

She hung back while Sid hugged their mother, then held out his hand to Sam.

'Pleased to meet you at last,' he said. 'Thanks for writing like you did. And welcome to the family.'

Sam pumped his hand.

'That's very generous of you,' he said. 'I've heard so much about you, I was beginning to be scared this would be some kind of inspection drill!'

'No need,' Sid grinned. 'I trust my mother's judgement. And I know my fierce little sister wouldn't have let you near Mum if she thought badly of you!'

'Fierce?' Sam winked at Lily, recalling their encounter in the yard. 'Too right, I've certainly heard her roar!'

With an arm round each of their shoulders, Sid led the pair off to a side table stocked with bottles and as Sam accepted a small whisky, Lily could tell they were going to get along.

Gladys and Bill and the twins arrived next, then Beryl, Les and Bobby. Lily had known they were expected, but when she glanced at the long table, the starched white linen already laid with silver and glassware, she noticed there were more places set.

She pulled Sid away from the throng and into the garden.

'What's this?' she asked. 'Extra places . . . you're not . . . don't tell me Jerome's flown over from America?'

Sid shook his head. 'Sadly not,' he said. He glanced back into the room to make sure no one else was within earshot, then added: 'I've got some news too, but it's not for general consumption, not today, which is all about Mum and Sam. He seems a really good bloke, by the way.'

'He is,' said Lily. 'Very much so. But what's this news of yours? You can tell me, Sid. You know I can keep a secret when it's important.'

A bee blundered past. They both watched as it settled on the well of a lupin and began to drink deeply.

'OK, then, I will. Brace yourself.' Sid went to reach in his pocket for his usual prop, his cigarette case, then changed his mind. 'Mum may not be crossing the Atlantic, Lily, but I am. I'm going to America.'

Lily felt her eyes stretch wide.

'No!' she gasped. 'I know you hoped you could, to be with Jerome, but how have you managed it?'

'I've spent the last six months trying to work out how.' Sid was deadly serious now. 'I knew I needed a work permit, so I had to get there in some official capacity, find a job that came with one attached. So I've been applying for jobs that would get me to America and finally it's happened. I'm joining the Diplomatic Service — the Foreign and Commonwealth Office.'

'The Foreign and Commonwealth . . . the Diplomatic Service? Oh, Sid!'

The idea of her brother Sid — her own brother — having risen so high, having gone so far, and going so far — Lily hardly knew what to make of it. But Sid carried on matter-of-factly:

'There was a job at the Embassy in Washington that I didn't get, then one at the Consulate in Chicago that I did, but America's a big place. The Yanks might think nothing of travelling hundreds of miles, but if I'm going there to be with Jerome, I want to be with him, and he's on the West Coast, back working in films, so in the end I turned it down.'

The bee, as unsteady as if it had been swigging wine, backed out of the cup of the lupin. It hovered for a moment as if getting its bearings before zigzagging shakily away. They watched it go, gaining confidence as it went.

'So . . . ?' Lily prompted.

'So finally a vacancy came up for a clerk in the Consulate in Los Angeles. I applied — and I got it. I've dropped a grade to go, but I don't care about that. I just want to be there.'

'Oh Sid!' said Lily again. She was devastated at the thought of losing him, but at the same time . . . if Jim had been half a world away, she knew she'd have moved heaven and earth to join him, and it was no different for her brother with the person he cared for. 'I — well, I'm very happy for you, even if I'm sad for me!'

'You'll have to come and visit,' he said. 'In time, I might even get a job in films myself, you never know.'

'What?' gaped Lily. 'You haven't been taking acting lessons?'

'Not in front of the camera!' scoffed Sid. 'I mean a job on the production side.'

Sid had always had a thing about the cinema: Dora still kept a stack of his old *Picturegoer* magazines. She used them for inspiration sometimes, if she got hold of a length of material, to make a dress for the shop.

'Can't you just see me in a loud suit, smoking a fat cigar?' Sid went on with a grin. Then, putting on a cod American accent, he drawled: 'Hey baby, wanna be in pictures? I can make you a star!'

Lily shook her head in exasperated affection.

'You'd do great in Hollywood, Sid,' she laughed. 'You always did know how to shoot a line!' Then, more serious: 'But no thanks. I'm very happy where I am.

And I want you to be as happy too.'

Sid gave her a look of intense gratitude.

'Thanks, Sis. I know you understand.'

Lily and Jim were the only ones who'd met Jerome and knew the truth of his and Sid's attachment. Jerome's name would never be mentioned to Dora — Sid's new job would be presented as a good career step, with the suggestion that it was a temporary move, and not a permanent one.

In fact, Dora was well aware that her second son was not the marrying kind. Though she worried for him, because his way of life was illegal, she was grateful that Sid had tactfully conducted his affairs well away from Hinton. As a result, even Jean Crosbie was indulgent about Sid's bachelor status — with his good looks, she proclaimed, why would he settle down when he could have his pick of the girls? Dora would smile to herself when Jean, usually such a hanging judge, delivered this verdict. If only she knew!

'When do you go?' Lily asked. 'You'll still be here for Mum's wedding, I hope?'

Sid pulled a face.

'That's the only snag. I'll have to leave sooner than that, I'm afraid.'

'Oh, but Sid!' Lily exclaimed. 'You can't! She was expecting you to give her away. Who'll do that now? I mean, Jim can do it, of course, but it won't be the same without you!'

Sid held up a wagging forefinger.

'As if I'd leave Mum in the lurch! I shall arrange a very suitable substitute,' he said.

'How could anyone substitute for you?' puzzled Lily.

'It's a tough call, I know,' said Sid, with his best swagger. 'But I think I've found someone who'll be up to the job.'

'Who? Have you asked Jim already? What are you talking about?'

The chief waiter who'd be looking after them emerged from inside the hotel and lingered nearby. Sid stepped aside to talk to him. Lily looked around. She breathed in the scent of the summer flowers, the lupins, the stocks and the roses. Before they were over, her mother would be remarried, Gladys and Bill would be gone, Sid would be gone. It really was all change.

Sid reappeared at her side.

'Food's ready,' he said. And, crooking his elbow: 'May I escort you in to luncheon, madam?'

They all took their places, Dora and Sam in the middle on one side of the long table, with Sid, Jim and Lily opposite. Before the others sat down, however, Sid asked for a place to be kept free on either side of Sam and Dora. The rest of the party took their seats, the children were settled, and, standing up, Sid said he had an announcement to make. Lily knew it couldn't be about his own plans, so what on earth had he come up with now?

'Oh, here we go,' called Bill, who knew Sid loved being in the spotlight. Sid ignored the banter.

'The first thing I said to Sam when I met him today,' he began, 'was to welcome him to the family. But the family's not complete without everyone being here. So, fresh from the aerodrome — well, not quite, they've had time for a wash and brush-up, I hope —' He turned towards the door and called, 'You can come in now!'

And in walked Reg and Gwenda.

★ ★ ★

267

'I can't believe it!' Dora kept saying all through lunch, and it was the same when they got up from the table. With Sam at her side, she couldn't take her eyes off her elder son and his wife, nor stop reaching out to touch them, as if she really couldn't believe they were there.

'It's all right, Mum,' grinned Reg, small and wiry as ever, with a new pencil moustache and a deep tan from his years in the African and Middle Eastern sun. 'You can take your hands off us! We're not going to disappear!'

'Oh, leave her be, bless her!' chided Gwenda, Reg's wife. She was petite and pretty, and tanned too, even on the back of her neck since her dark hair had been cut shorter. 'It's been long enough, Reg.' Her slight Welsh accent was as musical as ever.

Gwenda had served with the Military Transport Corps in the war. She'd carried on working, though in a clerical role now, during their time in Palestine while Reg, a sergeant, had overseen transport and logistics all around their base near Jerusalem. But they weren't going back — and suddenly Sid's idea of a 'substitute' to walk their mother up the aisle began to make sense.

'The extremists aren't going to let up,' Reg explained. 'They hate us Brits being there.'

'You never know where they'll strike next,' Gwenda added. 'It's why I switched to a desk job. You don't feel safe when you're off the base. And to be honest, we didn't always feel very safe there.'

'We knew about the attacks and riots from the news, but you always played it down!' Lily objected.

'No point worrying you, was there?' said Reg easily. 'Especially when we were digging our escape tunnel anyhow.'

'What do you plan to do now?' asked Sam. 'Are you settling back in Hinton, or . . .'

Sam knew about Gwenda's dad's garage in Welshpool, and that Reg was well qualified for a job there, if there was one. And it seemed there was.

'My dad's going to take him into the business,' beamed Gwenda. 'The petrol ration's about to go up again, so there'll be more car journeys, see.'

'Is it going up?' Jim asked.

'Yup, by almost a hundred miles a month by the end of the summer,' Reg replied, confiding that he had a bit of 'privileged information' about oil supplies due from the Middle East. 'That's a lot more pleasure trips. A lot more petrol to sell, a lot more punctures, and a lot more bumps and breakdowns.'

'But we'll only be an hour or so away,' Gwenda put in, worried that Dora might feel disappointed. 'A lot nearer than Palestine, so you'll be seeing plenty of us!'

Sid joined them in time to hear this last remark. He put one arm round his mother's shoulders and the other round his brother's.

'And the best is, Mum, I shan't have to fight our Reg for the honour of giving you away. The job's his — I did the honours with Lily, after all, and I concede to his superior position in the family!'

Sid shot Lily a look and she smiled back. She alone knew that Sid would be on the other side of the Atlantic by the time Dora and Sam were married. He'd be building his own new life just like they would be, like Reg and Gwenda in Welshpool, like Gladys and Bill in Weston and like herself and Jim rather closer to home in April Street. And there seemed a rightness about all of it.

29

Next day, after all the excitement, it was down to earth with a bump and back to work as usual. As was also usual at this time of year, that meant getting ready for the summer sale ('The Klondike in the Gold Rush,' as Jim put it). Boxes of special 'bought-in' bargains were arriving daily, and there were all sorts of oddments, discontinued lines and end-of-season items which could be marked down. Lily was doing just that on some grey knee-high socks left over from the winter when Nancy sidled over.

'Got five minutes?' she asked.

Lily looked around. It was still early, so there were no customers in sight. Miss Frobisher was conferring with Miss Kendall from Schoolwear; Mr Marlow must still be on his tour of the ground floor. Molly, the Childrenswear junior, had gone down to Despatch with a parcel, but Miss Temple was there if an early bird customer should fly in. Lily nodded.

'I've got some news!' Nancy began. Lily had to stifle an urge to say, Not you as well! which became even stronger as Nancy went on: 'I'm moving! That is, I'm leaving Marlows. I'm going to throw my lot in with Harry!'

Lily dropped the socks.

'What? You're getting married?'

'No!' Nancy's eyes signalled scorn, and amusement. 'I do like him — a lot, actually, but don't you tell him so! — but that's not on the cards, not yet anyway, if we ever do. But we're going to work together!'

'How? Where?'

Nancy leaned in confidentially.

'Harry's always wanted to set up on his own, and now he's got the opportunity. His dad's going to put up the money for him to buy into a pet shop.'

'A pet shop?'

'The one by the station!' said Nancy, as if Lily should have known. 'The owner's retiring and me and Harry are going to run it together.' As Lily gaped at her, she went on: 'Everyone wants a pet now, all those people who had their dogs and cats put down when war broke out. All those kids who've come back from the countryside and want a rabbit of their own, or a pet mouse, or even a rat! All those people who keep chickens and want a bit of fish meal or lice powder —'

Lily had to smile. Didn't this sound exactly like Sam's reasoning about the British and their love of animals when he'd been explaining the business he and Dennis were going to set up?

'I have to hand it to you, Nancy,' she smiled. 'You never cease to amaze me! Well, congratulations! You've always said you like change. And if you and Harry want a reliable supplier for your dog kennels and rabbit hutches, and' — thinking of all the cutting and sawing Sam and Dennis would be doing — 'actually, sawdust for pet bedding too — I know the very person!'

'Oh? Who?' said Nancy at once. 'Harry'll be very interested! He wants to review all the suppliers to make sure we're getting the best deal! And you've got a dog, haven't you? Ten per cent discount for friends!'

The two of them were so deep in discussion that Lily didn't notice Miss Frobisher's approach.

'I had no idea boys' winter-weight socks could

ignite quite so much interest,' she remarked. 'Are you planning to take some off our hands, Miss Broad? To sell as pan-holders on your department, perhaps?'

'No, Miss Frobisher,' Nancy said meekly. Even she quailed in front of a raised eyebrow from her former boss. 'I'll get back.'

'I think you should. I can see Mrs Mortimer contemplating that dressing table set that's just come in.'

Nancy shot off like a rocket. Mrs Mortimer was one of the store's best customers.

'Now, Miss Collins,' Miss Frobisher began, as Lily returned to her socks. 'I hope you had a good celebration at the weekend?'

Miss Frobisher was always astute, but Lily hadn't realised she was clairvoyant. She'd said nothing to her about Sid's party plans.

'For your anniversary?' Miss Frobisher continued. 'You've been married a year, isn't that right?'

Surprised and flattered that Miss Frobisher had remembered, Lily confirmed that there had been something of a family party.

'Thank you for remembering,' she added.

Miss Frobisher raised her sculpted eyebrows again. 'In all the excitement, another anniversary may have passed you by. It's five years this week since you started at Marlows.'

She was right, of course, Lily realised. Five years! Where had it gone?

'I hope you feel those years haven't been wasted, and that you've progressed as much as you'd have hoped?'

'Oh, yes,' said Lily. 'More so! Thanks to you, Miss Frobisher.'

Miss Frobisher gave one of her more enigmatic

smiles.

'On the contrary, I think it's been down to your own hard work. So I'm wondering — well, hoping would be more accurate — if you feel ready for a new challenge?'

Lily looked at her expectantly, but not without some dread. Was this what Miss Frobisher had been talking to Miss Kendall about? Maybe Miss Kendall needed time off to take care of a relative or to have an operation or something . . . Lily had been sent to run Schoolwear before during a hiatus, and though it had been good experience, it wasn't exactly an inspiring department, or one that you could do much with. It was all about essentials: there was no room for flair.

Miss Frobisher took a deep breath.

'The thing is, Lily —'

Using her first name! That was unheard of on the shop floor — what was she going to say? Lily didn't have long to wait as Miss Frobisher went on, rather tremulously for her:

'I'm going to be facing a new challenge myself. I'm expecting a baby.'

'Oh, Miss Frobisher! Oh! That's — congratulations!'

'Thank you.' Miss Frobisher dipped her head briefly to hide a broad smile — she was obviously thrilled. 'To be honest, I — we — wondered if it would ever happen. At my age, I'm something of an elderly mother. I — well, that's why I had a few days off unexpectedly in the spring, do you remember? I was feeling rather grim. But now I'm feeling much brighter, and it's confirmed, it can be common knowledge. I shall be leaving towards the end of the year.'

Lily had noticed a change in Miss Frobisher's shape

recently. Her figure had seemed fuller, and she'd definitely let her belts out a notch, but Lily had put it down to her contentment in life as Mrs Simmonds.

'That's wonderful,' she said warmly. 'I'm so happy for you. For both of you.'

And she was, even as she remembered that she'd have left Marlows herself by now if she hadn't lost the baby. The pain of that loss had subsided to a dull and very occasional ache: the wound had healed, but the scar would always be there. She forced her attention back to Miss Frobisher.

'Obviously this will create a vacancy,' she was saying, 'and it won't be a temporary one. I had enough of working all hours while John was small. I missed so much of his babyhood, his childhood, even. I don't want that to happen again.'

'No, I can understand that,' said Lily, wondering what was coming next.

'So . . . that challenge I was talking about . . . Do you feel able to step up to running the department? You'd only be graded and paid as a junior buyer to begin with, but Miss Kendall, with all her experience, will be on hand — not that I think you'll need her. I believe you're more than capable. What's more, you've earned it.'

'Oh, Miss Frobisher!' Lily's eyes filled with tears. 'Really? You've got that much faith in me?'

'I had faith in you from the moment you started,' smiled Miss Frobisher. 'Even though your first day went rather catastrophically wrong!'

Lily blushed, remembering the incident in the basement air-raid shelter when she'd slapped a customer — Violet Tunnicliffe, in fact. It had been to bring her out of hysterics, but an assault on a customer had still been a grave transgression and Lily had expected to be sacked. Luckily it had all worked out — after all, she was still here, wasn't she? She'd survived that, and she'd survived a lot of things, personal and professional, in the past five years. She squared her shoulders and stood up straight.

'I won't let you down, Miss Frobisher,' she said.

★ ★ ★

Naturally, the first person Lily wanted to tell was Jim, but having been caught in a huddle with Nancy, and already feeling the weight of her soon-to-be acquired responsibilities, she thought she'd better wait till her official mid-morning break. Cocking her head meaningfully towards the back stairs as she passed him, she waited for him to join her. He burst through the doors at a lick.

'Are you going to say what I think you're going to say?' he demanded.

'What am I going to say?' Lily asked.

'Miss Frobisher's leaving, you're getting a promotion — and it's good news for me, too!'

Light dawned. Lily had been so bowled over by what the baby meant for her that she hadn't even considered the wider implications.

'You — you're not!'

Jim nodded, eyes shining.

'They're scrapping the deputy post. I'm going to be first-floor supervisor!'

Blow responsibility, blow store rules, blow everything! Lily flung herself at Jim.

'I always knew you could do it!' he cried, hugging her tight and lifting her off her feet.

'I always knew *you* could do it! Oh Jim!'

'World at our feet, eh?'

He put her down so her feet felt that world. He bent his head to kiss her, but before he could, they heard someone coming up the stairs. They sprang apart as the top of a bald head appeared on the half-landing below.

'That all sounds most satisfactory, Miss Collins,' Jim said, straightening his tie and moving a good foot away. 'Thank you for bringing that to my attention, though.'

'Thank *you*, Mr Goodridge,' smirked Lily. 'Good morning, Mr Gilbert.'

Mr Gilbert, of Clocks and Pictures, nodded to them and passed through onto the sales floor. Jim promptly grabbed Lily again.

'Always finish what you started,' he said, and kissed her properly, this time.

★ ★ ★

At dinnertime, Lily got a pass out to nip to Wedding Belles to tell a delighted Dora — and Beryl — and that night, she and Jim went round to Gladys and Bill's to pass on the good news.

Gladys had started packing up a few things at a time whenever she could get hold of a box, and the walls were already showing brighter patches where pictures had hung. The front and back rooms were bare of the ornaments that Gladys had spent so many hours dusting for her gran: a treasure trove for the next WI jumble sale!

Bill was over in Coventry again and Gladys was upstairs putting the twins to bed. Lily and Jim wandered out into the backyard. Bill hadn't much spare time for gardening, and Gladys had more than enough to do — there were just a few runner beans vying with bindweed for light and some tomatoes straggling up a sagging trellis. Jim had much bigger ideas.

'I want a proper veg bed,' he said. 'Wooden sides'll do — Sam can get me the wood. I'm not sure about bringing the chickens now, maybe we'll leave those at your mum's. There's more room there, and Sam can fix them up with one of his deluxe henhouses. They won't want to leave that to come here . . . then again, we could get a couple of hens of our own . . .'

Lily looked critically at the yard. It was quite a bit smaller than the one at Brook Street.

'I'm not sure,' she said, 'about us ever having chickens. They take up a lot of space with their run and everything. We want to have a bit of room to manoeuvre.'

'You think you'll be sitting out here sunning yourself, do you?' Jim caught her round the waist and hugged her to him. 'There'll be no time for that, Miss Junior Buyer, what with work and darning my socks and cooking my tea!'

'I'm not thinking of sunning myself,' said Lily. She took a deep breath and looked into his eyes. 'Not yet, not for a while, but when the time's right, we need to save a nice sunny spot for the pram.'

Jim dipped his head and kissed her.

'Indeed we do,' he said.

Acknowledgements

The world has changed so much since I started the Shop Girls series. When I began, many family-run department stores had already been bought out by big chains — as had the small Midland store group Beatties, the inspiration for Marlows. But Beatties' new owner, House of Fraser, fell victim to changing shopping habits even before the pandemic, while Debenhams was finally seen off by the virus. It's not all bad news — the big department stores that have survived are cleverly straddling online and physical shopping. Some independent stores have managed to hang on too, like Bobby's in Bournemouth, Jarrolds of Norwich and Watson and Ling in Weston-super-Mare. (I'm sure Gladys could have got a job there, if she'd wanted!). And the Beales group, under new management, has revived three of its High Street stores.

The last two years have been tricky times in publishing too, so my thanks to those who've helped the whole series out into the world are from the bottom of my heart. That starts with my agent Broo Doherty for her constant cheerleading for me, my perceptive editor Lynne Drew and her assistant, Lucy Stewart, who's been endlessly helpful. Emily Goulding and Jeannelle Brew in publicity and marketing, and Isabel Coburn and Sarah Munro in sales have also all played their part. On a technical level, copyeditor Anne O'Brien and proofreader Franciska Fabriczki made sure my words looked their best on the page.

Former Beatties staff, those at Wolverhampton Archives and Weston Museum, the BBC's People's History archive and everyone who's shared their wartime memories ('nothing but carrots for years — in everything!') have all helped enormously, as have family, friends and fellow writers for their support and advice. There are far too many to list but I hope they know who they are.

Lockdowns meant no face-to-face meetings with readers, but thanks to some wonderful librarians, I Zoomed to areas of the country I might never have been able to visit in person. Lovely comments on my Facebook page from readers who feel like friends and warm reviews on Amazon and Goodreads really mean a lot to me — thank you so much. It's a great relief to know I'm not just writing these books for myself!

I shall be so sorry to say goodbye to the Shop/Victory Girls — and I hope you will too. Who knows, maybe they'll be back one day — as one canny reader suggested, can't you just imagine Beryl's Bobby as a Teddy Boy causing havoc in the 50s?

With love, Jo x